MAN OF CLAY

Center Point
Large Print

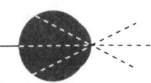

**This Large Print Book carries the
Seal of Approval of N.A.V.H.**

MAN
OF
CLAY

ALAN DEROSBY

CENTER POINT LARGE PRINT
THORNDIKE, MAINE

This Center Point Large Print edition
is published in the year 2022 by arrangement with
SpellBound Books.

The text of this Large Print edition is unabridged.
In other aspects, this book may vary
from the original edition.
Printed in the United States of America
on permanent paper sourced using
environmentally responsible foresting methods.
Set in 16-point Times New Roman type.

ISBN: 978-1-63808-343-6

The Library of Congress has cataloged this record
under Library of Congress Control Number: 2022933002

PROLOGUE

A cup of coffee, placed on a table next to the old recliner, kept him awake. Karl desired something much stronger, but the effects of liquor on his elderly body would send him off to sleep. And Karl did not want that.

Even after his wife made the decision to retire to the bedroom, Karl stayed, alone, in his thoughts and nightmares that arrived every evening. So much sadness and regret were embedded in his mind, even as simple memories like last night's dinner or the score of the ballgame, slipped through with ease.

Once the lights were dimmed and the sun began to set, shadows formed through window blinds; striped lines appearing on the floor and walls. Sometimes, when Karl left his jacket on the back of the kitchen chair, the stripes brought back awful images of forced enslavement with and by men long dead and buried. However, the shadows alone were not the entirety of his fear. It was where his eyes and thoughts went when he was alone; the locked cellar door that was next to the kitchen. Boxes and crates, filled with memories of Christmas past, graduations, and family vacations, lined the walls of the basement, every nook and cranny taken up. But there was something so much darker, hidden deep within the basement that scared him.

Sometimes, it was as if eyes were looking back at him, peeking through the tiny keyhole that kept the cellar locked. Other times, the howls and cries of all those who kept his dreams alive could be heard through the wind that swept through the screened windows on a light spring evening.

Eventually, Karl would go to his bed. He would rather be frightened next to the woman he loved than closer to what truly scared him. And though he desired to keep things secret, nightmares carried until death, Karl could feel the pull. He was destined to bear witness to his past, though everything in his being told him to avoid it. And soon enough, the great beast would return, and Hell would follow close behind.

PART I:
REVELATION

CHAPTER ONE

The school bell rang to end the day, and young men and women poured out of their classrooms and into the hallway, discussing plans for the long weekend with quick stops at lockers to grab any necessary supplies. Thanksgiving break had come yet again, and for the next five days, all schools would be off, celebrating another holiday season. Soon Hanukkah and Christmas would arrive, and the schools would again empty out for a long-needed winter break, both for the students and the teachers. Zachariah Auerbach, known as Zach to his friends, was more than ready to get out of the building, even if it were for just a few days. He'd be given a reprieve, primarily from the three seniors who used him as a human punching bag.

The room he waited in was dark. Zach's science teacher had let him hang out in her classroom after school. The custodian for the third-floor hallway knew it as well and swept around him, acting as though she was alone. The principal had even given Zach the approval to wait in there. Everyone knew the bullies who wreaked havoc on the young boy's life, as well as the lives of many other students. It was just that Zach got it the worst. It had been this way since the day he had walked into Kingston Regional High School, and it was apparent that it was going to last the entire school year.

Zach was sitting in the back of the room, laboring over a research paper he had no desire to write. He refused to wait until the last minute, a quality very few high school students had. Many of them stretched assignments until the last day, even praying for a snow day in October to extend their stay of execution. Writing on a laptop with the lights off was easy for Zach. Staying awake while researching King Philip II of Spain was making it a bit more complicated.

"Kid." A voice shook Zach awake. He had indeed zoned out. He was drained, running from his personal hell for the past few months. He couldn't talk about it at home. That's what brought it all on. And here, if he spoke too much, it would get back to them.

The boy looked up, seeing the kindly face of Jerri Lee, the custodian hired to clean the classrooms. She had already swept and emptied the trash cans in most areas, leaving this one for last. But as the winter slowly crept in on this sleepy town in Rhode Island, the darkness came with it. After the time change, it wasn't shocking to see the sun go down by four in the afternoon. The boy didn't need to be sneaking home in the dark either. That was just as dangerous.

"Time to head out. I can give you a ride home if

you'd like. Sure your pops wouldn't mind," Jerri smiled. She liked the kid and felt bad for him. But her life could be made that much worse by crossing the wrong families. If any of the three found out she was helping out the Auerbach boy, she might find extra work needed to be done in trashed bathrooms or destroyed lawns.

Zach started to load up his bookbag. "Nah, I'll walk. If I sneak out the back, I'll be alright. Chances are they went home anyway." He wanted to believe that.

"You know, you can't keep running forever. If you just let your dad handle it, then maybe they'd stop." Jerri knew this was wrong. Those boys would never stop until their own sick, twisted needs were satisfied.

"Last time I mentioned something to him, I had my nose broken. I'm thinking I just keep waiting it out until next year when they graduate and move on. Then I can stop hiding." Zach put on his jacket and flung his bookbag over his shoulder. "Have a great holiday, Jerri. See you Monday."

It was hard to slink out of this place since the district rewired the school for safety. A rash of break-ins forced the school board to put in cameras and motion-sensor lighting that came on when someone walked close to it. Any sign of life in the school would give away his location. Zach tried to hug the walls, but those damn sensors were too powerful, practically announcing his exit from the building. When he made it to an exit facing the teachers' parking lot, he scanned it before even opening the door. It was completely empty except for the cars belonging to the custodians and secretaries. Slowly opening the door, the young boy stuck one and then both feet out, holding the handle of the door so as not to make a thudding sound. He was now exposed, and his anxiety rose.

"Here we go, Zach," he said, trying to talk himself into running the few blocks to his grandparents' house. He had to cross the parking lot, go through a wooded trail and come out on the other side, with a mere two-minute walk to the front porch of his home.

Zach counted to three, using one hand to hold his bookbag in place. He bolted from the door, running down a small path that led to the parking lot. His legs took long strides across the tarred lot. He wanted to slow down and walk. If anyone was around, they would see him and laugh. But no one truly understood the terror these bullies had placed in him.

The opening to the trail got closer and closer. Once Zach was there, he'd be home free. That was the demarcation line. Safety was just beyond that path. When he finally stopped at the woods, he looked around one last time. The only thing that he could hear was the rustling of falling leaves in the woods ahead. He stepped in and took the trail home. This was the safest place of all. He walked, taking in the quiet, except for the occasional chirping of a bird in the distance or the sound of tree branches dancing in the wind. He wanted to whistle, patting himself on the back for a successful evasion, but it was temporary.

"Little boy? Little boy, where are you?" The voice was followed by giggles.

"Shit." Zach was trapped. The seniors had been waiting for him the entire time. If he just kept quiet, maybe they wouldn't find him. He looked around for any bush or tree close by he could hide behind, but the trail was as clean as a paved road from kids using the path ever since the school had been built. He could run either left or right into the more secluded area, but he would be found. Two of the three aggressors were athletes at the school. Vern was just given a full scholarship to a Division I university, just because he could throw a baseball ninety-five miles an hour.

"Come out, come out wherever you are." The catcalls were getting closer. Footsteps came towards him from the trail, as well as to the sides.

"LEAVE ME ALONE!" Zach didn't want to beg or plead. The fifteen-year-old in him did that quite willingly, even though his brain fought against it.

"Nope. Tell your daddy to leave us alone, and we'll do the same. Until then, you know the rules." To the right, Peter Saunders approached. He was overly broad for a high schooler. Diabetes and a heart attack were in his future, but at eighteen, he was built like a brick shit house.

"SURPRISE!" Fred screamed. He stood on the edge of the trail.

Fred was the weakest of the bunch but the most sadistic. His parents indulged him with money and pumped him full of aristocratic beliefs that he was above the law. He was willing to do the most harm, but only if his two companions were there to back him up.

Zach ran towards him anyway, but before he got far, something hit him in the back of the head. One of the boys had caught up with him, landing a massive fist against the skull of the freshman boy. As he crumpled to the ground, Zach heard the laughter of the bullies who refused to stop. Everything went black.

CHAPTER TWO

Time seemed to tick by slower with each passing day. Karl Auerbach, who recently celebrated his eightieth birthday, knew his life was on the final leg of its journey. Memories seemed to be more prominent now as if every past event wanted that last moment to be remembered before the light went out for good. Karl would rather avoid these moments, but his memory was too damn clear, though his body was failing. Frequent naps seemed to happen whether he desired them or not. It was then that his past haunted him, following him like the Boogeyman. His enemy was all too real, however.

"Karl. Karl. Wake up. It's almost five o'clock, and Zachariah still hasn't come home." A withered hand shook her husband's shoulder, waking him from his nap. Shirley had looked outside to find it dark, realizing that her grandson should have been home at least an hour ago. She had come from a traditional Catholic family, always looking to the husband to take care of uncomfortable moments. This was one of those times.

Karl looked around, allowing his eyes to adjust to the light. Many chilly fall afternoons resulted in a nap, followed by a family dinner. Bedtimes tended to be quite random. Some days he had

15

no problems falling asleep while other days he was kept awake by the dread of dreams he had no desire to have. This nap had brought him back to his childhood, where he saw the same faces wearing the sad masks of death. It should have comforted him that while those people faced death, they were freed from the memories. Only death would release him now.

"Alright, alright. I'll go out and drive around a bit. You give Steven a call and have him send someone out to look for him." Karl had no sooner finished lifting himself off the chair when the front door opened and slammed shut. Loud footsteps were heard running up the stairs and into a bathroom.

"Damn it." Karl walked towards the base of the steps and looked up. He and his wife had lived up on the second floor most of their lives. It was there he and Shirley had made love on their wedding night. Only time forced them both to restructure their living conditions. Now his son and grandson lived upstairs while the two elderly people were stuck sleeping in a converted den. Karl was pleased as punch to have Steven and Zachariah residing under the same roof. It was Father Time that pissed him off.

Slowly, Karl pulled himself up to the second floor. It may have been only a minute to get to the top step, but it felt like forever with his knees. He could hear the water running in the sink and went to the bathroom. His generation always respected space and privacy, but to hell with that; his grandson was his business. With a shaking hand, he knocked.

"Zachariah, is everything alright?" Karl said. He could hide his Central European accent except when calling out the boys' names. He knocked for a second time.

"I'm ok, Zayde. Just stayed after school." The boy only called him his Yiddish title when he was either in trouble or needed something. It wasn't cool for a high school boy to call his grandfather a weird sounding Jewish nickname. Lately, it was "Gramps." Sometimes, when feeling particularly brave, he'd even address him as "Karl." But that would get him "the look," the one that said this shit must be cut.

"Clean up then and come downstairs. Your Bubbe is worried sick. I'm sure seeing you will reassure her." He knew his grandson was lying. Those bastards got to him again. But he needed to act like he trusted Zachariah. He never wanted the boy to feel weak. Instead, once the child was in bed, Karl would have a discussion with his own son. Though his age was advanced, Karl knew Steven could handle things. The only problem was that that was what got his grandson in trouble in the first place.

Dinner was set and ready by the time the teenager came down the steps. He had tried to hide any sign of injury by putting on a sweat-shirt, hood pulled over his head. He knew his grandmother would make him take it off, as it was not polite to be at the dinner table with a hat on. He had to try and hope they felt bad enough to let him leave it on. They might be old, but they knew what was going on at school.

"Take it off, mister," Shirley said before her grandson even stepped into the dining room. It wasn't too fancy a dinner that particular evening, just some Reubens with Israeli salad, but that wasn't the point. It was the fact that the dinner table was the place to respect your family and share about your day, and that was what Shirley wanted.

Zachariah pulled the hood off his head, not even attempting to argue. If his grandparents didn't find out now, they would when his father got home. Maybe by doing this, he could lessen the shock. He couldn't have his dad overreacting and going to the school to complain because it would get back to the other boys and keep this cycle going. His right eye was swollen, and there was a welt on the side of his head, by his temple. A cut went from his ear to his chin, the likely result of a dragged fist with a worn class ring.

"Oh my." Shirley put her hands over her mouth. The beatings were becoming increasingly more violent. It had started with a black eye or bruising, but the boys were ramping up their attacks. It would only be a matter of time before her grandson was hospitalized. And then what?

"Bubbe, stop. It's fine. We can clean that right up." Karl went to the fridge to grab some ice and wrapped a towel around it. He handed it to Zach and motioned for him to press it to his temple. It had been a brutal attack, but overreacting helped no one, neither his wife nor his grandson. He would talk to Steven once the boy had gone to bed, but at the same time he knew that his own son was both the problem and the solution. He'd heard why Zach believed this was happening, picking up on partial phone conversations.

"You gonna tell Dad?" Zach couldn't have his father march into the school. If anyone saw the cruiser pull into the parking lot, it would get back to Peter, Fred, and Vern. Then it was lights out, the party's over for him.

"Nope, you can tell him. You know what I think about those little shits. One day, a reckoning will come to them. Always does. Sometimes, it's best to wait out the storm and look for the sun to shine." Karl had lived at least three lives and was forced to look forward. He wanted to share his past with Zach, but it was too dangerous. His own son knew bits and pieces, and his wife knew a bit more than that, but the whole story, top to bottom, was his alone. Everyone else that was a part of it was dead, many years ago. Perhaps it would be best if his tale died entirely with him.

CHAPTER THREE

Steven hated working late, especially when he knew his mother expected him home for dinner. After the death of his wife, Steve and his son moved in with his parents. Steve had tried to make it work, living the same old life in the same home his wife had died in, when cancer destroyed her brain. He refused to sleep in the bed where she took her final breaths and only went into that room to grab clothes from the closet. It wasn't a shrine, like some people created, unwilling to let go for fear the memories might fade. It was just too painful to accept that everything needed to change. He had taken residence on the couch, lying to his son about a bad back, just to avoid the bedroom. But most nights, when sleep finally came, Steven could hear the moans of a woman who was no longer there. He didn't believe in ghosts or restless spirits. Instead, it was the residual memories that haunted him. He would dream of those last few days when hospice came in to care for the final moments of his wife's life. A nurse stayed throughout the day and night, standing by in case Rachel passed. It took a week to succumb to cancer but, in the process, leaving behind a lifetime of memories and echoes of her cries of pain. When he closed his eyes, all he could see was the strange stare she would give him once her speech no longer worked.

Tonight he'd known almost immediately that something was wrong with his son. Steve had called to check in with his mom, just like he always did when he had to stay a bit later than usual. Tonight, there was a sick call that required him to stay at work until just before midnight.

"Make sure you have a nice long discussion with Zachariah when you see him. He has something he'd like to share with you," Shirley had informed her son.

What this indicated was that Zach had had another altercation at school. This wasn't the first time he'd received these kinds of messages. In fact, they were becoming frequent occurrences. Maybe things were picking up because this would be the last year any of those boys could hurt his son. All three would be going on to college, becoming deviants in whatever town they chose to live in. His son was the target only because Zach was the child of the Chief of the Kingston Police Department. Transferring here wasn't merely to get away from the past but to get a fresh start. Now, it seemed, the beginning wasn't a good one for either of them.

Steven had spent his adult life working as a cop, many years in some of the rougher places in Rhode Island. For several of those, he roamed the streets of Providence with partners who quickly realized the big city wasn't for them. He liked feeling like he made a difference, and though it was not easy, it was rewarding. After his wife passed, his mind wandered more, with morbid curiosity about what would happen if he was injured on duty, or worse. His son needed to be his first and only priority. The problem was his role as a chief in a new town, one where he was forced to discipline angry young males, had only made things much worse for Zach.

CHAPTER FOUR

The young girl had no desire to be stuck in this house any longer than she already had been. Gretchen had already spent the entire afternoon tidying up and spending "quality" time with her grandfather. That's how allowances were earned, and though her parents told her how good it would be to get to know Grandpa, it was not as easy a task as it was made out to be.

George Clement sat at the kitchen table, drinking his black coffee and smoking unfiltered cigarettes. Sometimes, depending on the time of day, the drink of choice would switch to a brandy. If his family thought he was ornery under normal circumstances, just wait until he had a few glasses of his favorite liquor on the rocks. George liked the way it felt, giving him that freedom to say whatever came into his head. Most of the time, they were insults thrown at his daughter and knucklehead son-in-law. He tried to avoid being too harsh to his only grandchild, though that wasn't how he was with his own children. Unfortunately, his only son had long since moved out west to separate from his father. That was fine with George.

Each room in the home had its own distinct smells, none of them pleasant. Gretchen would always tidy up the kitchen and the living room, and clean the bathroom, even though her grandfather no longer inspected them as he once had. Gretchen had been forced to scrub until her knees bled. Once she had completed her task, Grandpa would check the entire area, wearing a white glove to test for stains. If he was unhappy for any reason at all, he'd fill the bucket back up with the necessary items and force his granddaughter to do it all over again.

Gretchen was much too bold to put up with that anymore, even if she was scared of him. She had just turned fifteen, a pretty young girl with long, blonde hair that she sometimes put in ponytails—though recently she'd realized that most high school girls might not do that. Her grandfather liked her to appear young and innocent. The child's growing changes made him feel old and weak. The older she got was an indication that he was also getting older, something she noticed bothered him. She'd be forced to listen to his stories of living in Germany before the war and what life was like as a young boy in Munich. Gretchen knew he left when things got bad and that he refused to go back, even to see it one last time. It still made her uncomfortable because while he enjoyed telling stories, he declined to answer questions. She wanted to know much more than George Clement was willing to share.

"Who were your parents, Grandfather? I'm

working on an ancestry project for history class," Gretchen asked, knowing the response.

"Why do you wish to know about them? They both passed many years before you were born. Their names won't help your studies." George would change the subject before any prodding continued. There wasn't a need to dredge up the past. He might demand she clean something or just send her back home.

Gretchen once tried to push a bit too much, not accepting his lack of answers. She followed him, prodding, reaching out for more.

"Grandfather, please tell me. Why won't you share? Every time I ask, you refuse to say anything. If you'd just . . ."

George Clement spun around on his heels faster than he had moved in many years. His eyes looked devoid of emotion yet beneath them, pockets of tears were forming.

"You need not be a nosy girl. I have no desire to dredge up the past. If you cannot accept that, you'll not be allowed back here. I will not have you constantly beg for me to discuss something I refuse to talk about. Now leave!" He pointed towards the door, not looking her in the eyes.

Gretchen told her mother, who affirmed that she too had had this conversation with him at one point. It was fruitless to poke and prod.

She mentioned this to a teacher at school, who gave her an article he found on the internet.

"Maybe the reason he doesn't share is it's too painful. Many people suffered in Germany and all over Europe. What do you really know about his religion and family?" the teacher asked her.

Gretchen knew so little. Her family wasn't religious in the least, but perhaps there was a reason for it. Her grandfather had forbidden having any religious items in his home. Until she went with a friend, she had never stepped foot into a house of worship.

"A Jew in Germany during the war was not something I'd want to be. He said he came to America before the war. But what about family and friends? Sometimes a loss can be so painful that talking about it only dredges up memories best buried forever. Give him some space. Even if he never decides to share, he might have things hidden that could answer your questions." The teacher was correct. He had listened to enough survivors to know that while they were willing to share stories, many wanted to avoid it.

That made so much sense to Gretchen. She had never thought that her family had Jewish heritage. Once, she'd heard a Holocaust survivor speak and wondered how that man could tell his tale over and over. She'd wait until her grandfather was ready to talk to her. There was no need to make him relive his past.

CHAPTER FIVE

The holiday ended without incident. Zach was able to talk his father down from approaching the school administration in response to the recent attack. He hated all three boys, of that he was sure. However, it seemed as though any discussion by his father carried further retribution.

It hadn't always been like this. Zach's first few weeks at Kingston went without much of a hitch. He didn't stand out or cause a problem. He never got involved in the drug or sexting scene that had swept through the halls. And the bullies, his bullies, never even knew of his existence. Zach tried not to blame his father, knowing the man was just doing the job the city paid him to do. Part of him wished that his dad could have waited one year to make an impact, just long enough for the three boys to graduate.

"How could I live with myself by not teaching them a lesson?" Steve had said to his son, on the way home from grabbing Chinese food.

That was the first time Steven went into Kingston. It was not as an officer but as a concerned parent of a teenage boy. The incident itself wasn't as bad, especially in comparison to what it had become. At least it wasn't physical; they'd hurled racial slurs at his kid.

Officer Auerbach's first real introduction to the three occurred with a schoolwide assembly in response to the desecration of stones in the graveyard, which drew the ire of Peter, Vern, and Fred, clearly the focus of the reprimand. Most teens would mope, piss and moan but move on, not wishing to perhaps hurt their chances of playing sports. But these boys were different, very different. They went back to the cemetery, spray-painting swastikas on Jewish stones. Steve wanted to put up cameras to catch them in the act, but this upset his own people, who had been through so much at the hands of a Germany that no longer existed. And many wealthy Jewish community leaders were equally as angry, but not enough to take the necessary steps.

"I'm not happy with the situation, either," a well-known Jewish businessman said when discussions with local leaders went nowhere.

"Then, let's do something about it. If not to right a wrong, then to teach a lesson. Our people have been through enough without some assholes pulling a prank like that," Steven said.

"Most of the time, I'd agree with you. But the Ripkens are powerful. If I stand up against them, my time in Kingston comes to an end. No one will shop here. Damn, Steve, I'm retiring in a few years, and I plan to hand this place to my kids. It's not worth the risk over defacing property with a symbol."

Everyone knew it was more than that, but Steven didn't wish to push it further. His father was a survivor and recognized the importance of the lesson that young adults needed. But even Karl attempted to talk his son into backing off.

"Sometimes, your heart does more thinking than your head," Karl said. "I understand what you are looking to do, but it will only create problems. You're dealing with people who don't know the importance of history, except their own."

"But Dad, we shouldn't have to always go through this. How many Hitler salutes or bent crosses do we Jews have to see before it's too much?" Steven was angry. He hated having these discussions of such a sensitive nature.

"We? So, it hurts your sensibility as a Jew to see stupid teens acting as teens do? Son, I lived it. I was there when it was much more than a childish prank or some backwoods hillbilly posting comments on the internet."

Steven didn't listen to the community or his father. He attempted to set up a meeting with Mr. Alfred Ripken II, owner of the largest scrap metal plant on the East Coast, but ran into lawyers. No one took any ownership of the damage though the Ripken foundation donated money to the community to clean up and restore the gravestones, as well as sent a sizable check to the local synagogue. That didn't end the situation. In fact, the mere mention of the incident to Fred's father sent the boy into a rage.

"Stupid Jew. Go back to Israel." Fred's verbal assaults on Steven's boy hit the mark. Steven wasn't told of the incident until weeks later when the mention of the large donation came up in dinner conversation. He drove to the school the following morning, demanding a meeting with the principal. He received the same ineptness that he'd run into again and again.

"What would you like me to do, sir?" Principal Wendy Collins said, exasperated after way too many emails and phone calls from Steven that preceded this interaction.

"I want you to punish them. That's not too much to ask, is it?" Steven was hoping this would be an easy fix, but it seemed as though it wasn't going in that direction.

"For what, exactly?" Collins knew the man was correct, and she so badly wanted to come down on those arrogant bastards. But she was on a lifeboat with no oars. No one on the school board would support her.

"It's a God-damned hate crime. What Freddy Ripken said was hate speech." Steven could feel his anger boiling.

"Which the family paid for with significant contributions. How can I punish the child who has already been punished once before? How is that fair?"

"You and I both know that Daddy wrote a check and wiped his hands of the incident. What does this teach the boy about respect? Do you know how often we deal with those kids once they leave here?" Steven wished to avoid using the cop card to get somewhere. All too often, kids like Fred found themselves in trouble with the law, especially when Mom or Dad could no longer buy people off.

"That's good, then. You get your pound of flesh when Freddy leaves here. If we both know that it's just a matter of time, wait, and exact true justice." Collins stepped from behind her desk and closed her office door.

"Listen, you and I both know the boy is an asshole. His two buddies are just as bad. Not a redeemable quality amongst the three. But please understand my position. For four years, I've dealt with these boys. I fully support the law coming down on them, but my hands are tied. As soon as I send out a suspension slip to the Ripken residence, I'll have several costly lawyers here to expunge any record of the incident. And if I can indeed break past the men in suits, I will have a school board bought and paid for by Ripken money to work against." The principal looked like a weight was lifted off her shoulders by the mere admission of the issues she had dealt with.

"So, we just sit by as my son gets terrorized? I understand the position you're in, but you have to understand mine. I need to protect my child," Steve said.

"And I will do the best I can to assure that happens. We can work together to get these yahoos out of here, and then you and the legal system can nail them. Until then, please trust me. Let me find ways to make sure your son is safe." Collins assured him and tried to stay true to her word. She had guidance transfer Zach into classes that Fred Ripken, Vern Watts, or Peter Saunders weren't in and safe spaces for him to go. The lunchroom had other faculty on duty, and teachers stood outside their doors during passing time. That didn't change much. She couldn't truly protect the child any more than his father could outside of the school walls. Kingston High School was a dangerous place for a young man who could never run far enough to avoid his enemies. And the changes wouldn't go unnoticed, especially by the three very angry teens.

CHAPTER SIX

Three boys sat in the sunroom, passing around a joint to help keep them subdued. Mr. Ripken had read them the riot act, letting each one know the ramifications of their actions, especially this close to going to college.

"You stupid fuckers have no idea how much this cost me. And for what? To piss off a cop." The large man's voice resonated throughout the entire first floor. He didn't care who heard him, whether it was the help or the Jehovah's Witness at the door, attempting to save their souls with a random and unwanted visit.

"Come on, Dad. It was harmless fun," Fred said, who had a way of minimizing any incident. He did this often whenever trouble was close by. Stealing a car wasn't his fault; he was playing a prank on a friend by moving his car across town. Not showing up to practice or coming to a game high was merely a misunderstanding. Nothing was his fault.

"We didn't mean to cause any problems. Honest, sir," Peter said. He was too stupid to realize that perhaps he should keep his mouth shut.

"Problems? Want to know what the lawyers were saying? Hate crime. You idiots committed a hate crime. You're lucky I have pull in this town. Some of the most prominent people in this town are Jews. And you feel the need to desecrate their resting places with Nazi symbols. Then you heckled the kid for being a Jew. Jesus Christ, Fred. You are better than this. You're a Ripken." Fred Senior was none too pleased. The only reason the other boys got out of any jams was because of his wallet.

"They're all too sensitive. That shit happened years ago. No one cares anymore. I don't even think they teach that shit in school anymore." Peter refused to take the hint that it was better to say nothing.

"How about this? Next time you pull a prank like this, you let your own daddy foot the bill. Think they could do that? If it wasn't for me, your dumb ass would be in some alternative school already. You've got the best lawyers in Rhode Island free of charge because of my acts of kindness. Pull this shit again, gravy train stops, and you two get off. Neither of you is my responsibility," Big Fred said.

"Sir, don't listen to Pete. Thank you for doing that for us. I'll pay you back. . . ." Vern tried to play a peacemaker. It wasn't successful.

"When, Vern? When will you write me a check? When you make the majors? Big draft bonus? You don't keep your nose clean and your grades above a D, you'll have no shot at sniffing a coed slow pitch softball field, much less a major league one."

Once Fred Senior was done, he pulled his son into another room and continued to chew his ass. It was loud enough for the others to hear yet not enough to make out what was said. The discussion about finding new friends wasn't uncommon, but all that did was overlook the more significant problem of his own son's involvement. He had no idea his own child was the mastermind behind most plans.

Later, when alone, the boys discussed the issue at hand. They weren't talking about payoffs, as this wasn't the first time it had happened. Instead, the conversation came down to the father and son who they believed had created this hostile environment for them.

"Maybe we just leave the kid alone. It's not his fault his dad's a douchebag." Vern tended to take the path of least resistance. He had no desire for this problem to escalate more than it had. Out of the three of them, he had the most to lose. His family was not wealthy in comparison to his friends. His father worked the same mill jobs his grandfather did. There was never a week when a paycheck didn't arrive on time, but it wasn't something a person could retire on. In fact, Vern would be the first Watts family member to get an education after high school, and most had never even made it through the 8th grade. While the other two friends had white privilege written all over their faces, Vern struggled with skin color. It wasn't many years ago that Pete Saunders hurled insensitive racial comments at him. The difference was that he fell into line instead of fighting back. He was the background player in this group of three for sure, but that didn't make him any less culpable.

"Leave him alone? What the fuck, dude? We got in trouble because of them, and you want to let them win?" Peter said, not accepting responsibility.

"Come on, Vern. Don't be a pussy. We got caught. Shame on us. Next time, we don't get caught." Fred handed the joint to his friend, who took a long drag. "But there's no way I'm letting this one go. When we get hit, what do we do?"

"Hit harder," Pete yelled, slamming back a beer and crushing the can down against his massive thigh.

"Fuck right, we do. We're playing a game of chess, and our enemies made a good move. Now it's our turn." Fred remained unfazed. His family had too much power and money to worry about the short game. The end result was that he would win this battle. There was no concern about how this would affect the lives of his friends.

"Read you loud and clear. But I can't lose this scholarship. If I don't have it, I can wave bye-bye to LSU or Division I baseball. Man, I love you like brothers, but I don't have anything to fall back on." Vern thought with his head and not his emotion, more so as he approached graduation.

"You won't have to worry about that. I've got it covered. Our mistake was bringing the fight to the community. I should have realized the reaction that Nazi shit Peter drew would get." Fred was not concerned with how inappropriate the symbols were. It was more about how people viewed it.

"Screw off, Fred," Pete said, tossing a throw pillow at his friend. "Those fuckin' Jews have run this country far too long."

"Come on, stop that," Vern said. "Turn off those conspiracy documentaries and stop trolling the 'net. That shit belongs in 1945."

"My dad says . . ." Pete started in again, about his beliefs in race wars and white power. He avoided Klan talk not only because of Vern but also because his ideas had changed with the times. His focus was no longer what he saw as the violent, uneducated black community. Now it was the immigrants and foreigners coming into the country to take jobs, rape women, and steal money from the hard-working white man. The beer and pot helped the other two boys listen to Pete ramble on without genuinely caring what was being said.

"From now on, we keep our focus on the boy. We can't go into town, causing problems. Local law enforcement will be a pain in the ass for us if we do." Fred had thought about this. "If we keep it in school, they'll be no problem. My dad has enough pull with the school board, and Principal Collins isn't protecting the cop's kid over us. She knows where her bread is buttered. His dad can come in all day long, but if it's a school issue, the school alone will have to handle it."

Though Vern wasn't entirely on board, he agreed. He'd do what his friend asked. It wasn't the first time that the young pitcher would do what was asked of him, but those decisions were coming to an abrupt end.

CHAPTER SEVEN

Karl sat in his recliner, listening to the most recent issues at school. He understood his son was venting, not really looking for concrete answers to the problems currently facing Zach. The reality was that nothing would stop the attacks from happening. It was beyond the help of an administrator or school resource officer. The money that flowed from the hands of one of the parents was too much, and the pockets too deep to make a dent. His worry was that at some point, someone involved would snap, whether it was Zach or one of the boys. Once that line had been crossed, there would be no going back. It was at this moment that he decided that he did indeed need to share his tale with his grandson, one Karl had kept bottled up and hidden deep within the recesses of his mind.

It was a story his own wife and child knew little of. They had heard pieces of it, the parts Karl felt were important enough to share. He had met his wife after 1945, moving from a war-ravaged Europe to the United States in hopes of a fresh start and a bright future. Like other immigrants from places such as Poland, Austria, and former Czechoslovakia, Karl came into New York Harbor, spending several days at Ellis

Island before being released into a very new and scary city. He knew no one because all those he had once known were dead. His entire family was killed. His extended family was murdered. The friends he made during the war: dead. His belongings were in others' hands, stolen both during and after the war. All Karl had to his name when first entering New York from the Island of Hope was the clothes on his back, a small sack thrown across his shoulder, and a wooden box, 7 inches by 5 inches by 14 inches. It was checked when he first got on the boat in Italy, almost stolen by a younger gentleman who regretted the decision, and checked finally upon entering the United States. Each time, he was viewed with the tiniest bit of distrust. That didn't stop him from telling anyone who asked that they were the only items he had left from his time in Germany. However, that was not the truth. The box, and its contents, were to be watched closely at all times. It could not fall into the wrong hands.

Karl Auerbach met Shirley Moore while working at a 2nd Avenue deli. He was given a job, immediately fitting in with the Jewish culture in America and fully embracing every aspect of Yiddish life. He had explained parts of his story to the owners, much like he explained parts with everyone. Karl was captured in Poland as an active resistor to the Nazi scourge. He had been in Buchenwald camp and forced to do jobs no normal man desired to do, even if it meant saving lives. But secrets were kept by him, even from the rabbi of the synagogue he attended. Throughout the courting process, Karl discussed the war years but in generalized terms. His wife might have viewed it as something too painful to talk about: the dead bodies, the smells, the sounds of screams in the night.

The next time he was alone with Zachariah, everything would be on the table, including the war and the wooden box locked away in the basement. His only hope was that valuable lessons could be taken from it. Nothing good came from retribution and vengeance. A haunted past followed you until you died, if not beyond.

CHAPTER EIGHT

Life was better during the spring sports season. Vern Watts and Peter Saunders were both on the varsity baseball team, though Peter was there only due to his friendship with Vern, who was the real standout. At every game there were significant league scouts, talking into phones and jotting down notes. In the past few months, the words "draft pick" and "potential first-rounder" flowed in the articles of the local sportswriters. He was the prototypical five-tool athlete, harnessing the skills of speed hitting and defense, and teams were willing to gamble on him. That meant Vern had to be on his best behavior, though he still gave glares and shoulder bumps in the hall when he encountered Zachariah Auerbach.

The three boys had been called into Principal Collins's office and read the riot act several times since the incident at the graveyard. They had made it their mission to find ways to pick on Zach without getting his father involved. The most recent one was a bullying session that went just too far, with Peter punching the young Jewish boy in the stomach. Any more targeted attacks on the young Auerbach boy would cause the immediate suspension of the two baseball players. The third boy, Alfred Ripken, would receive no such warning because he wasn't the focus of the complaint. All three boys knew that was an untruthful statement. The chief of police might not care who Alfred's parents were, but the school sure did. Even if it meant punishing his two friends, the boy born with the silver spoon in his mouth would slide on by, as long as he didn't do anything terrible.

"Just leave him alone. He's not worth your time," Principal Collins said, attempting to smooth things over. "In a few months, you'll be gone and doing greater things than this. Why stain your reputations by going after this kid? Besides, it's not his fault his father is coming after you." She refused to place personal blame on them at all in fear of Fred Senior.

"You have bright futures in front of you. Do you want to go through life with a record? Now that you're all eighteen, your parents can't prevent the Kingston police from pressing charges and making your lives hell. I can, however, assist you now by begging you to be on your best behavior until graduation."

Vern could see Fred sitting back, his feet kicked up on the edge of the principal's desk, and understood his cocky attitude. His friend had nothing to lose here. Even if they kicked the ever-living piss out of the freshman, only two of them would get into trouble. The funny part of that was Vern accepted it. That was the nature of the way things worked. If it was between his future and Fred's, you could bet your bottom dollar that Mr. Alfred Ripken II, multi-millionaire, would assure his son's reputation was intact and clean, regardless of who fell on the sword. And it was that attitude that had bailed all three boys out on more than one occasion. If it was just Pete and Vern, their gooses would have been cooked years ago.

"What if we keep doin' what we've been doin'? What's gonna really happen?" Pete used to be the silent one, avoiding confrontation with adults. Since he became close friends with the others, he puffed his chest out more, willing to test limits.

"Well, Mr. Saunders, you can kiss baseball goodbye; I can tell you that. I know football is your wheelhouse, but your friend here relies on the bat and ball. The thing is this, you three don't understand the dangerous waters you're wading in. With a click of the fingers, Mr. Ripken will be over here toot sweet with a lawyer to bail you out. That's going to end, though, you know that. One day, Daddy won't be able to come to your rescue. And think about this very carefully, all of you. A name is forced on us, but a reputation is built. Just because you have money backing you don't mean the court of public opinion backs you as well. Your names will be run through the mud, taken up by the media and hounds of justice. Then what are you going to do? Parents can't hide your names, and any time you apply for a job or go for a bank loan, a simple online search will reveal your crimes in the court of public opinion." Principal Collins leaned forward over her desk to stare at the boys. "Does that answer your question, gentlemen? So cut the shit and fly right. I promise you that things will go smoother if you don't cause any more trouble. Now get out of my office."

The boys waited until they were out of earshot before talking about what had just occurred. For now, they needed to be on their best behavior. Vern needed a sharp end to the season so he could get the hell out of Rhode Island and into minor league camp. And the other two had to make sure they kept their noses clean. As long as Zach Auerbach left them alone, maybe they'd leave him alone . . . maybe.

CHAPTER NINE

The next few weeks were some of the best that Zach had in the Rhode Island school system. The attacks were no longer happening. Sure, he still got the looks if he glanced at the back of the classroom, but even those were minimal. Would he ever become friends with any of those guys? Not a chance. However, there was the small glimmer of hope that an unpeaceful alliance could be formed just to make it through the last part of the school year. They would graduate and move on to berate and bully other people, but they wouldn't have to worry about little old Zachariah and his cop dad from a small town in the smallest state in the union. Any decision those boys made could now follow them to college. Zach wasn't one hundred percent certain any of them understood that, but even if it was explained to them, it wouldn't matter in the least.

Another development made going to school that much easier. Her name was Gretchen Clement. They were just friends at the moment, but it was a friendship he hoped would quickly blossom into more. She had transferred in at the start of the year as well, a sophomore who came from Scranton, Pennsylvania, with her parents. She was shorter than Zach, standing about 5'2", with long, blonde hair and crystal blue eyes. It was purely by chance that they talked at first, being put in the same large group to work on a project for history class. It wasn't until recently that more was said between the two. Mr. Martin, their U.S. History teacher, allowed the students to create their own small groups to do a project explaining the short- and long-term effects of the conferences at Tehran, Yalta, and Potsdam.

It was a shock when Gretchen raised her hand and informed Mr. Martin that she wanted to work with Zach Auerbach. He was more than excited, turning around to look at her, just to make sure that he heard it correctly. He received a smile, followed by blushed cheeks. His mind wandered as to why this girl had any interest in working with him. He could assume, reasonably correctly, that she knew he'd do the work. He loved history and had shared his grandfather's basic story of survival in the camps on more than one occasion.

Once Mr. Martin was done explaining things, he gave them the rest of the class to review the project, sharing the rubric and scoring guide on their school accounts. Zach stood up and walked to the back of the room, where Gretchen was waiting for him. He was nervous; his hands were sweaty, making it hard to hold a laptop. What if he dropped it right in front of her? What if his breath smelled terrible? Questions rolled in his head, and before he knew it, he was sitting down next to her. The talk was light, nothing too intense for the moment. He read the document aloud while she took down some brief notes of ideas on how to approach the project. To be honest, it made no difference what she said. If she decided on doing something, no matter how outlandish or off base it was, she was going to get her way. She was smart, though. Zach could see that from the way she jotted things down regarding how to attack this project and cover everything appropriately.

"Do you have a cell phone?" Gretchen spoke softly. She held out her hand. "I can put my number in, and you can text me with any ideas. Might be easier that way." She smiled, refusing to look up in case he had no interest. She felt something in her hand, which allowed her to relax. She wasn't sure where this was going, but Gretchen knew the boy was cute and very nice and a loner like her.

After the class was over, Zach sat by his locker, staring at the newest number on his phone. It wasn't the first girl's number on his phone. He had some friends' names from his old school. He also kept his mother's number on his phone. He wouldn't get rid of that, even though he couldn't call it again. On the walk home, later in the day, he took his phone out, still staring at Gretchen's name. Bravery wasn't his strong suit, but something said that he should initiate conversation. Hitting the text button next to her name, he typed, "Thanks for wanting to work with me" and sent it off. Within moments, he received one back. Just a simple, "No problem," but the face with a wink spoke volumes.

The evening passed with texts, back and forth, discussing the project while at the same time flirting as two young adults do who have no experience with the opposite sex. Zach received tons of affirmation to any joke he sent, with a simple "hahaha" or "lol." Was she really laughing out loud on the other end? He wasn't concerned with that, only that she was enjoying herself. By the end of the evening, only a mere outline of the activity was actually planned. Most of the night was talking about and to one another. The messages didn't end there. Gretchen sent one in the morning, wishing him a good day and several more texts throughout the school day.

Throughout the day, Zach and Gretchen could be seen walking the halls, talking about U.S. History. They weren't fooling anyone, including the three boys who always took a very active interest in everything Zachariah Auerbach did.

CHAPTER TEN

Up until that moment, Zach never once thought about retribution towards Vern, Peter, and Fred. He and his dad had many discussions about bullies and how to stand up to them. Frequently, showing bravery in the face of fear did the trick. His father believed calling someone out on their poor behavior stopped said behavior. His father should have known better, considering the trouble the boys had been in with the police, even if that had been buried by wealthy parents and fancy lawyers. Drunk driving? Buried. Breaking and Entering? Buried. Disorderly conduct? Buried. Desecration of gravestones? Buried.

It never mattered about Zach's own well-being. He was a fight or flight sort of guy, and the fleeing seemed to fit him to a tee. One-on-one, he had little chance of doing much damage. On a good day, Zach might be able to beat Fred, but the ramifications would be immense. Not only would he have to deal with the two more intimidating and much scarier individuals but also with the school, who would surely come down on him for retaliation. And once his father caught wind of an issue, things would only get worse, much worse. Whenever his father pushed, the boys pushed back.

The cause for concern was not for his own safety, but only when others were dragged into it. He was angry when the guys made jokes about his zayde and his Jewish heritage. After responding to a racial statement with an outburst, Zach was sent to the office and reprimanded for inappropriate language. All the while, the others sat in the back and laughed, knowing they had goaded him into it. This incident on a Friday before a long weekend pushed him harder than he had been in a long time. He and Gretchen had been talking for weeks now, and though they hadn't been official, most knew they saw one another. There was a lot of giggling, handholding, and messaging. Zach had been a bit nervous about moving forward with a kiss, but he wanted to.

"Check this out." Gretchen sent a snapshot of a text she had received. She was well aware of the behavior of those who bullied Zach and every other kid in the school. No one could ever say, "That's too bad what happened to that poor boy. Those three were always so kind and innocent. If I'd only seen warning signs."

"Hey, cutie just wanted to say hi. I was wondering if you had plans this weekend? If you don't, my boys and I are having a party. You're invited. -Fred"

Zach bit his bottom lip, not realizing he had drawn blood. He could feel the anger welling up in him, causing a hot flash across his entire body.

"YIKES!!! What are you going to do?" Zach was pissed but couldn't show it. He had to remain calm.

"I'm going. :)" Gretchen texted back.

"Oh, ok, cool." Zach was brokenhearted. It was only a matter of time before she moved on anyway. He always thought she was out of his league.

"Dummy. Of course, I'm not going. How about we do something instead?" Gretchen sent it almost immediately after, not wanting her new friend to have a moment of doubt.

Zach was taken aback. His stomach had dropped and raised in a matter of moments. He felt like he had clicked to the top of a roller coaster before dropping. He was glad his texts didn't show his excitement but he was over the moon.

"Sure. We can do that. I'll call you later," Zach said. He rushed off, beyond happy with his life in this new school. A few hours later, he received another text, this one less positive.

"Just received this. What do I do? -G"

"Bitch, how dare you don't answer me. I ask, and you say yes unless you're with that Jew-Bastard. Don't fuck with me because I fuck back harder. -Fred"

Zach called her, and they talked for what seemed like hours. He tried to comfort her, tell her everything would be fine. But he knew that wasn't true. If past experience meant anything, Fred would come back with a vengeance, and unlike Zach, Gretchen had no recourse. She spent most of her time with an elderly grandfather, who, by all indications, didn't know the time of day. Zach felt like he was her only lifeline and her knight in shining armor. Something had to be done.

CHAPTER ELEVEN

Karl could see his grandson was steaming mad as soon as he laid eyes on him. Something was wrong. This was different.

"How was your day, kiddo?" Karl asked, hoping Zach would share. Like always, things were "fine," no more, no less. It wasn't believable.

"Spill the beans, mister. I can tell something's going on with you." Karl went into the kitchen, motioning his grandson to join him. He grabbed a beer from the fridge, something he didn't often do, and sat at the table, folding a paper towel to put under his beer. The last thing he needed was Shirley bitching about water stains.

"It's nothing, really," Zach said, though he followed his grandfather into the kitchen and sat next to him. Just a slight prodding would do the trick.

"Nothing? Come on. I can read you like a book." Karl passed his beer to his grandson to open it, even though he still had some strength left in his body, which had been slowly breaking down due to age and wear.

"It's those guys at school. Until today, they've just targeted me. I know you have told me to turn the other cheek, Zayde, but this time it's not about me. See, I've been talking to this girl . . ."

Zach blushed, knowing that once it was out, the taunting and the jokes would follow. His grandfather's body might have been old, but his mind was fresh and sharp as ever.

"A girl? Who else knows? Have you told your father? What's her name?" Karl had so many questions, never thinking his grandson would have girl troubles. This could save him the discussion he felt he needed to have. He'd rather bury that past with himself. Even if, upon his death, his family broke the lock to *that* part of the basement, they'd find no more than a few papers, random knickknacks that meant little to most, and a wooden box, just large enough to put a pair of shoes in. Even the secret in the box was nothing to the untrained eye.

"That's not the problem, Grandpa. Not even close. Her name is Gretchen, and no one else knows about her except you. I mean the kids at school do but no one in the family. It's the fact that now Fred Ripken is harassing her. I have to do something. No one else will. My dad can be a pain in the backside, but at least he has my best interests in mind when he goes to see Principal Collins. What makes me the focus of their attacks also protects me most. Gretchen doesn't have that protection. I need to do something. If I tell the principal, she'll call in Fred and then it will get much, much worse. If they hurt her, I don't know how I'll react or what I'll do. Zayde, what should

I do?" Zach fought back the tears, not one to cry in front of his family, especially his grandfather.

The old man drank from his beer, tipping it back to get every single drop. He hadn't felt this alive in years. His only grandson came to him for help. While he couldn't provide it in any physical form, perhaps he could extoll some words of wisdom to allow Zach to cope with the current issues at hand. The last thing he wanted was for Zach to use violence to solve this problem.

"Meet me here after Bubbe goes up to bed. Your father is working tonight, so we don't need to worry about him, either," Karl said, flattening out the tablecloth with a shaking hand.

"What are we going to do?" Zach asked.

"I think it's time I told you my true story."

CHAPTER TWELVE

Night came quickly as if something was forcing things to progress. Zach waited by his bedroom door until he heard the shutting of his grandmother's down the hall. When he went into the kitchen, his grandfather was waiting for him in his pajamas, robe, and slippers, a pot of tea boiling on the stove. From the moment Zach laid eyes on Zayde, there was something out of sorts. Zayde looked to be much older than he was, as if carrying a burden that weighed down his soul. He asked a few times if things were okay, each instance met with a mere wave of the hand.

"Do not worry about me. It will be better when it's over."

When the tea was done and seeped properly, Karl handed both hot cups to Zach. He motioned to the basement door. "We'll need to go down there. That's where I'll tell my story. No one else can hear it." Karl grabbed the handle, ignored the coldness, and opened the door wide, reaching around the corner for the light switch on the wall.

"Be careful going down. Grab the handle, please." Karl stuck his right hand out, squeezed against the banister and slowly, step by step, made his way down. His grandson didn't heed the warning, with a cup of tea in both hands, but made it to the bottom just fine.

"Just around the corner, here. You'll have to help me in, though." The old man made his way down a dingy hallway, past boxes and totes of things not viewed in many decades. They walked by all of it, past the collectibles, old furniture, and boxes marked FRAGILE or DO NOT OPEN. Occasionally, he grabbed on to one for balance, but it didn't stop his advance. He stopped in front of an old coat rack, hanging from it some jackets, blankets, and a few leis from a luau party held in the '50s.

"I need you to pull that rack to the side if you could. We need to get behind it." Karl waited patiently, taking a cup of tea from his grandson so the item could be moved. Many years ago, when he was younger and stronger, Karl could do it himself. It was only the bad dreams that had stopped him from visiting this place finally. Early on, he remembered the heroics, not the pain. Acceptance of who a person was and who they became wasn't easy.

Behind the rack was a small door, like a crawl space. There was a simple latch on it, shut tight with a padlock. Karl reached into his pocket, pulled out a key, and handed it to his grandson. His hands were shaking too much, and opening it would have been quite the feat. He took the key back once the lock was opened, slid it into his housecoat, and pushed the door open.

"Zach, I'm going to need a bit of help getting in. Just steady me and make sure I don't hit my head going through. I wouldn't be able to explain that to your grandmother, and she'd have me at the hospital in no time flat." Karl made his way in through the door with little help, motioning for his grandson to follow. Using a flashlight, he led Zach into a much larger area. There was a simple table in the center of the room; on it was a candle, a glass, and a bottle of something brown that might have been whiskey many years ago.

"Put the tea on the table, shut the door, and grab some of those metal chairs out from the corner if you could." Karl barked instructions, ensuring things went the way they needed to. He waited for Zach to sit, but Karl did not. Wandering off, Karl returned minutes later with a wooden box. He placed it on the table, pulled his chair closer, and sat down.

"What I say here today must never leave this room. I am not asking but demanding. No one knows my story, not to this extent. I tell you this for a particular reason, and that is vengeance. You're angry and confused. I hear the rage in your voice. It's against your father, against your enemies, against the institution that allows the injustice to continue. You bottle it all up, always turning the other cheek. But this girl puts a new wrinkle in things. Love can make you do crazy things, things you normally wouldn't. I can't let any of that happen. I can only hope you listen to my cautionary tale of revenge and what it can do. I will tell you my past eats at me every day, and I fear that even when I pass on, it will haunt me. I do not share this for you to carry my burden but to teach you what happens when one lets emotion take hold." Karl drank a sip of tea, not noticing his hands were no longer shaking. "Do you promise not to repeat a word I say?"

Zach sat still for a moment. He had no idea what was happening, but the look on his grand-father's face was different than he'd ever seen. "Of course, Zayde. Not a word." His hand was quickly grabbed by the hands of the man across the table.

"Look into my eyes and tell me you won't ever say a word about this." Karl's eyes filled with tears.

"I will never repeat this . . . ever, ever, ever. I promise," Zach said.

"Good. You're a good boy." Karl adjusted himself in his chair. "So, I guess I'll start at the beginning. My name wasn't always Karl Auerbach." He took another sip of tea, wetting his throat just enough to speak what hadn't been spoken since the end of the war. "I was born Karl Adolf Krueger."

PART II:
THE WAR

CHAPTER ONE

The German nation had often changed course based on events in which they actively participated. In 1870, the Franco-Prussian War pitted German states, who wished to expand and create a formal country, and France, who feared expansion by these smaller kingdoms into a much larger power, into war. A year later, the nation of Germany was created with the defeat of the French, placing Kaiser Wilhelm I on the throne. Wilhelm and his chancellor, Otto von Bismarck, spent years creating alliances with countries bordering their enemy, believing the only hope for their new nation was through military expansion and might. They saw it as their destiny, their German right, to continue this path, so too by training the grandson of the Kaiser, Wilhelm II, to one day take the throne with similar ideals. At the death of Wilhelm I and a very brief stint as king by his son Kaiser Frederick, a pacifist, Wilhelm II ascended the throne as the second and last king of Germany. He continued the trend brought about by his grandfather, building up his navy in response to a growing British navy. Wilhelm II also formed alliances, defensive ones, with Austria-Hungary, one powerful empire on the verge of collapse, and the Ottoman Empire. Archduke of Austria-Hungary, Franz Ferdinand, and his wife, Sofie, were assassinated by a Serbian terrorist organization known as the Black Hand. It was the German Kaiser that pledged his full support in hopes this quick war with Serbia could bring about riches and new territory. It did not.

World War I, at the time known as the Great War, dragged countries across Europe, Asia, Africa, and North America into a four-year-long showdown as to who could hold out the longest. By 1917, close to thirty-two allied countries fought against Germany and what was left of the Austrian army. Later that year, Russia, due to poor leadership and economic disaster, pulled out after going through an abdication by the Romanovs and a full revolution led by Vladimir Lenin and the Bolsheviks, also known as the Communists. By the end of 1918, Germany had exhausted all options. After convincing Kaiser Wilhelm II to step down from power and go into exile, German military leaders signed an armistice on November 11, officially ending the fighting on the battlefield. This did not stop the political fight, however.

In early 1919, the Big Three, Woodrow Wilson of the United States, David Lloyd George of England, and Georges Clemenceau of France, arrived in Paris. The goal was to create a finalized treaty, one that would not only formally end this war but also prevent any future chaos that would wreck the world. Almost immediately, problems arose. Countries had their own agendas, pushing to incorporate as much of their own plan as possible. While the United States, and to a lesser extent, Britain, wished to punish Germany but in a way that would allow them to rebuild and avoid a communist revolution, France, who was the focus of German might, wanted the country brought to its knees. The end result was the Treaty of Versailles, 440 articles designed to punish the defeated nations and build a better future for everyone. Germany was not included in the process until they were forced to sign at the Palace of Versailles. It disabled their economy, forcing reparations of $33 billion U.S. dollars. The war destroyed the German economy. Their natural resources were taken from them in response to the damaged resources of their neighboring countries. Germany lost all overseas colonies and, with them, their ability to make the resources to sell for money. They were left unprotected, with no fortified walls, military-style weapons, or submarines or any vehicles that could be deemed part of the military. The army was reduced to 100,000 men; their job was to police the country and prevent revolutionary threats, nothing more.

The Weimar Republic, the new government of the German nation as adopted, struggled to dig itself out of the economic hole it was in. Attempts to pay back the treaty continued to yield little results due to tariffs placed on German goods. Many blamed the Allies and the men who signed the Treaty of Versailles, known as the November Criminals to revolutionary groups within Germany. Even when positive changes occurred in the mid-1920s, such as social reforms and an attempt to align cultural norms with the rest of Europe, many older Germans viewed this as selling out the strict culture and order of the German people.

One of the organizations created to question the new German order was the German Workers Party, out of Munich in the Bavarian region of the country. A young Adolf Hitler, recently out of the war, worked for the German army as an informant. He attended a meeting of the German Workers Party to report if they were a legitimate threat to the status quo of Weimar. Hitler became enraged while at this meeting and stormed out. Due to his passion, members of this organization sought Hitler out, asking him to join. He became the 55th member of the German Workers Party and, in 1920, it aligned with the German Socialist Party to become the National Socialist German Workers Party, also known as the Nazi Party. The party itself was a mere caricature of revolutionary groups at the time. Angry, downtrodden, unemployed men met to discuss changes that needed to be made to rebuild a destroyed German nation.

In 1923, Hitler and the Nazis attempted to overthrow the government in Munich by staging an armed revolt at a local beer hall. After a brief shootout, several were arrested, including Hitler. Though many journalists believed this was the end of this cartoon figure, it had the opposite effect. Hitler became more popular, using the trial to showcase his beliefs of the government, the Treaty of Versailles, the November Criminals, and the various groups that held the ethnic Germans hostage, like the Communists and Jews. He was found guilty of his crimes and sentenced to five years, a death sentence to a party that would fracture and break without Hitler, though he was to only serve nine months. In Landsberg Prison, Hitler wrote his book, *Mein Kampf*, outlining his goals of building Greater Germany and ridding it of its enemies. He left prison a hero to the German people, who looked for someone to recreate the past lost after World War I. With men like Ernst Hanfstaengl, Hitler gained popularity not just with the uneducated and unemployed masses but among the German elite and middle class.

By 1930, many German men and women looked to Adolf Hitler to save them from the internal and external threats facing their own country. Dieter and Ilse were no different.

CHAPTER TWO

Dieter Krueger was a byproduct of a world at war. Born at the turn of the century, he lived through a war that ravaged his country. There was an attempt to join the German army in 1917, but Dieter failed the physical due to a limp caused by flat feet. Instead, he stood on the sidelines while his country was embarrassed by the Allies. The post-war years were no better. Dieter married, had a son, moved from unskilled job to unskilled job, looking to make a quick dollar while overestimating his own skills. Eventually, his wife desired to start a new life without her husband or child, unable to be with someone with no future. It wasn't until 1927 when Dieter found his real purpose.

If Dieter hated anyone, it was the Communists. They single-handedly overthrew the Russian monarchy and created chaos and discontent in Eastern Europe. They had become a presence in Germany and had significant power in the Reichstag, one half of the German Parliament, along with the Reichsrat. When he heard that there was to be a Day of Awakening rally at Nuremberg, Dieter found transportation so he could attend. Here he witnessed the nationalism and pride in the German nation he had long hoped for. Brown Shirts, also known as the SA, marched in the streets, yelling their commands to cheering crowds. Hitler and other top Nazi officials spoke of the threats to Germany, including the Jews, who started the Bolshevik Revolution as part of a more massive Jewish conspiracy. To be present at such a rally, where swastika banners decorated various buildings and bright red armbands with bent crosses were worn with pride on the arms of patriots and visitors alike, Dieter realized this was something he could believe in. He cheered as Hitler spoke to the crowd and sang along as Brown Shirts belted out "Horst Wessel Lied," the official song of the party. And it was at this rally that he met his wife.

Ilse Fischer didn't remember much about the Great War. She spent her youth living the life of a socialite with her parents and grandparents on the outskirts of Leipzig. It was old money, not finances gained through hard work and dedication. It was passed down from generation to generation, at a time when working for one's money was still frowned upon. Her father was called to serve the country in 1914, but Grandfather called in a favor and, with a quick and sizeable donation, kept the entire family together. Here, Ilse learned to ride horses and read and write, never attending public school, instead learning from private tutors. The end of the war brought about pain for the entire country, and this time the social status of the family could not save them. The mark, the German currency, had stabilized directly after the war. However, unpaid reparations caused the Reichsmark to be worthless, and by 1923, a single U.S. dollar was worth over four trillion marks. Like many wealthy families who carried their status like a badge of honor, this dramatic change destroyed the lifestyles of the elites, and the Fischers were no exception. All money was lost, necessitating the sale of the large home outside Leipzig. A smaller home was purchased in Nuremberg through the sale of several expensive items sold outside of the country. The war did not completely break the Fischer family, and though Ilse no longer could live like a princess, she was able to get things most Germans could not afford.

Art, jewelry, and land outside of Germany kept its value and, in time, would allow the Fischers to regain most of their wealth. However, it caused the family, like many others, to hate the Weimar Republic. When Hitler spoke, the elite also listened. The Fischer family was no exception. Ilse agreed with most of the rhetoric though the antisemitism was new to her. Her family had many Jewish acquaintances who had contributed much to German society. Perhaps a closer look would help. She also made her way to the Day of Awakening rally to gain a better understanding of what this Herr Hitler spoke of. Not only did she come away from that day a loyal and rabid Nazi, but she also met the man she'd marry in Dieter Krueger, a hardworking and dedicated German who brought with him a two-year-old son, Hans Ulrich. A year later, on August 19th, Ilse and Dieter officially became man and wife, not only proclaiming loyalty to one another but to the German nation and its leader. The happy couple announced to their families they would be helping the process of rebuilding Germany by giving their country a healthy Aryan child. In April 1931, they gave birth to a child of their own, Karl Adolf Krueger. While both children were brought up with strong Aryan ideals, their lives branched in very different directions.

CHAPTER THREE

Living in Germany during the early 1930s as a German was like a dream. Since the end of World War I, the country had struggled to maintain any kind of power on the world stage. Their economy ebbed and flowed with the years, dropping hard after the U.S. Stock Market Crash destroyed most economies in Europe. All the while, the Nazi Party grew and grew until the 1932 election, where Hitler lost to Paul von Hindenburg for the presidency. However, the results showed the world that the party wasn't going away. Adolf Hitler gained millions of new members, and the Nazis became the largest in the Reichstag. Soon, Hitler was given the role of chancellor and used it to gain full control of the government through nefarious means, such as burning down the Reichstag building and suspending all Parliamentary control under what was known as the Enabling Act. When Hindenburg died in 1934, Hitler slid into power, never allowing another election for the presidency and never relinquishing control until his own death in 1945.

Karl Krueger didn't know much about life before the Second World War. He was born just a year before the 1932 presidential election. His entire early life was centered on the party and the only leader he'd ever known. From his earliest memories, Karl knew Adolf Hitler was someone important. On the wall, behind the kitchen table, hung a picture of Hitler, given to the family by someone famous, though at the time Karl didn't know who. In fact, he knew very little about the inner workings of politics. At night, he said his prayers, but it wasn't to God. It was for the country and to the support of his Führer. His father frequently would quiz him on his German history, demanding much of a boy so young. His first real memories were of the move to Berlin so his father could be closer to the heart of the government.

"I work for my leader and my country," Dieter would proclaim when questions of the move came to him. His family and friends lived in Nuremberg. The children had been born and gone through their early lives there, creating bonds and friendships as well. When the call came from Heinrich Himmler, head of the security services known as the SD, with the request to work for the Schutzstaffel, or the SS, Dieter and Ilse answered with gusto. It wasn't just the honor of the call but the ability to finally be part of something bigger. There was no family discussion as children were better seen and not heard.

Karl watched as people came in and packed his stuff up over two days. They rarely spoke to him, occasionally asking him whether to keep something out of storage or not. The men seemed to like his father, who would receive salutes whenever they approached him. It made him giggle to watch their hand go straight as a plank of wood and utter, "Heil Hitler," as if his father was the man himself. Even sillier was that his father would return in kind with the exact same wave and response, calling them "Heil Hitler" as well.

"Father, why do you say this?" Karl once asked, not realizing once he got into school, he'd be saying it as frequently as he'd say "hello" or "good day."

"It is to show our thanks for how fortunate we are to have him in our lives. He provides us this freedom, the food on our table, and the great German nation. It is the least we can do to honor him with this simple request." Dieter smiled at his son, but behind the smile was something more sinister. "And those that don't do what is asked of them, especially naughty little children, can be sent away to awful places where you'll be forced to do terrible things, like work with Jews. You don't want to do that, do you?"

Karl thought about the question sincerely. At that moment, he had answered "no," but that was only because he knew that was the answer his parents expected. There were no Jews close by, only the rhetoric his parents said about them. He'd be entering kindergarten this fall, his first year in school. Perhaps he would find a Jew there. But there wasn't. Not a single Jew in sight.

CHAPTER FOUR

Karl's family moved into a charming five-bedroom villa roughly twenty miles south of Berlin in the city of Potsdam. For a few weeks, Himmler and the ranking SS decided that Dieter would be best served in the position of Untersturmführer, an officer's rank in the SS, and the first of many of his steps to the top. It was apparent members of the party saw his father as a potent force, one whose loyalty to the party and the leader came above all else. His mother was quite happy with this prospect and showered her entire family with hugs and kisses, realizing the opportunity to go back to a time when having the last name Fischer meant something. His brother Hans was also ecstatic. His father's rank said that he was also something, the son of an Untersturmführer. Opportunities for his family were to be plentiful by the start of the Thousand-Year Reich. He and his mother both saw the opportunity, though Karl didn't understand why.

"Do you know what this means for us?" Hans said when his brother showed less interest than average for a five-year-old child. "This is a real chance for all of us to be more. One day, Father could be the head storm leader, a real Haupsturmführer." Titles meant little to the young child and, most likely, very little to Hans. He overheard his mother discussing this with neighbors who came to the house to introduce themselves. Over the next few weeks, many men in fancy uniforms came to visit, say their "Heil Hitler" before locking themselves in a room to have an adult conversation. Hans and Karl were not allowed to attend the meetings but were commanded to be waiting afterward to give a salute and introduce themselves as fine little German boys were expected to do.

That fall, Karl and Hans were enrolled and attended their first schooling in Potsdam. Since Karl was five, he was going into school for the first time. His older brother was almost ten, so his education would be quite different. Hans was close to the age to join the Hitler-Jugend, also known as the Hitler Youth. Since his father was becoming someone of importance within the party, his children would be as well. Karl had no desire for any of it: the talk, the uniforms, the salutes. He wanted to meet children his own age, friends he could play hide and seek with. Of course, reading and writing were essential to him. He loved it when his mother read to him, but lately, the books were miserable. That didn't change once he got into school. The talk of Jews was everywhere, in school and on the playground. Everyone hated them. And he didn't even know what a Jew was. He saw pictures in the schoolbooks: men with long noses. Sometimes they were rats. And they were always hurting someone. He frequently thought about what it would be like to meet one of these creatures.

"Oh no, you must never come in contact with one. If you do, you tell your father or me immediately." Ilse took her son's arm and sat him down on the couch next to her. "Karl, you are a nice boy. So sweet and innocent. I can only hope your schooling helps with this education. Would you like to hear a story?"

Karl nodded. He loved stories, though less so than when he was younger. The boy enjoyed an excellent folktale like Hansel and Gretel. The witch scared him, and many nights after hearing the story, he woke up screaming for his parents. His mother and father would come, not to protect, but to scold. There was no such thing as witches, they'd tell him. No such thing as monsters in his closet or under the bed. No Krampus gathering up bad children during the holidays. Those tales were fables.

"Many years ago, my own father and mother were rich beyond your wildest dreams. I haven't told you of your grandparents, have I?" Ilse never shared much, especially stories of her own past. That was also too painful. The scourge of the enemy cut deep.

"I had a very happy childhood, much like yours now. Instead of going to school, I had teachers come to my house to educate me. I learned so much about other countries and had such a passion for it that my mother and father sent me on trips to Paris, London, and Rome. I ate new foods and learned new languages. I visited the Eiffel Tower, the Statue of David and Windsor Castle. I returned after a month away, bringing with me stories of what I saw. I never knew why my parents sent me away. It wasn't to see the world. It was to go somewhere else while they figured out how to restructure things. I had no real idea as to what the Great War was and, because of my family, I was never exposed to it. No one went off to war. No one lost anything. I only learned from it because it took everything away from us. My trip and the people sent with me to show me these beautiful cities; it was a ruse to try to hide items, so my parents didn't lose them. Would you like to know why they did that?" Ilse didn't wait for the answer.

"My mother and father did that because of the Jews and the war they started. Jews stole my home; they took everything from me, including my own father. I never told you what happened to your grandfather. He could not stand all he lost. The embarrassment was too much for him, and all his old friends disappeared when the secret was revealed. When my own mother died of breast cancer, he was left alone. When I left for Nuremberg and met your father, it wasn't just because of curiosity. I had no one. Your grandfather took his own life in a tiny apartment that we shared. I went out for an evening with friends to return to his body on the ground. I don't tell you this to scare you, Karl. That isn't my intention. I just think you need to know how much the Jews affected our lives. They took everything from my family and me. If it wasn't for meeting your father, I'd have no one. The witch isn't really in your story. She is a cautionary tale as to what happens when you deal with evil." Ilse grabbed her son's hand in hers and squeezed tightly.

"Promise me, if you ever meet one, you must tell me immediately. Jews have ways of making you think they are good. They aren't." Ilse wiped some tears from her eyes, kissed her son on the head, and walked out of the room, leaving him alone to sit and think. Karl was scared. He'd never seen his mother so upset before, and now the possibility of running into a Jew made him nervous. Would he be able to notice the difference?

CHAPTER FIVE

lse's nightmare had come true. It wasn't something brought up by her young son, now approaching his tenth year and who still hadn't met a Jew. Karl saw many in the streets performing tasks that seemed logical. Roads needed to be shoveled, and it was necessary to have clean sidewalks. He didn't understand why they were cleaning the dirt off with toothbrushes, as there had to be a more efficient way.

"Mother, I need your help for a project I am to work on as part of the Jugend." Hans had been accepted into the youth program, led by loyal Nazi Baldur von Schirach, spending the first two years learning what all good German girls and boys must know. Now, at the age of fifteen, he was awarded another job. The task given to youth members was to look into their own family past. It was customary for all Aryans to prove their blood was clean, not tainted with the blood of a Jew. It was a way for the party to self-police, making all Germans join in the fight against the foreign invaders.

"I'd love to help you. Anything for the Fatherland." Ilse was proud of who she was, a strong, devoted wife and mother of the German nation. She was willing to do whatever was necessary.

"Reichsjungendführer Schirach has asked we look into the bloodlines of both you and Father. It is a skill required of all those in preparation for a future at the party." Hans slid a pencil and paper towards Ilse.

"Father has all the paperwork, and Reichsführer Himmler personally looked into our background. That should be enough for your instructor." Ilse wasn't angry. It just seemed like a waste of her time.

"Regardless, it is not a mark on you but more so how to look into the backgrounds of those wishing to join the German nation. We cannot allow anyone to infiltrate what is being built," Hans said. He was just doing what he was supposed to do.

"If that is what is asked, that is fine. Just know, your father might be upset to know Schirach or anyone else is commanding you to do a job already done." Ilse led her stepson to the attic, pulling a box to the forefront.

"In here, you'll find all the paperwork on my family. In the crate next to it is your father's papers. There, you can look back at three generations. Your father has more detailed records somewhere, as Himmler commanded." Ilse walked away to tend to her other son, not recognizing the threat before her. The self-policing of children against their own family was the first significant step in the indoctrination of the German youth by the Nazi leadership.

The rest of the afternoon passed by as most did. Ilse tended to her son until lunch when she set a meal for both children and her husband. Several times, she called for Hans to come down from the attic to eat, but he was too busy to waste time on food. Eventually, Ilse made him a plate and carried it up.

"Did you know your parents were not German but Austrian? You said they were German, Mother," Hans said, more interested than shocked. He knew this would not be a problem, but it felt as though he uncovered a deep secret.

"Well, once you are done combing through the files, my little spy, come downstairs for a spell. The attic isn't the best place for a young man on a nice day like today." Ilse kissed him on the top of the head and left. Though she did not give birth to Hans, the close bond the two shared made it as if the boy had been her own. She had raised him since he was a boy, and now seeing him as a robust German youth made her proud.

"Mother?" Hans came walking into the kitchen area, a handful of paperwork tucked under his arm.

"Your family was from Leipzig, correct?" Hans sat down on a stool, looking across at his mother, who was enjoying her afternoon tea.

"Of course. My ancestors were there several centuries back. It's quite an old family," Ilse said, not seeing where this conversation was headed. She had trouble reading people.

"Perhaps I am reading a misprint, but this says the last name was once Fischel, not Fischer. Isn't that a Jewish name, Mother?" Hans said in an accusatory tone.

"How dare you? A Jew in my family? That's unheard of." Ilse tossed her cup across the room, shattering it. "Besides, your father passed my paperwork through the proper authorities."

"That's the thing. This wasn't in your box; it was in Father's. He'd hidden it." Hans took a document out of the pile and slid it across the table.

"And here's the one he passed to Himmler. He only goes back two generations, which is what is asked by the party. Grandfather might never even had known he was a Jew . . . unless." Hans reached across the table and snatched the papers back before Ilse could damage them.

"I think it would be best to wait until your father came home." Hans slowly stepped away, never taking his eyes off his mother.

Ilse sat, unable to move. She was not a Jew. That was a dirty word, one that would not be spoken. Eventually, she broke into tears, not wanting to accept something that made sense.

Dieter walked in an hour later, quickly approached by both his wife and first-born son, each one wanting to get the jump on the other.

"Honey, clear this mess up for your child, please," Ilse said, getting in the first word. "He's under the impression that we are Jews."

"No, you are wrong, Mother. I said *you* were a Jew. Father and I come from good German stock. It's you and Karl that have the blood of the invader in you," Hans said, handing over the found paperwork to Dieter.

"A drink, please," Dieter asked as he carried the file into the living quarters and took a seat on the couch. He didn't even open it, instead waiting for his scotch which he downed in one sip. Holding up the glass for another, he lit a cigarette and took a long drag off it.

"Where did you find this, Hans?" Dieter asked, not in a commanding tone but one of curiosity.

"In the attic. The sheet with the mother's information was in your folder. How could it have gotten there?" Hans looked at his father with distrust, something he had been taught to do quite recently.

"I would advise you to watch how you speak to me. Obviously, this is an error. I, as well as Nazi officials, combed through both of our family histories." Dieter had received his second drink, this time alternating between that and his tobacco.

"All that is required is to go back a few generations. But if it was investigated further back, it would have been seen that Mother is a Fischel and not a Fischer. Fischel is a Jewish name. That means Grandfather was a Jew, which makes Mother and Karl Jews as well." Hans was correct in his statement if he followed Nazi ideology.

"A paperwork mistake. That is all it is. I assure you that your grandfather was a great German patriot. He was one of the most powerful men in Leipzig, all due to the hard work and dedication of the Fischer family," Dieter said, clearly uncomfortable with the conversation, wanting it to end.

"But, Father, it says their name was originally Fischel, and they were from Austria. In school, we learned the Jews swarmed into our country in droves from neighboring areas." Hans knew he was correct. It was a feeling, perhaps intuition, that his father knew he was not wrong.

"Hans, this discussion is over. Your mother and brother clearly aren't Jews. Do you believe that Heinrich Himmler would have signed off on the marriage if he knew your mother was a Jew? Do you believe I would achieve the rank of Untersturmführer if the nation didn't view me, and us, as necessary to the continuation of the German ideal? Your mother bore this country a strong Aryan boy who will go on to serve it any way Hitler sees fit. She is the perfect wife, mother, partner. Your questions are an insult to her, to me, and to Himmler," Dieter said, a bit more forcefully.

"I am sorry, Father. I apologize to you and Mother. Perhaps Reichsjungendführer Schirach can clear this all up," Hans said. He approached his father, sticking out his hand to take back the information he had.

"Schirach will not be involved. No one will be involved. I command you to drop this subject immediately. Do you not understand the embarrassment this will bring to our name if an investigation is opened into your mother's past? Though your claims will be baseless, the Fischer and Krueger names will be dragged through the mud. The SS is one of the most powerful units in this country, and I am working up the ranks. The stain of the Jew, even an unsubstantiated one, will ruin us." Dieter stood, walked to the empty fireplace, and took out a lighter. Holding it underneath the page with the Fischel name on it, he lit it and tossed the remains into the furnace.

"I have looked into your claim and find it unnecessary to proceed further. This is an order not from your father but by a ranking member of the Schutzstaffel. I do not want this to ever be brought up again. The repeating of these rumors will result in grave punishment. Do I make myself clear?"

"Yes, Father. I'm sorry," Hans said, bowing

his head in shame as he scurried out of the living quarters and to his room.

"Dieter?" Ilse waited until her son was gone to talk.

"It is not true. Your son is mistaken," Dieter said, not looking at his wife. He couldn't make eye contact. Lying to her face was not something he prided himself on.

"Are you certain the claims are false?" Ilse was crying. It was not just the thought of her family being dishonest. Parents often kept their secrets. But the Jew was the enemy and performed the devil's work. It was put on this earth to cause chaos and destruction. It was here to steal Aryan children and use their blood for ritual sacrifices. The Jew was a rat, vermin, not fit to walk the earth. That pill was hardest to swallow. She was no different than her husband or any other German mother.

"It is not a rumor to concern yourself with, my love. You are not Jewish. I did not marry a Jewish woman or have a Jewish child. I married a strong, beautiful, caring, and dedicated Aryan." Dieter grabbed his wife, hugging her hard. She cried into his shoulder, and he let her. Emotions were not something he dealt well with, but that afternoon, he thought with his heart and not his head.

"Now, why don't you have yourself a drink and go lay down. I am sure this has been a trying day for you." Dieter kindly ordered her off. He needed to think. If Hans left things well enough alone, all this could blow over. If the youth leader entered into the discussion, things could get messy. He had burned the one piece of evidence he had, but it would take Himmler's top investigators only days to come up with enough reliable proof that his son was correct. Ilse was a half-Jew, born to a Jewish father. Dieter had hidden this secret for years. He knew the SS would look back only a few generations, not enough to see the Fischel name. That was written by Hermann Fischer himself while looking into his own past. That document was not given to the proper authorities, tucked away in his own paperwork after its approval.

Now, everything he'd built was to be destroyed if this got out. His career as a valued member of the Nazi Party and the elite SS would be in tatters. His belief system, something he preached to his wife and sons and anyone who would listen, would be a lie. And his family, the one thing he was prouder of than anything he'd accomplished in his life, would be gone. Maybe Hans will think better about the situation and let sleeping dogs lie.

CHAPTER SIX

Hans did not let it go. That wasn't in his nature as a young man instructed to look into the past. It was just like the Jew to hide in plain sight. That is what Baldur von Schirach told him, and those orders came down directly from the Führer himself. To believe that his mother was, in fact, a Jew did not concern him in the least. Hans did feel sorry for his brother. It was not Karl's fault he was lied to about his heritage. The issue with his father was another story. It bothered him that Dieter let himself fall prey to this mind control. Not only was he convinced that the woman he married was Aryan, but he was also subconsciously forced to burn the only evidence by the evil Jewess.

"It is good you came to me, son," Schirach said, handing off the information to the proper authorities. "This is indeed a difficult circumstance. Does your father know the truth about your mother's past?"

"Only what I brought to his attention yesterday. He claims it is untrue, but that could be the spell." Hans believed a little white lie was necessary. He loved his father, and to consider

90

this secret was known to Dieter before yesterday was inconceivable.

It did not take days for Himmler to find out proof of this claim; it took less than twelve hours. Everything was there, proof that Ilse Fischer was of Jewish heritage. Her father was a Jew, as was his father and so on and so forth. By the next morning, the top brass of the SS was in the offices of Dieter Krueger to discuss the situation. There was no customary period of introductions or small talk. Everything was put on the table almost immediately. The punishment for this crime could be significant, especially if it had been hidden from the proper authorities by one of their own.

"How was I to know she was a Jew?" Dieter asked, hoping to avoid any serious repercussions. His concern was now his livelihood and the life of his son Hans. He loved Ilse and Karl, but was it better to all fall or merely a few of them?

"You could not tell the difference between a Jew and a non-Jew?" The authorities wrote every answer down in great detail to be able to process through it again once the interrogation was completed.

"I must have been under a spell. Jews can do that, you know." Dieter found it easier to lie than he imagined.

"Regardless, there is much at stake now. This situation could create issues for many people within the party, some of them with much power. Even if this was unknown to you, it leaves us with the question as to whether you could properly perform your duty as an Untersturmführer." The men asked many questions after this, looking to poke holes in any story Dieter gave. They found nothing but apologies for not realizing sooner. The SS would need to reward Hans for bringing this to their attention, but for the officer that was duped, it was another story entirely.

"Please, give my deepest apologies to Reichsführer Himmler. I, in no way, wished to sully the SS or his good name." Dieter begged. He knew they'd want to hear this.

"That is of no consequence now. What is necessary is to make a decision on how the situation shall be handled. You will be hearing from us soon, Mr. Krueger." The men left his office, ready to report back.

Dieter waited an hour or so to assure he wasn't being watched before going home. He loved his family, his wife, and his youngest son. They would need to be warned of the storm that was coming their way. There was nothing he could do to save them now.

CHAPTER SEVEN

The house was silent, except for the weeping of a woman who hid her face into a pillow. The news she was given by her husband was much worse than she imagined.

"How dare you hide that from me?" Ilse whispered, not wanting her children to hear. "My life is a lie because of you."

Dieter sat next to her, placing his hand on her back, attempting to console her. Nothing he could say or do could make this any better. She was correct. He'd known of her Jewish origin soon after he met her. While it wasn't customary to look into pasts, he did so on his own. He'd fallen instantly in love with this woman who shared the same passion for the party as he. Much like his son, he too noticed the last name of Fischel was not a typical German surname. He followed his future wife's genealogy back to Austria, where many Jews immigrated across Europe to avoid persecution.

Love has a crazy way of making people do unusual things. In most cases, Dieter would have turned in a family with this past. Instead, he hid it. The girl's father didn't kill himself for losing money. Whether Ilse knew it or not, her family name still had finances in Switzerland and the

Americas. He was once one of the wealthiest men in Leipzig. Grandfather had killed himself because of his hidden secret, a Jewish heritage. As a rabid anti-Semite, Ilse's father refused to accept his own fate, something he'd lied about his entire life. By attacking other Jews, he could play it off and keep his family happy and wealthy. Only when someone close to him mentioned his potential heritage did he decide to end it. If he killed himself and left a note blaming the economy, he looked like a good German who suffered at the hands of the Jews. His legacy would remain intact, and his family would continue to be safe.

There was nothing Dieter could say to calm his wife down. He refused to mention the death of her father. Nothing good came from bringing up the facts of that situation. Instead, he sat back as she shot insults at him, never once questioning her behavior.

"What are we to do, Dieter? Our lives are ruined. We will have to leave Germany a disgrace." Ilse was beside herself. This new reality was a shock to her system. For as long as she could remember, there was never a time when she looked favorably on the Jewish people. No one in her family had done so either. Now to find this out was beyond comprehension.

"Perhaps I can talk to Himmler and explain the situation. If I only get an opportunity to council with him, this can all be swept under the rug, and we can move on as if this never happened." Dieter knew that this was not something that would be allowed. He, as well as anyone, understood the gravity of the situation. To have one of the higher-ranked officials married to a Jew heiress would be the ultimate betrayal to the Reich.

"And our son, God, Dieter, our son. Poor Karl, what will happen to him? Even if your friends agree to forget my past, how can they forget him? His tainted blood can still be spread with those of an unwitting Aryan woman." Things seemed to be lost on Ilse. She talked as though this new secret did not belong to her. She struggled to grasp the realization of her own origin.

Dieter was shocked but not surprised at his wife's reaction. She was a strong German mother, providing children who would stand for the same country and ideals she did. There was no concern for the child's well-being or a showing of love from mother to son. Dieter had and could look past the history of his wife's family. In his heart, he was an opportunist, doing what was necessary to profit from it. The war brought him more power and money. He had no real care. His wife was Jewish, and his son Karl was Jewish. As an atheist, the faith intrigued him. The strength, community, and commitment to one another based on religious affiliation was something he could have quickly rallied behind. How would this be perceived? What would happen to their station in life if a Jewish heritage was established?

"We've been put in a challenging situation, my dear. Even if I can discuss things with Himmler, I can promise that Karl's life will be much different." Dieter took a small velour bag out of his coat pocket and placed it on the small bedside table.

"But what of my legacy? If the world finds I am a Jew, it would be humiliating to my name, the country, all the way up to Hitler himself. If specific steps are taken, could you assure this will all go away?" Ilse asked.

"To avoid public perception, I know Himmler would rather bury this story than release it. One of his officials married a Jew. That would show the process did not work, and he would rather not have his superior find out that secret either." Dieter couldn't care less about her legacy. It was his that was important. If something did happen to his wife and child, he could play it off as being deceived and perhaps even face a promotion for doing what was right by coming immediately to the proper authorities. His son Hans would be rewarded for choosing country over family, the ultimate sacrifice of a young Aryan.

Ilse was left alone to collect her thoughts. It seemed like she was in the room forever, making decisions. Dieter was patient, sitting downstairs on a couch. He knew what his wife would do but was curious as to how far she would take it.

"Karl, dear, could you please come to see mother for a moment?" Ilse's voice rang down from the top of the staircase, sweetly asking for her youngest son.

Dieter smiled, though there was sadness behind the expression. Both he and his wife knew that neither Ilse nor Karl could survive in Germany as a Jew. They must be sacrificed to save the family name and the Reich. He could hear the light footsteps of his son ascending the stairs to answer his mother's call. Part of Dieter wanted to follow his son and pull him back, scream at him not to go to that bedroom. He knew what awaited Karl. But if he did that, he and Hans would also pay the price. This scandal could be kept hidden if only his youngest son did the climb to the top alone.

CHAPTER EIGHT

Karl could see his mother's bedroom door was open, ever so slightly. At first, he wondered if he imagined that she called him with as sweet a tone as he had heard. He never remembered a time where it was gentle and loving. That should have warned him that perhaps something was wrong, but it didn't occur to him. He was a devoted son to his parents, so when they called, he listened and reacted.

"Mother?" Karl said, pushing the door open slightly. He peeked in, noticing the lights in the room were off, and the shades were drawn.

"Oh, my sweet boy. Please come in and sit next to your mother. We need to talk." Ilse's voice set off red flags in Karl. His mind was screaming for him to turn around and run far away. Something was wrong. Instead, he went into the room and did as his mother said.

"Karl, I have an important question for you. How much do you love this family?" Ilse asked in a voice that now sounded drunk.

"Very much. You know, I do," Karl responded.

"And how much do you love this country? How is your bond with this great nation and our Führer, Adolf Hitler?" Ilse wanted to convince him but was willing to use force if necessary.

"I love Germany. As soon as I am ready to join the Jugend, I shall take the oath to defend the Reich and fight for Hitler." Karl was merely spewing rhetoric. He was too young to show allegiance. Many of his friends talked of fighting and dying for Hitler, but he was not as willing.

"Germany asks you to take a courageous step. If the Führer himself asked you to do something, would you do it without question?" Ilse never sat up, her head laying back on a pillow as she stared at the ceiling. She'd had an opportunity to accept her own fate.

"I guess I would," Karl answered, though he had a bit of trepidation. Something was wrong with his mother. He could clearly hear it in her voice.

"What if Hitler asked you to die for him?" Ilse asked.

"Why would he want me to do that? Can't I provide more if I am alive?"

"In some cases, men and boys provide a great deal to Germany. They fight the wars, they work in the factories, they keep the streets clean of foreign elements. They are here to benefit the whole nation," Ilse said. She was careful in her wording of the foreigners in comparison to the word "Jew." Even though she was in no way a Jew mentally, it was in her blood.

"Like Father?" Karl said.

"Yes, like Father and like Hans. But we don't

all provide that same service to the Reich. Some can show their support and devotion by willingly giving what is most important to them. You and I can do that as well. I want to give myself up to Hitler to ascend to greater heights with the most loyal followers. Would you do that with me? I don't want to do it alone." Ilse was ready.

"Mother, I don't understand. Wouldn't I be better served fighting in the war? What purpose would I serve, giving myself up?" Karl asked her, curious as to what she wanted. He was much too young to realize what his mother was asking him to do.

"Sometimes, we are asked to give our lives to benefit the nation. We would serve in Hitler's army in the great beyond. Would you do that?" Ilse said, holding her hand out to him. In her palm was a glass pill.

"I don't want that." Karl now knew the obligation his mother asked of him. He had heard that Germans would rather die at their own hands than at the hands of the enemy. Though he'd never seen it, his father also had one tucked away for each of them in case of necessity.

"You must. I cannot do this alone. I'm scared, Karl. The Jewish invasion is closer than you think. It's at our doorstep, breathing down our throats." Ilse pushed her hand towards her son, hoping guilt would force him to take it.

"Please, don't," Karl said.

"Damn it, take it now, Karl." Ilse jumped towards her son. She was going to force the cyanide down his throat, even if he didn't want it.

"NOOOO," Karl screamed, hoping someone would come to save him. Little did he know that his father had no desire to help. In fact, his father wanted him to make the decision that would benefit the family name.

Ilse had her son by the wrist, pulling him closer. When her hand was in a tight enough grip, she used her other to force the pill forward. "Take it, Karl. Take it and join your mother in Hitler's eternal war."

Karl wanted to scream but refused to open his mouth. He could feel his mother's fingers pressed against his lips, the cold glass pill trying to slide its way between them. He wished his father would intervene.

"Wait, wait, wait," Ilse said, pulling her hand away. She was desperate. "Look, son. How about we do it together?" Ilse took a pill that was sitting on her bedside table and held it in front of her lips. Before she could be stopped, she slid it into her mouth.

"Now take yours. We can bite at the same time. Let us die together." Ilse held her hand out, letting the pill sit in her palm.

"Ok, Mother. I'll take it." Karl swiped the tablet in her hand and put it in his mouth. "I'm ready."

Ilse smiled. She tussled his hair, grabbing his hand in hers. "Let's do this together."

Karl nodded. He watched as his mother bit down on the pill before mimicking the process himself—instead, tucking the pill under his tongue. He saw his mother die. She fell back almost immediately, the sides of her mouth filling with foam. She choked and gagged, reaching out to him, unable to realize that her son wasn't committing suicide with her.

The death of his mother, the look on her face as she passed, was enough to haunt him forever. He sat in the room with her body for many hours, unable or unwilling to move. Eventually, his father entered the room.

"Karl? Karl, what happened?" Dieter asked, shocked to see him alive.

"Mother is dead. I don't want to be dead." Karl was crying. He ran to hug his father but was pushed away.

"Why are you still alive? Karl, you needed to go with your mother. Do you know what will happen if you are found alive?" Dieter shook his son by the shoulders.

"What will happen?" Karl asked. He wanted to know why his father was upset but had little time to question him. There was a loud knock downstairs. The SS was at the door.

CHAPTER NINE

The SS waited for no one, not even Dieter, one of their own. On orders from Himmler, this issue was to be immediately investigated. They'd found that the young boy Hans was indeed telling the truth that the wife of one of their own was an enemy in plain sight.

"Where are they?" the officer asked, walking around the room, looking for the criminal he was sent for.

"The woman is upstairs. She could not live with the news that was given to her and decided to take her own life." Dieter had already moved on from calling her his wife. It allowed him to separate himself from the crime.

"Typical Jew. Wanting the easy way out." The officer lit a cigarette, taking a long drag. "It will make the paperwork much easier for us. So, tell me, Mr. Krueger, how did you find your wife was lying to you?" This was now an interrogation.

"My son Hans informed me. He is very loyal and dedicated to the Reich," Dieter said.

"This child, Hans, is he a son borne to Miss Ilse Fischer?" The officer was looking down at his notes, checking things off, and jotting ideas down.

"No, he was from a previous marriage, long

before my devotion to the cause. My first wife left the child and me. I can inform you she was of one hundred percent German stock. The SS looked into this before accepting him into the Jugend. Schirach himself signed off on it," Dieter said. He had already had the paperwork handy in his living quarters. He freely handed it over.

"Thank you, Untersturmführer. The help is very much appreciated. However, I cannot merely check a box and move on. You see, Heinrich Himmler is most displeased that this has happened. He views it as a personal attack on him." While the one officer talked, the others walked around the home. Two went upstairs into the bedroom to find the dead woman, foam built up along the sides of her mouth. They did nothing to the body, since there'd be no need to properly dispose of it. It was not an Aryan, the only peoples worthy of burial. The body would be burned, and the ashes tossed away. There would be no memorializing this creature.

"Please apologize to the Reichsführer. If I was aware of the lies, would I have freely tried to join the SS and bring my family into it as well? Hans did exactly as was commanded of him. He looked into his mother's past, came to me, and then reported it to the youth leader. Why would I want to sully my own name by having him do so?" Dieter was good at lying. It was one quality he did not struggle with.

"Himmler will be pleased with her decision to take her own life. It makes things less . . . messy. I must say, I do believe you. How would you know of her lies? And why would you put yourself out there to be found? And your son Hans, he will be held to a high standard for all those too frightened to do what is right," the officer said.

"There is one other issue before we leave. It says here that you have two sons. The older one, we have already concluded, came from strong German stock. But this other boy, did he not come from the loins of the woman that lay dead upstairs?"

"That is correct, sir." Dieter did not even lose a step. He answered as though his wife wasn't his wife, and his son was a stranger. "He was born to me by Ilse."

"Is it safe to assume that he is somewhere close by?" The officer leaned in close, his hot breath wafting onto the man across from him.

"He is in this house at the present time. He is not as smart as his mother, however. She was certain that once we found her secret, suicide was her only option. Karl is still very young and does not know what awaits him." Dieter closed his eyes, took a deep breath, for the first time questioning if he could give up his youngest.

"You will find Karl in his room." Dieter pointed towards the hallway.

"And does the child know he is a Jew?" the officer asked.

"No. Karl is unaware of who he is. He's spent his life as a Jew in an Aryan household. He does not know why his own mother killed herself. I was hoping he would do the same and take the honorable way out. Unfortunately, even when given the option to do so, he chose to live."

The officer stood up, patting down the wrinkles in his coat. "You know what I must do, do you not?"

"Yes, I do," Dieter said.

"And before I do that, do you wish to talk to the child one last time? Though he is a Jew, he is still your son." This wasn't something customarily offered to someone who unknowingly hid the enemy. It was a courtesy given only due to the man's rank.

Dieter thought for a moment. Could he save his son? He could beg for more time and sneak the three of them out, though Hans might refuse to go. The choice was between his firstborn and Karl. The entire time he was with Ilse, Dieter knew of her past. Only now, that knowledge could doom them all.

"No, please take him immediately. There's nothing I can say to him. He'll try to use his powers to stay here. It would be better if he were removed so my Hans and I can rebuild our life in this ideal Germany." Dieter did not feel too badly about the situation. He could save his older son's life by giving up the other. If not, they all died. Instead of waiting in the living room to see his son dragged off, Dieter excused himself and took to the backyard where he enjoyed a smoke. Through the open windows, he could hear the screams of his child, demanding to be let go without knowing why they were taking him. Karl called for his father and for his brother. In confusion, he called for the woman who attempted to murder him. No one responded or came to his aid. Dieter waited until he heard the front door slam before entering the house. He walked towards the door and watched as the cars drove away, never to see Karl again.

CHAPTER TEN

For days, Karl Krueger cried for his father and brother. Every time a guard walked by, he demanded to see them. Each time, he received the same answer.

"They will not be arriving. Jews don't get guests." The younger guard was much worse than the older gentleman. He'd sometimes toss a plate of food into the cell, ruining his meal. There would be times when he was incredibly generous, talking to him for hours, never once bringing up the lie he was a Jew. Other times, Karl'd be chastised and told the only reason he was given this treatment was that his father was a ranking member of the SS.

"Soon enough, you'll be sent away. Then you can be with all the other vermin," the younger guard said, laughing at him.

Karl didn't understand why he was being called a Jew. It made no sense. His family was prominent, hard-working, dedicated Germans. He was to be a member of the youth program as soon as he was of age. His parents hated the Jews. Now his mother was gone, and his father hadn't come searching for him.

One evening, awaiting transfer to what he

was told was a "more permanent location," Karl asked the older guard why he was here.

"Karl, how old are you?" the guard asked, taking a drink from a metal cup.

"I'm going to be ten, sir," Karl answered.

"So young. Do you know I am jealous of your youth? You've never known a time without our great leader. When I was a child, monarchs of all sorts ruled these lands, many times unqualified for what needed to be done. Kings and queens all fell because of their own stupidity. They fought unnecessary wars and caused harm to those around the globe. They allowed countries, like ours, to be inhabited by the foreign invaders. And one by one, each person was overthrown by the winds of change. Germany, my Germany, was saved by Adolf Hitler, a man of the people. Others, like Mother Russia, succumbed to the Bolsheviks, led by the Jews and deceivers who wished to cause chaos and spread it across the continent. Those were uncertain times." The man closed his eyes, harkening back to a much different era. He refused to let the thoughts of doubt creep into his mind that perhaps this führer had made poor choices.

"I could always see my enemy because he was in front of me. I cannot imagine if I was the enemy but did not realize it." This was not an attack on the boy but a matter of fact.

"I'm not an enemy. Why do people say that?"

109

Karl was clearly upset. Certain inappropriate words had been thrown at him these past few days, very hateful ones that he'd heard his brother use when discussing the Jugend.

"Ahhh, no one told you, did they?" The guard did feel bad, not wanting the child to continue being blind to what was directly in front of him.

"You're a Jew. Your mother was a Jew. That's why she killed herself. People had found she had been living a lie, trying to incorporate herself into our society," the guard said.

"NOOO!" Karl screamed, not holding back the tears that had come. In his heart, he knew this was true. He could see in his mother's eyes a dark secret that she attempted to keep hidden.

"Unfortunately, it's true. You should be proud, though. It was your brother who brought this to our attention after stumbling on information about your mother's past. A clerical error on the part of your father, though I don't see how. However, the SS and Himmler seem satisfied with the conclusion of events."

"Is that why my mother tried to poison me?" Karl asked, not caring the man answering hated him, not for who he was but for a label.

"Ahhh, perhaps. You should have let it proceed. It would have been a much more honorable death. There is shame in what happened in your home; the Jewish secret kept locked away. Your mother no longer carries that burden. Your poor choice makes you the loose end that must shoulder the weight of this unfortunate incident." The guard excused himself. He'd spent the evening emptying and refilling his cup many times and needed to clear his bladder.

Being completely alone, in a dark cell, with nothing but his own thoughts allowed Karl to think back. He had never met his grandparents on either side of his family though he consistently heard stories of their devotion to National Socialism. If it was indeed a fact that there were Jews on his mother's side, no one gave any indication of such. Mother had done nothing but spew hatred towards the Jew. Father seemed indifferent towards them, only speaking ill of them when around people of opposing views. Even as a family, while Hans attacked the Jewish people, his father would look over at Karl and roll his eyes, giving a slight smirk.

"Tell us what else the Jew does, Hans," Dieter would ask his oldest son, egging him on. Sometimes, it would be just him; other times, Ilse would chime in, speaking her own truths on the matter of the Jew.

"Do you not agree, Father?" Hans questioned Dieter when he felt he wasn't being listened to.

"Oh, of course, son. Your professors have taught you well. But as they focus on their enemy, do they talk of the greatness of this empire? Do you not cover art? Literature? How often do you need to hear the Jew is bad before you believe it? From your rhetoric, I see you know it in your heart. Maybe I shall bring it up the next time Schirach comes into the SS office."

"Please, do not do that. That would be a great embarrassment. Besides, unless taught who the enemy is, Hans might not live to see those great works of art you speak of." Ilse furrowed her brow, clearly angry at her husband's sarcasm.

"What kind of art?" Karl said. He was more interested in the beautiful universe his father mentioned.

"Oh, none, my fine young German." Dieter snickered. "You see, if the Jew has his way, you will never lay your eyes on the Mona Lisa or stand in the presence of greatness of the Sistine Chapel. The Jew will take it all away because not only does he hate us, he hates perfection and beauty as well. They shall steal our priceless artifacts and hide them in their camps."

"Dieter, that is enough!" Ilse yelled. She slammed her napkin down on the table and left the kitchen.

"I think I better go talk to her," Dieter said, shaking his head. He followed her into the living room. Soon, the boys heard yelling.

"Why is Mother so upset? He was just joking," Karl asked his brother, who never stopped eating. He'd been told it was necessary to grow up big and strong to fight for the Reich. Eating as much as possible, along with physical activity, would go a long way in achieving that.

"Father isn't supposed to mention the camps. They don't think we know about them, so even bringing them up sends Mother into a frenzy." Hans didn't even look up from his plate. He continued to shovel food into his mouth.

"What camps?" Karl had never heard of them before. His mother was correct.

"You don't know?" This time his brother put the fork down. "Oh, you never want to go there. It's filled with the evilest, dirty, disgusting monsters ever." Hans grinned, showing all his teeth.

Karl ran into his room and slammed his door. He had no desire to hear about a place where they kept monsters, like a zoo. It must have been quite bad there because Mother refused to allow it to even be mentioned.

"Wake up. It's time to go!" The cell door opened, and the younger of the two guards stepped in, kicking at the boy. He must have dozed off, his mind still swimming with questions.

"Where are we going?" Karl asked, hoping it was back home to see his father and brother.

"We're taking a trip to Ettersberg, my little Jew. There's a special place for people like you there."

CHAPTER ELEVEN

Karl wished he was dead now, but it was too late. Instead, he stood in front of this cattle car at a station. He wasn't going on a vacation; that much was certain. Ordinary people wouldn't travel this way. But this wasn't a usual trip, and he wasn't a regular person anymore. He was a Jew, or that was what he was told.

The large wooden car he stood next to was for him, but not for him alone. Guards unlocked the door, pulling the handle to the side. The smell emanating from it was intense, and Karl put his hand over his nose to block it. It was dark inside, and he was scared.

"Get inside, Jew." A guard pushed the young boy forward, forcing him into the car. Before he could fight back, the door closed, locking him in.

Karl's eyes took moments to adjust, seeing only darkness. Soon, his vision picked up on the grates that let in small bits of light. He could hear things around him, the loudness of guards screaming at people, forcing them onto other cattle cars. But that was the least of his worries. Karl could hear movement around him, the chattering of voices so close. If he reached out his hand, only slightly, he knew he'd touch those moving closer to him.

"Who's there?" Karl asked, hoping that no one would answer. It would be much easier to accept if there was no response. Instead, he felt a hand on his shoulder, soft and kind.

"It's alright, son. You're safe in here for now," an elderly voice responded. "Paula, bring the bucket over. This child needs some water."

Karl could see more now that his eyes had become accustomed to the darkness. He felt something pressed against his hands.

"Drink, child. You will need to have some if you are to make this trip." The voice was caring and loving in a way he'd never heard from an adult.

Karl did as he was told, pressing an end of the bucket against his mouth. The water tasted disgusting, and though his mouth wished to spit it out, his body sucked it down. He tried not to be greedy and took only a few smaller drinks.

"Thank you," Karl said, wiping his mouth with his forearm.

"Of course. It's our job to look out for one another, especially for someone so young." This time the voice was followed by a darkened face as the man came into view of the light. He was old in a way that Karl pictured a great-grandfather would look. He was haggard, tired looking. A long beard hung from his face, though it seemed unkempt. His hands shook as he placed his over the boy's, holding them tightly.

115

"I thought all the Jews in this area were gone. Where'd he come from?" a woman asked in the darkness.

"Stop, Paula. Don't forget, we hide well, like rats." Another woman giggled slightly.

"Ignore them. Please come sit while we still have room in here." The old man held onto the boy's hands and led him over to a corner.

"Introductions might be wise for our new travel companion. I'm Rabbi Berger, but you may call me Abel if you wish. And you are?"

"Karl. Karl Krueger." Karl did not know where he was headed, but he quickly understood what was in this car with him, Jews. Even days ago, it would scare him. Not so much anymore.

"It is very nice to meet you, Karl. When we get to our destination, you'll be able to get to know the others with us. Say hello to Ittel, Salomon, Paula, Hirsch, Chaim, Harta, Jakob, Magdalena, Frieda, and Samuel."

"Hello, it is very nice to meet all of you." Karl did not wish to meet any of them, but the response seemed custom. He received hellos from ghosts he could only hear. He didn't want to see faces; it would make the situation more real than it already was.

"How'd you stay hidden for so long?" A young boy came into view, taking a seat next to Karl. He was roughly the same age, it seemed, though much more weathered and aged.

116

"Samuel, we do not ask those questions. It is not how we got here, but what we do with the time we have remaining," Abel said.

"It's fine," Karl responded. "I wasn't hiding. But it's a long story . . ."

"And we have time. We are many hours out of our destination and are in desperate need of a good story." Abel was just as curious as his companions. This entire group, except their newest traveler, came from cities in the west. This child came from the heart of the Third Reich.

Others gathered around, taking seats close to the boy. They'd all shared their tales and would hear new stories once they arrived at the camp, but for now, everyone needed a distraction.

"I guess I'll start at the beginning. I'm not a Jew, or I didn't know I was," Karl said. For the next hour, he told his story: the lies, deception, acceptance. The boy still hadn't fully grasped the circumstances, and though the idea seemed more comfortable to take, it didn't mean Karl understood what that entailed. He didn't know what a Jew ate, how they spoke, or how he was supposed to act. Throughout his story, Karl could hear gasps and moans when discussing the potential murder-suicide his mother wished to commit. Occasionally, someone would reach out, touching him just enough to let him know he was cared for. Once he was done, he sat back, himself using this cathartic opportunity to take in everything for the first time.

"Your father is a fool," Samuel said, not thinking how that comment might sting, which it did.

"Perhaps, Samuel, but if he was not, we wouldn't have met our new friend." Abel was correct. The others agreed.

"Are you afraid of us?" a female asked him.

"No? Yes? I don't know. Since I can remember, I learned how bad and scary Jews were. But you don't seem like vermin to me." Karl was honest. His interaction with Jews was viewing them from a distance or within the German schoolbooks. This was his first meeting with a person of the Jewish faith.

"No, we aren't rats," the woman said, snickering slightly.

"I'm sorry. I didn't mean it." Karl felt guilty.

"Please, do not apologize. It is your father and mother who should for the way you were taught. It is the German state for filling your head with propaganda. A child should not be blamed for listening to what they are told. In time, you will see that those were lies." Abel felt nothing but sadness for the boy. Everything and everyone had left him, along with secrets that he was moved to unearth.

Moments later, the cattle car stopped yet again, and more people with their own sad stories came on. Soon, there would be no room to sit anywhere. Bodies would be crushed together, for long distances, without food or water. The elements took their toll on the weak. Those of advanced age or riddled with sickness or injury struggled to successfully make the trip, dying along the way. Many times, there was nothing to do with the bodies, so they stayed, held up by the pressure of the living smashed together in close quarters.

Karl could no longer hear the sweet voices that had made him feel at ease during this trying time. In its place were the cries and moans of those wanting to get off this car, not knowing where they would be going. Once there, at Buchenwald, they would desire to be back on the train. It would be much better to deal with that than deal with what awaited them at camp under the command of Gunter Müller.

CHAPTER TWELVE

Gunter Müller did not generally like to drink in the morning. It made him lethargic the entire afternoon, and he still had several shipments of Jews coming into Buchenwald, all needing to be processed. The paperwork was far more involved than it had to be, but the Reich demanded numbers. It was about efficiency, especially from a camp that held such high prestige that the party wanted, and with the SS using it as a training ground, Müller was always monitoring.

The bedroom in the villa was outfitted with the most elegant furniture in the area. Gunter had seen to that. The king-sized bed, taken from a wealthy Jewish home, was in the corner of the room. Also, much of the living quarters were adorned with items from the same place. A beautiful, brightly colored oriental rug lay on the floor, the one thing he had purchased legally. Art from museums hung on the wall, compliments of the previous commander, who met an untimely end due to stealing money. Taking from the Jews was one thing but committing fraud against his own country and the party was quite another. A show trial and hanging followed soon after.

The only thing missing was his family, which Gunter left behind. Some associates brought their families to live on camp grounds, but that seemed like a feeble idea. His wife knew little about what he did for work, and his kids knew even less than that. Young adults needn't see the horrors war brought on, especially when it was something not understood. Gunter sat his own down many times to explain the problems and solutions necessary to make the German nation grow and prosper. Camps, much like this one, required a more in-depth discussion than a simple one on the ills of the Jew. Things happened here that couldn't be explained away as quickly as he wished. His wife wouldn't understand, hating the rhetoric. His young daughters both would struggle if he told them of the death and destruction that occurred behind the fences. It was best to leave them behind. Dresden, while still very National Socialist, was away from the killings.

Müller stood 6'3", frequently towering over everyone else. He was an imposing figure with a long scar going from his right eye down to his chin, a gift given to him during a street fight with Communists. His hair was slicked back, always cut clean around the neckline. Facial hair was unappealing to him, so there was never a day that he wasn't shaven. Once in peak physical condition from hard work in sculpting the body in the image of the ideal Aryan male, Gunter had lost the cut of a young Nazi SS member, even though he only just turned twenty-seven years old. Something about the task at hand required a lot of smoking and drinking and more drinking. His choice was American whiskey, though that was harder to come by as the war progressed. Fortunately, someone in his position was able to procure it.

"Sir, when you're ready, the new stock has arrived." A young woman, waiflike and worn, came to Müller's bedroom door, not daring to step in. She only had to break the rules once to know what was and was not acceptable practice. It had been innocent enough, entering to lay some clean clothes on the dresser while the commandant was busy. Ester Demsky hadn't even been seen in the commandant's quarters. But the man knew as soon as he came home, and he made sure she understood what it meant to enter his room. Ester was beaten severely, suffering a black eye and cut lip that refused to heal correctly.

"Ahhh, yes, more Jews. That's just what I need here. Every day, they come. It never stops. Tell me, Ester, when was the last time we didn't go without a new shipment? Try to remind me of that day because I clearly do not recall." Gunter wanted to make changes at Buchenwald. The last man in charge left it a mess, no order at all. Guards were killing freely without regard for protocol. People were accepting bribes and stealing for their own benefit. Buildings were run down, and the crematorium wasn't equipped enough to dispose of the bodies. Gunter promised Himmler he'd get this place back in working order, but up to now, he spent his days taking in new Jews from all across Europe, a task that was becoming increasingly difficult.

Ester hated this man, the one she was subservient to. Many nights, he'd rape her after an evening of drinking. He'd stumble into her room and do what he wished, only to act as though he had no recollection of it the following morning. The physical pain; that she could deal with. Every time she was beaten, the young girl marked it down. She would make sure this devil would be repaid for each and every strike. The psychological torture was much worse.

"Sir, I do not remember a day that a new trainload did not arrive. It seems as though it is every day and sometimes several times a day, at that," Ester said, answering the commandant's question. She could see he was frustrated and quite hungover and did not wish to anger him further.

"And yet they still come. From the west. From the east. What am I to do? I cannot fix this camp if I am bombarded with those rats," Müller said, not worrying that Ester was a Jew as well.

"Perhaps if the National Socialists stop shipping Jews, you will have time to rebuild and restructure," Ester responded. The commandant did not pick up on her passive-aggressive answers.

"Agreed, yet the elite tell me I am too important to the state, and my services are required. I was trained in Hartheim for this very purpose, and they overload me with this shit." Gunter stood up, tucked in his tee-shirt, and grabbed his suspenders to hold the pants below the enlarged belly.

"If you please, have my breakfast ready, so I can start the day off on the right foot. It will be good for those Jews to wait for me. Standing at attention for a few hours builds character." Müller smiled at her, happy he'd convinced himself of his importance to the Reich. He was a cog in the wheel that was necessary for it to turn.

CHAPTER THIRTEEN

The travel was excruciating, and even though the journey was merely a day with stops, many died. The car baked in the sun, with no way for any airflow to enter freely. Bodies were packed, crushed against one another. During the trip, several, too weak from the mistreatment, died, still held up by the living. There were attempts to create a pile of corpses off in a corner, but there was little room to do so. Eventually, people gave up on the idea altogether, hoping only that death would not come to the next.

"It's so hot!" a voice screamed, stating the obvious. There was nothing to allow even the slightest bit of air in the car. No one had water, except urine, which occasionally ran on the floor. Soon, that was joined by excrement as well.

"Perhaps we should open the windows," a person answered, getting a series of snickers and giggles.

"Enough, enough." Abel didn't want people to argue. It was essential to keep solidarity. He'd heard about where they were headed, and if it was even a tiny percentage as bad as he'd been told, everyone would need to work together.

"Karl, and how are you doing, my son?" The rabbi checked on the boy as much as possible.

None of them had any relatives with them, all individual Jews riding the same car to Hell, but they had the bond of their faith. This boy, a poor child, had been thrust into this situation. Until days ago, he'd lived a life much different than the one he was living now. The child had remained quiet most of the trip, which worried him.

"I'm fine." Karl gave the same answer each and every time he was asked the question. He wasn't okay; in fact, he was feeling quite awful. Karl was so confused about so many things. Pain and anger kept bubbling to the surface, but now was not the time to let it free. He was in a situation that required keeping a level head, and even though he was very young, Karl locked his personal feelings in the back of his mind to revisit at a better time.

Some of the people in the initial group were quite nice to the boy, accepting him as their own. Here was the child, alone and scared. But not everyone felt that way. Salomon and Jakob were both distrustful of him. They'd been schoolmates, at one time enemies fighting over the same girl. Now, they were best friends, not able to be separated. They called it safety in numbers, but both boys were scared of what was to come, and it was easier to find comfort in a familiar face.

"I don't trust the boy," Jakob whispered to his friend. It was hard to trust anyone, to begin with, much less someone who just days prior labeled themselves a National Socialist and supporter of the Aryan movement. Was he a spy sent to learn secrets? Was he a traitor, being punished for crimes against the state? His story, while quite sad, didn't add up. A boy who never knew he was a Jew. His father, a high-ranking Nazi in the SS, didn't realize he married a woman with that past? None of it made sense. Something was wrong. However, now was not the time to interrogate the boy.

"How long until we get there? My legs hurt," an older gentleman cried out, not used to being forced to stand, crushed like sardines in a can. The elderly were affected the most. Some had lived in luxury, never forced to endure such physical and mental strain.

"Shut up! Complaining doesn't help at all." A woman answered his cries with nothing but contempt.

As the day wore on, more echoed the gentleman, crying out for help, for water, or for death. At one point, it seemed as though the destination had been reached. It was not to be. Shunted from one station to another, it would be days until they unknowingly arrived at Buchenwald.

CHAPTER FOURTEEN

How many?" Müller asked as he walked from his villa to the drop-off point for new prisoners. In his mind, he added and subtracted, thinking of all the ways to keep his numbers down. There were options of sending the weak to Auschwitz or Bergen-Belsen, whichever was able to take on the load.

"This car has fifteen hundred, Commandant," Ivan Kravets responded. Ivan, a Ukranian soldier who was here because of his efficiency in Eastern camps, was transferred under orders of Müller himself. This was never a required role to take on, and while most went in with gusto, the pressure of death wore down most. Soon after arriving, alcohol and debauchery would enter the equation, making a new guard less useful to the state. Kravets never wavered, a trait that made him very important to the mission at hand.

"Can we assume they are all fresh, able-bodied workers?" Müller knew this answer already.

"We cannot, sir," Ivan said, holding a clipboard, ready to record even the smallest detail. Everything was to be written and kept for posterity, so future men and women of the German nation could see what was put into creating this nightmare.

"We will have older people that are unable or unwilling to work. I don't remember a shipment that didn't have them. Also, children, very young ones, will be present." Ivan had seen many cars come into camps, each time having the same scared look. It delighted him to see the faces of the newest arrivals, the combination of shock, pain, and fear. Some would ask him where they were or why they were here. He never answered them as one would speak to a real person. A simple shrugging of the shoulders or acting as though he didn't understand the German language were two ways that he started his cat and mouse game.

Gunter took a sip from his coffee cup, one he carried around with him all morning. The thick black liquid and constant smoking stained his teeth a bright yellow. He hated the Jews like every good German was supposed to. But this wasn't about emotion; it was about getting the numbers down while not showing weakness.

"I would like to rid myself of two thousand here before the train arrives. It will be nice to have a brief cushion, at least until Himmler interferes.

"I want one thousand collected and sent to Bergen-Belsen. I don't care who, but please attempt to clean out the ones we cannot use anymore. Next, ship five hundred to several of our subcamps, maybe in blocks of one hundred or so. Any of those officers might be upset at a new shipment, but those feelings will go away when they see the small number getting off the train. It's all about appearances." Müller smiled.

"That leaves us five hundred," Ivan said, looking down at his papers. He had already listed the subcamps he was going to use.

"Send two hundred to medical as a gift from me." Müller enjoyed making others around him happy; it made everyone work harder.

"I want the remaining number brought here. Shoot everyone after unloading the cattle car. Let the new prisoners bear witness to what happens when someone does not properly follow orders." Müller showed his cruelty at times, though he didn't label it as such. He merely viewed this as a part of the job, a task that had to be done.

Ivan grinned at the prospect. He enjoyed a proper introduction to the newest arrivals into Buchenwald. They needed to know who was in charge. And while they would despise the camp commander, they would come to fear him, Ivan Kravets, the Mad Ukrainian. He enjoyed this. Until the war broke out, he was a town drunk and doofus, not respected by anyone. Due to the heavy drinking, Ivan was unreliable and unable to hold down a job for very long. Here, in this environment, he was a king. He was feared unlike any other guard at the camp. And it was quite easy for him. The death of a single prisoner, seen by all, would automatically make every other walk away from him.

"Once I've completed that task, how should the bodies be disposed of?" Ivan knew this was a problem for every commandant of any camp. The bodies just piled up. It never ended. But it wasn't always from the kinds of mass executions that his superior ordered. Every morning, there were fewer people at roll call than the previous evening. Ivan would make each Jew stand at attention, sometimes for hours on end in the hot sun, as he waited for the remaining numbers to be counted. It was quite easy to send guards into the barracks to find the dead, but that wasn't the only reason to do things the way he did. It broke the spirit of the Jew, which was necessary for him.

"You know the official stance on the disposal of corpses, Ivan. To leave them lying, rotting for others to see would be the wise thing to do. The Romans used to line the Via Appia with crucified Christians, warning all others who wished to practice that it was not a wise decision to do so in their Empire. That was a cruel and brutal time. We don't do things like that anymore. It's about efficiency, not proving a point." Gunter waited for his train car to arrive, his mind a bit less fuzzy than when he woke this morning. He knew how psychotic Ivan was, and the stories of raping and murdering prisoners were not lost on him. It was hard for him to deal with. Müller didn't consider himself a violent man. He hunted only for food and hated fighting unless it was a necessity. But times were different now. He wasn't fighting for himself but the survival of the German people. If that required him to line every street in the German Empire with the rotting bodies of their enemies, so be it.

"There is the other issue of disease, Ivan. We were brought here for a particular reason, were we not?"

"Yes, sir." Ivan agreed.

"The last commandant of Buchenwald used it as a playground for him and his wife. That didn't go unnoticed. Because of that, the camp was rife with typhus and smallpox. This place is not only to corral and execute Jews. Very prominent businesses rely on us to provide them able-bodied workers. We cannot allow this camp to fall into disrepair again. The work I've done to rebuild is not yet complete."

"We shall go with a mass shooting. After, I will have some of the less desirable workers carry the bodies to the crematorium. Once the dead are thrown in, we can shoot the others. That would also help bring the numbers down a bit before the next shipment." Ivan wanted only blood.

"I trust that you make that decision for the benefit of the camp, so I fully support you if that's what you decide is necessary." Müller understood the psychology of this man. It was what he'd always been good at; reading people. His parents always told him the same thing. He could tell if a friend would be a positive influence or not. Studying at university, he surrounded himself only with fellow students who would help him advance in whatever avenue he chose. It was here, during the war, that Gunter was able to hone his craft. He saw snakes all around him, men and women using the system to get ahead. Some used it for power, sex, or financial gains. Even some of the most potent Nazi elite, such as Göring, lined his pockets with money from the dead. Others were supporters of Hitler's beliefs, but not as many as Himmler would like.

Ivan did not look for financial gain and cared little for the accolades that came with the job. What he enjoyed was the power over others and the reaction he received when he made sure to take care of a problem. It got him this far, sending him from camp to camp when things needed to fall into line.

Ivan bowed and rushed off, excited to get the day started. In less than an hour, a new car would arrive, and the psychological torture would begin.

CHAPTER FIFTEEN

Karl seemed to remember everything that happened to him from the moment he was forced onto the cattle car until things ended. He couldn't recall much that occurred in his life before this time, and though he had no clue as to where this was headed, something told him it was essential to keep track of every detail: every smell, every sound, every face, and name.

The car came to a stop, and everyone shifted suddenly, though there seemed to be so little room to move throughout the entire trip. It had done this several times before, waiting on the track before moving on to the destination. But this seemed different. The car waited. Outside, screams could be heard; Germans commanding people to move this way or that. The door opened, shooting in a blinding light, one that hit the eyes of everyone looking in that direction.

"Be strong, my young friend," Abel said, grabbing Karl's hand. "We shall face many perils, but if we stay active in our faith, nothing can defeat us."

"I don't know what my faith is," Karl said. Before he could receive an answer, he felt someone from behind push him out of the car. He tumbled down on the ground.

"GET UP, JEW!!!" a man screamed, yanking him by the arm to his feet and tossing him towards others he had traveled with in the car.

Karl was helped up by some strangers who pulled him into a huddled mass. He recognized a few of the people he had met when first entering the cattle car. Dogs were barking, demanding to attack the newest prisoners. Only collars with chains attached stopped them from doing so.

"Welcome to Buchenwald," Gunter Müller said, stepping out from the crowd. He did not yell and scream at them like the other guards were doing. Later, many would mistake this demeanor for kindness, a quality Müller did not possess.

"You have been sent to me from far away to a place you did not know existed. Here, we have choices, much like each and every one of you. The decisions you make, while here, will determine how you survive this awful war." Müller had no desire to allow any of these vermin to live. However, a full-on riot wasn't the way to deal with any new and strong-willed prisoners. He'd need time to break them of their will to live and to fight.

"For the women, I shall give you a chance to say your goodbyes to your men. For the time being, you shall be sent to a neighboring camp. This is a work camp for males only, except for a few women, for housekeeping purposes. That being said, all but for two, you have a moment before re-boarding the car. The trip will not be long." Gunter had pulled Frieda Aumann and Paula Reiss to the side. He would use them as he saw fit. The younger ones were more malleable. He had no desire to break a strong woman.

Once the women boarded and the train car left, the remaining men, along with Frieda and Paula, were forced to stand in a line. Müller walked up and down, looking over each person briefly. He would occasionally stop, smile, or ask how a person's trip was and move on. When he came to a person that looked too old or feeble, he would ask them to step forward from the group.

"I welcome you all to Buchenwald. Unfortunately, I do have matters to attend elsewhere, so I shall leave you with my friend, Ivan. He will see to it that you receive a proper introduction." Gunter did a slight bow, holding his hands out.

"Ladies, if you will, please follow me. I will show you to your quarters." Müller's charm worked, both women giggling and taking his hand.

Ivan waited until the commandant disappeared from sight. The first few assaults were to be without him around. Ivan was okay playing the bad guy anyway. He started by calling over the men that were made to step forward in the line. He brought them over to his right; fifteen or so, not bothering to make them stand at attention. There was no need.

"The commandant has asked me to introduce you to camp life. He may be diplomatic with his statements, but I am not. You have two choices; do as I say and live or disobey and die. Those are your only options," Ivan said. He motioned towards the barracks, and soon, several guards led out a large group of men wearing prison uniforms. They were stopped just in front of the group.

"These men here made the decision to not follow the rules here at Buchenwald. For that, they shall face the punishment of death." Ivan held his hand up and then dropped it. Guards pointed the guns and opened fire on the huddled group of men. Screams and cries came, not only from the victims but the newest prisoners, who could only stare in horror at this mass execution. The air was filled with the coppery smell of blood and the burning of the gunpowder.

"If you refuse to listen when spoken to, you will die. If you try to steal even an extra morsel of food, you will die. If you talk of an uprising, you will die." Ivan motioned for the guards to surround the new men and lead them off to start their life here. The fifteen or so that had been called out of line were required to load the dead bodies onto wagons and push them to the crematorium. Once that task was complete, each of those men received a bullet to the head. They were some of the lucky ones, never forced to spend more than a few hours under the command of Gunter Müller and his monster, Ivan the Horrible.

CHAPTER SIXTEEN

We cannot let that break us." The rabbi spoke to the men who had congregated in a smaller area of the barracks. It would be a tight fit with all of the other Jews that were forced in the small enclosure.

"Break us? We just watched them kill innocent people," Hirsch said. He was still shaking from what he'd witnessed an hour prior. He'd seen death as any man had who spent time in the army as he once did. But never that. Never a massacre on such a scale.

"That is true. What we have seen shall not go unpunished. There will be a time that those men will have to face their own creator and explain their actions. But as a united front, we must stay strong. It's our will that those men are attempting to destroy. Once that is gone, we are nothing more than mindless souls, hoping for a way out." Abel was just as disturbed and angered as any of his friends. The death of innocents shocked him. He always struggled with mortality; not being able to fully explain God's plan of when someone is taken. When his people lost their rights, Abel prayed. When his synagogue burned to the ground during Kristallnacht, he found another place, and he prayed again. When his brother and

139

his family were murdered, he prayed. The rabbi accepted God's will, but it was becoming harder, considering the circumstances.

"They shot them. Why would the Germans do that?" Karl couldn't wrap his mind around it. Weeks ago, he was considered a future functioning member of the Nazi Party. In a few years, he would join Hitler Jugend, just like his brother. He'd been force-fed the rhetoric of the party, made to repeat the hate-filled propaganda. It was never something he truly believed, unlike Hans, who sucked it all in, repeating it as it was told to him. Up to now, it was just talking. Karl never thought about how those words affected others, especially the Jews in his community. His father, a big proponent of the party, spoke of ridding the world of the vermin, not only Jews but homosexuals, Jehovah's Witnesses, gypsies, and those with disabilities. The child had never uttered those phrases, but Karl never stood up to his brother and all the hateful speeches Hans gave.

"I can't answer that question, Karl. Only those men know why they made the decision to pull the trigger. However, what we can now attest to is that their words are backed by violence. It's not just hateful speech." Abel walked to the young boy and put his hand on his shoulder trying to calm him down. The child pulled away.

"We're all dead. There's no hope," Jakob said,

no longer concerned with the actions of the strange boy added to their group.

"There is hope. There's always hope. As long as your beliefs stay strong and you never cross that moral line, there's hope." Abel didn't believe what he said. He wanted to. He wished that all it would take was a prayer, and that would solve the problems they faced.

"How can you say that? It's a lie. You're lying to all of us. I cannot imagine those men lost their will to live or their dedication to God. Yet, they are all dead." Jakob was having none of it. He was afraid.

Samuel stood up and stepped between the rabbi and the man, verbally attacking him.

"You need to stop this talk immediately. Do you think the rabbi wants this to happen? He has no more answers than you or I do. Stop blaming him for the situation we are in. We have no chance at all if we are divided."

"It's alright. Jakob is scared." Abel smiled at his accuser. "We all are. If I had all the answers, we wouldn't be here. But God chose us to be here for a reason. And Samuel is correct. If we don't stay together, we'll be picked off one by one. More good can come of our combined imaginations than a single person looking for answers alone."

The rabbi was correct. In the coming weeks, things would get much worse as the war ramped up, and more and more Jews were sent to places like Buchenwald. Pure evil would show on the faces of guards and commandants, and at any point death would be imminent. Karl had never witnessed death except his mother's, who took her own life to avoid this torture, both the physical aspect of camp life as well as the mental fight over being a Jew herself. His father hid him from everything. All things related to death were kept a considerable distance from the children. He could claim there was no indication of this form of violence, but in retrospect, all the signs were there. He was just too young and too naïve to really grasp the concepts.

It wasn't long before the barracks filled with sick, tired, and hungry Jews; men dragging themselves into the one place they could speak more freely, though still in whispers. It immediately became overcrowded. Over a thousand men filtered in, not recognizing who was new and who was no longer with them. It was a daily existence in which one did what they had to do to survive on their own.

"Move it," a rough voice said. A short, stout man pushed past the newest prisoners and made his way to a bunk area, sliding on what was meant to be individual beds. Soon, others did the same, making their way past Karl and his friends without even noticing them. It took no time at all before many of the beds were filled, not with one man but two or three per bunk.

The image of all those men bothered Karl immensely, but what was worse was the smell. It filled the entire barracks, and in no one corner could he escape the foul scent. It was a sour mix of sweat, piss and shit, and the unwashed masses. But that wasn't the only scent that filled the noses of all those close by. It was death. It was the smell of a man slowly rotting away until nothing remained. It was typhus. It was starvation. It was desperation. And that smell, no matter where he went in the camp, was always close by.

For the afternoon, the newest prisoners stood in the center while the other men relaxed and regained a bit of strength to go back out to work yet again. No one made formal introductions or gave them a hearty welcome. It wasn't necessary. By the evening, places would open up for them to sleep. The neighbors from the morning or afternoon might not be neighbors by lights out. It was the way life would be now.

CHAPTER SEVENTEEN

Gunter had wasted no time in raping the two young girls that he led back to his villa. The appearance as the gentle giant was unnecessary now. Paula and Frieda would never again see their friends and stories of his cruelty getting out was no longer a concern. Once he had finished with them, Gunter handed them over to Ester to clean them up and show them to their quarters located below. The villa was a vast place with many rooms, but he had no desire to even give the appearance of sharing a home with Jews. Let them sleep in the basement with the rats.

Lunch was served, which he had no problem finishing. The morning hangover was long gone, and his stomach had rumbled upon smelling the cooking of steak, his favorite meal. He had no issue with eating, something that was a struggle for other guards in the camp. Many complained of the smell, a thing he didn't enjoy either. It was all about compartmentalizing. He wouldn't last five minutes if he felt any sort of guilt or pain from what was done or what he asked others to do in his name and for the party. There was no denying the fact that Valhalla was in his future. He'd stopped being a religious person many years ago, well before the Nazis came to power and showed him the truth. The concept of Heaven and Hell, with a single being ruling both, did not appeal to him. No one chose his path, much like the path of his leader. And he did what he did, not for personal gain, but to assure a robust German nation for his children and his children's children as well. When he did pass, it would be as a hero for the right cause. Those beliefs gave him the strength to fight through the tiny inconveniences he faced now. The smell wouldn't stop him from continuing forward on his fight.

"Commandant, one of the girls will not allow us to clean her. She refuses and stays huddled in the corner of the room," Ester reported to her master. She had no desire to get anyone in trouble, but if Müller entered and saw his orders weren't properly followed, there'd be hell to pay for her as well as the other two.

"Give her to Ivan." Müller wasted no time at all in making the decision. He'd been prepared to make this the moment he picked two of them instead of just a single girl. It was also the reason he convinced himself that raping them early would weed out the weak. Girls like Ester were compliant. He was under no false pretense that any of the women cared for him. Even someone like Ester, one of the safest women in the camp, loathed him and would gladly put a bullet in his head if she had one. Regardless, he needed loyal and hard workers, a woman that would fill all needs.

"Yes, sir." Ester bowed and walked away, not arguing. She'd been with Gunter since the beginning and understood what made him happy. Keeping him content made others safe. It was much easier to find the tiniest of victories if he was in a good mood. The killing of a young girl because she was frightened wasn't acceptable in any culture but here. Ester could refuse to listen to orders and argue but that would save no one. In fact, it could result in the death of all three women.

It took no more than a minute, as Gunter sat back, digesting his meal. It never took all that long, as Ivan was a quick worker. Moments later, a single shot rang out, echoing through the halls of the villa.

"I'm happy to report the task is done; however, the basement must be cleaned." Ivan rushed right up to disclose the murder, splatters of blood streaming down his face. The young girl had refused to move, he said, and the execution had to take place where she sat.

"Excellent, get help removing the body and burn it. Have Ester and the new girl clean up the mess. It will be good for them to see what happens to those that don't follow orders." Müller ushered the Ukrainian out, wanting him to leave. The blood made him a bit nauseous after a big lunch. He went on the porch to get a bit of air.

A gentle cool breeze blew in but with it the smell of burning bodies. Müller was happy he only had to order the killing of Jews. Before Buchenwald, Gunter had spent time as a member of the doctoral staff at one of the many T-4 centers, euthanizing those that served no purpose to the state. Experiments were tried and perfected, and this allowed him to continue those same tasks here. The difference was delegation. Now, he only had to give the order, and men like Ivan did it without question. Even the disposal of the bodies was done by prisoners, which was quite the system. He profited from giving orders. After several minutes of serenity, Gunter exited his home and made his way to the barracks to meet the new prisoners.

"Good afternoon, my newest workers. I thought after that unfortunate incident earlier, I felt I owed you an explanation. You see, here at Buchenwald, you are asked to perform tasks. You must work hard and provide for the German nation, even if, at times, it seems like you have nothing left to give. You may complain of provisions or your stay, but please remember, it all depends on how much we profit from the war. The more we give to the war effort, the better it will be for us all." Müller walked up and down the line of men. By this time, he could predict who would survive the longest. Children had a short shelf life, usually contracting an illness that rendered them useless. The older men, ones that barely made the cut, fell to the wayside. There was a nice mix, ones that he could work with. They all seemed shocked as to what they had seen, which was the purpose of it in the first place.

"Here, my desire is to get the most out of your abilities. I demand hard work and reward it with life. However, my guards do not always feel the same as I. The Ukrainian seems to have an issue with laziness. That scene from earlier was a taste of what happens when Ivan does not get what he wants from his workers. Understand, I do not like to see that. It is a necessary evil. You don't provide the labor we need; you cannot stay here, and there's no place for you to go beyond these walls," Müller said.

"Oh, a rabbi. Welcome," the commandant said in a sarcastic tone. "We will need to get rid of this immediately." Müller grabbed Abel's beard in his fist. "It's not personal, believe me. Sanitary conditions require us to shave all hair. Lice can spread quickly in a place like this." It had nothing to do with that. While lice were an issue, that wasn't the primary reason for it. For one, it would be humiliating. This man of the cloth, someone who had spent his life studying the Torah and spreading its word, was forced to lose the symbol that separated him from other Jews. Secondly, once his hair was gone, like all the others, the rabbi lost his identity. He would be a number, one of many thousands that lived and died here.

"If that is what you have to do, so be it. My beard does not define me," Abel responded. It was true. He was not about to risk the lives of all the others here over a symbol. Hair could grow back, and God would understand.

"Good, good. Fall in line. You know, rabbi, you might survive this war." Müller enjoyed the banter, which was rare. Too often, people were surprised, shocked, saddened. Defiance wasn't as typical as it once was. Ivan's display upon their arrival usually squashed that.

"And you, how did you make it here? A bit small." Gunter stopped and looked down at Karl. Most children of his height and age were sent to immediate liquidation. They usually provided no usefulness to the camp.

"The child does not belong here." Samuel stepped forward.

"Of course. None of you do. Is that correct? If I had a Reichsmark every time I heard that, I'd be a wealthy man, indeed." Müller laughed at his own joke. No one else did.

"It's true," Jakob said. "He's not a real Jew. He's the son of an SS officer."

"SS? Child, is this true?" Müller could hear

Himmler screaming at him now if this was accurate. Imagine the controversy if he was to kill a German child over a minor misunderstanding.

"My parents are Dieter and Ilse Krueger and my brother is Hans Krueger. My father is an officer in the SS, and Hans is a member of the Hitler Jugend," Karl said.

"Oh my, we must get you back home immediately." Müller could feel sweat forming on his brow. This could be disastrous to his career, one he worked hard to perfect.

"But I belong here, with these people," Karl answered, fully accepting his fate. "I am a Jew, as was my mother and her parents before her." He was proud, though he had little understanding of what he was doing.

"Well, Karl Krueger. I shall check on your story immediately. If this is your game to garner attention from parents who pay more attention to the preservation of the state than you, there will be severe consequences, including ones to your companions." Gunter hated games, especially ones with such high stakes as these. He turned heel and returned to his office, where calls would be made to corroborate this story. Because of this turn of events which now required his attention, he'd give Ivan the pleasure of getting these people started.

CHAPTER EIGHTEEN

Time ticked by, and days meshed into one another without an end in sight. Over weeks that turned into months and then years, the small group of men that met on that railway car stayed alive, as many others around them disappeared. It soon became clear to all involved that there was no way out. Death came to them randomly and without purpose. Prisoners being publicly executed in front of new workers was not an uncommon practice, though Müller had attempted to pass it off as such. Abel lost his beard as well as all other hair on his head, but his resolve remained intact. Samuel still fought when it was necessary, several times facing extreme punishment. His once muscular frame was gone, now a mere living skeleton, like the others. Skin hung loosely on their bones, stomachs hidden underneath their rib cage, that stuck out.

Karl Krueger's situation was much worse than the others. It seemed as though his story checked out, the authorities looking into all aspects. In his hometown, his brother had become a hero of National Socialism, choosing party over the family. Dieter had survived the onslaught only due to his son's bravery. Karl knew he was kept alive because of his family influence, but how long would that truly last?

By the early-1940's, the tides of war had turned against the Nazis. The Germans were no longer dominating as they had once been. A failed invasion of the Soviet Union had cost money, lives, and armaments, showing the world the Nazis could be defeated. People within the country began to question the role of leadership. Hitler, once seen as a savior by the general public, disappeared from view, hidden away to only his close colleagues. Like rats on a ship, there was talk of dissension and assassination. Top Nazi officials lined their own pockets and planned their rise in the party as well as their own eventual escape. Camps became havens for death and disease at a much larger scale. Buchenwald was overcrowded more than ever and nothing could stop the trains from coming in.

"How do you expect me to continue at our rate?" Ivan Kravets asked Gunter over a drink. He wasn't one to share his thoughts, but the alcohol loosened his tongue. "Barracks are filled to capacity, yet we continue to receive shipments several times a day."

"Satellite camps, Ivan. We have so many." Müller knew of the smaller camps near Buchenwald. "Load some cars and send them there. Let our problem be their problem."

Ivan finished his drink and poured another. He

had become more brazen and bolder in front of the commandant during his time at the camp. It was he that kept this place running effectively. The orders came down from on high, but he always completed them. The blood was on his hands, forever his.

"Nothing works. That is the nature of the beast. There are sacrifices we all must make, but wouldn't it be easier to focus on the war effort, and once that battle is over, continue with the extermination of the Jews." Ivan was logical when he was forced to be.

Müller slammed both fists down on his desk, standing up, looming over his little guard. "Those words shall never leave your lips again, under penalty of death itself. Hitler himself creates the orders and to ignore those or to merely question them is traitorous." The commandant sat down, quickly realizing that this bravado went nowhere with Ivan.

"Listen, you must understand that this plan, the entirety of it, is not just something that happens overnight. It's a vision. I admit I don't understand it all myself, but an order is an order."

"Sir, it's not that I disagree. I'm fully on board with Hitler's plan. I was just thinking about allocating our forces differently, that's all. If he demands I kill a million Jews for his German nation, I do so willingly." Ivan knew he had pushed his vitriol a bit too far this time. Alcohol had a way of doing that to him. He'd lick his wounds, take his leave, and find some innocents to take out his frustration on.

"Completely understood, Ivan. As long as we are given orders, we will complete them to the best of our abilities." Müller smiled. He knew everyone was being taxed lately, especially with the news of the turn of the war.

"And Ivan, before you leave, one more thing that you must remember. The word extermination must not be used. This is a solution to the Jewish problem." Gunter had been given orders to not use specific terminology. In January of 1942, he was given a mandate by Reinhard Heydrich himself to push for the Final Solution of the Jewish question.

Müller waited until alone to smoke. He'd tried to quit numerous times, understanding the damage to the body. It wasn't a doctor that told him either, though all men and women working camps received physicals. Exercise, while necessary, wasn't a commitment for either he or any other commandant in any field.

The war had brought more Jews and criminals from all across Europe to camps like his own. It was a double-edged sword. Hitler needed to build this empire off of fallen countries, such as Czechoslovakia, Poland, Austria, and others. In fact, he welcomed it. And Müller realized their importance to the Reich, which was to last one thousand years. However, each time a new country was incorporated, their Jews were also added to the Reich, which meant he and others like him needed to clean up the problem. Yes, in ten years, this would be a minor bump in the road, and he could look back and see the good he'd done. But now, the stress was too much. Drinking became daily, even hourly. Alcoholism was a problem in all camps, and he didn't need a doctor or a wife to tell him he had a problem. He had gained considerable weight since he started this job, his clothes fitting tighter, and his belt forced to loosen a notch. His physical well-being was secondary to the work needing to be done here. One day, he could refocus on himself and his family. For now, it was Hitler's Germany.

CHAPTER NINETEEN

*W*ake *up!!! Outside in five minutes!!!"* A voice rang over the loudspeakers, filling the camp with the horrible sounds of the young loyal German that made the announcements each and every morning. He'd never been seen by many of them, but his voice was recognizable to all.

"Sam. Sam, wake up." Karl made sure all his friends were up for roll call. He'd grown tall since he arrived in Buchenwald, but it wasn't just his physical body that had changed. He'd fully accepted his Judaism, something once feared, now wearing the Star of David proudly. Due to war and his connections made in the camp, Karl welcomed the transformation as much as the situation allowed.

"These are trying times for our people. Do you not wish to wait until this all ends? Perhaps it would be much easier to convert when the time is right. Rash decisions can become future problems, my son." Rabbi Abel was more than willing to help his young friend become a Jew in the religious sense of the word. The child was already labeled as such by the state, but in God's eyes, it was much different.

"Why wait? I am here with family," Karl said.

He meant it. Karl's first family used hateful speech and rhetoric. He'd had a mother who showed little physical love and a father who spent more time worrying about impressing dictators than being a good role model for his son. He had a brother who spoke vile things about the Jews, even upon finding out his own brother was one. Now, he had a spiritual family. These people took him in when they didn't need to and nourished him back to health. He had been empty, sitting in that jail cell, awaiting his new routine. All he'd known was wrong. Up was down and left was right. He was a pile of clay waiting to be formed. It was the rabbi and his friends that did that, creating the being he was today; a strong, independent young man who was forced, all too early, to see the horrors of war and the mistreatment of the Jews.

"There may be a better time to convert. That is all I am implying. Once the war is over, you might feel differently," Abel said.

"Look around you, rabbi. Every day, we see people dying from disease and malnutrition. And those that make it past that don't always survive. Since we arrived, how many mass shootings have we been forced to witness? How many thousands of men disappeared from these barracks, never to return? Are we to assume they are in a better place? By the grace of God, we have survived living in this personal hell. I do not know if it is someone's plan if we're being punished or there's something greater after this world, but I live day to day. When I wake up in the morning and see the sun rise, I do not assume I will see it fall that evening," Karl answered.

"You know, you're very wise for your age," Abel said, putting his arm around the young boy's shoulders. "This place made you grow up much quicker than most children should. If your wish is to become a Jew, then to the best of my abilities, I will help you achieve it."

For months, the boy and the rabbi studied together late in the evenings when lights were out. Abel exchanged rations with another man in his barracks to give up his area of the bunk next to Karl. In hushed whispers, the two men would discuss the Torah, the Jewish faith, and the transformation from a boy to a man. There would be no bar mitzvah, as there was no time. Karl was correct. His day and all their days were measured in minutes and hours, not by months or years. Certain aspects would have to be pushed aside so the rest could be accomplished. And it all had to be kept quiet. Few people knew of Karl's German past. His friends and Gunter Müller knew the secret. If any of the other prisoners found out, there could be dire consequences. They might not be as willing to accept him as the rabbi did. In fact, it could result in the child becoming the focus of attacks. People in pain might take their frustrations out on the son of a Nazi SS member.

"I'm glad we are all here to see this night," Rabbi Abel said to the collection of men that had come to Buchenwald together, now sitting in a circle in the back of the barracks late one evening. Salomon, Hirsch, Chaim, Harta, Jakob, Samuel, Abel, and Karl were lucky. No sickness had befallen any, and while all other men lost their lives, this group stayed strong. Others became numbers, fighting for their own survival. These men had different goals to make sure all others but themselves lived to fight another day. There had been beatings, hunger, and emotional pain beyond what anyone had witnessed. Chaim lost two toes to frostbite but kept it hidden from the doctors. That deformity would have signaled his end, but he and his friends made sure it was a secret.

Jakob had once hated the young German and all he stood for. He had the hardest time accepting Karl into their community. Jakob's family lost everything; their home, their business, and soon after, their lives. He watched as his grandparents were arrested. His mother and father were shot in a raid of the ghetto they were housed in. His brother died of a typhus outbreak there. Nothing good had come from being under the German thumb. The fact that Karl came from a family that helped in the murder of innocents, like his own family, did not sit very well. But he'd seen the strength Karl showed, on numerous occasions, to protect his friends. Living in the camp was not easy. There were many enemies around you, and not all were German. Within the barracks, gangs were formed, and men gained power through that. All too often, a new group would enter the camp, and some Jew would step up to take control. The gang leader would frequently use this to gain favor among the others, obtaining food or other forms of trade to barter for specific amenities. This did not concern the group of eight that stuck together. They had been in this barracks the longest, having seen this act play out over and over. While they worked hard and kept their noses to the grindstone, hoping to make it out of this alive, others were looking for power. On occasion, that made the rabbi and his friends a target.

"Those are ours now." A large man walked over to the area where the eight were lying. His name was Isaac, and he'd just arrived from Munich. Until 1942, he'd hidden away thanks to the kindness of friends and neighbors. Once an art dealer, with ties to influential friends, he was forced to go on the run. Art was better than money to be sold all across the continent, and as long as it could be used to keep people quiet, it worked. It was only when he could no longer pay German civilians off that he lost his usefulness. Isaac's big mouth and his poor behavior toward those that stuck their necks out for him were no longer worth the consequences of death if captured. He was turned in by a local grocer who required a new storefront. Now, he was at Buchenwald, just like every Jew that was in here. The difference was that Isaac didn't grasp the gravity of the situation. In his mind, he was still a powerful man.

"I'm quite sorry, my new roommate. We've been here for many years, and these have been our sleeping bunks." Abel stood and confronted the man with kindness. He, like many others here, understood this wasn't a sprint but a marathon.

"I think it's time you changed then. You might not know who I am now, but in time you will." Isaac fell victim to his own self-importance, something that wasn't ideal for this situation. In time, he would speak these words to a man with a gun. That man would not take as kindly to his statement of fact.

"Unfortunately, who you were isn't who you will be. Your past in no way dictates your importance here." Abel said his most outward acts of defiance were through words.

"Fuck you, old man. Get out of the bunks before my friends and I remove you." Isaac got in the rabbi's face. He had no desire to argue with a rabbi who didn't know his place.

"How about you back off and find a new

place." Karl stood up, stepping between the rabbi and the aggressive gentleman.

"Jesus, we have ourselves a hero. May I ask what you plan to do about it if I take what is mine?" Isaac put his hand against the boy's chest and shoved him. Karl fell back into the rabbi's arms.

"Now's not the time or place, young Karl. We don't use violence," Abel whispered in the boy's ear. It was true. If this became an incident, there was no telling what the Germans would do to them.

"Sir, you and your friends may have these bunks. If your wish is to sleep here, so be it." Abel waved to his friends, who moved off without so much as an argument otherwise. In most circumstances, younger men with more testosterone would question why they hadn't done more to fight for what was once theirs. But this group knew better. They trusted one another unequivocally. If any of them wanted to do or not do something, the others fell in line and did the same. The trust in Abel was real and just. If the rabbi thought it better to move than fight, then so be it. There were other places to sleep, farther away from the areas with windows. In the back corner, where no one wished to go, the eight claimed their new stake in sleeping arrangements.

"Karl, I'm proud of you," Abel said. "You

showed more courage by stepping away than by fighting."

"That man won't last long in here anyway," Chaim said, snickering. "With that mouth and attitude, he'll be dead in a month. Then we have our bunks back."

Chaim was wrong. The man was dead in two weeks.

CHAPTER TWENTY

Ester held the body of Frieda, the girl on the verge of death. She had been around longer than most and fought hard, but eventually, everyone was broken by Gunter Müller and his sick, twisted mind. Ester knew one day her time would be up, and she too would break, but that was not today. Today, that belonged to someone else.

"Frieda, I need you to take this. It will help with the fever." Ester tried to shove a pill in between the dry pursed lips of the dying girl.

"No more. Leave me alone. I want to die," Frieda whispered, hoping no one would hear her. She lay on a mattress in a dank, musty basement, rotting away from the inside. Could she survive this bout? Of course, most could with the proper care and desire. That was the problem; the will was broken. The girl had no reason to live anymore.

"If you die, I'm alone. Do you really want to leave me here by myself? With that monster?" Ester tried everything to just get this girl to fight. And her comments were accurate. While she did want the girl to live, it was for selfish reasons. If she was the only girl here, she'd face the wrath of Müller more often. She paid her dues and had bided her time, taking it for years. It couldn't be her turn again.

"I'm sorry. I can't do it. I hurt too much." Frieda wished she could see her family and friends again. There was only one way to do this; it was through death. The girl heard stories of murder and the destruction of Jews from her time in the villa. She was told stories late at night by Ester and a few of the Jewish prisoners that delivered items from the camp to the home. The smell wafting in through the windows was constant. Even closing them did not work. The scent of death snuck in through crevices and cracks of every corner. It sickened her; the smell made it difficult to eat, though the man she worked for had no trouble enjoying an excellent meal and drink.

"Why does it matter? We'll all end up in the same place." Frieda spoke the truth. She knew her outcome.

"Don't say that." Ester sat the girl up, now able to get her to swallow the pill. "We *must* make it."

"You really think we have a chance in hell of making it out of here alive?" Frieda said sarcastically.

"I don't know. But even if there's only the slightest chance, I have to fight for that. Look around us? Our people are dying at the hands of these monsters. You know, Paula wasn't the first girl I saw shot under the orders of the commandant. Sure, he never did it on his own. Didn't want to bloody his hands. Instead, he called in his personal assassin to do it for him."

"Poor Paula," Frieda cried. She had tried to forget seeing her friend slumped in a corner, begging for death to come. One rape, one violent attack, destroyed Paula's spirit. Frieda had been able to block it out. Whenever Müller wandered into her room, drunk and stumbling, Frieda closed her eyes and imagined being somewhere else. Back in Czechoslovakia, she worked in a pastry shop, selling bread and sweets to the locals. During these situations, she thought of that life. The smells of the warm loaves coming out of the oven, the sticky sugar on her fingertips. Frieda thought of that and smiled. Most nights, the commandant only lasted a minute inside her, but that was often followed by a severe beating. He'd blame her for seducing him. She'd lost teeth, her nose set to the side after numerous breaks. Frieda could no longer hear out of her left ear. A bottle swung at lightning speed to the front of her face saw to that. Sometimes, she'd look in the mirror and wonder what it would take. At what point would she become so hideous that she was no longer desirable. Would that be the worst thing in the world? To become so ugly on the outside that she would be left to clean toilets and fold laundry. It might also mean her death if she was no longer sexually attractive, but that was a chance she was willing to take.

"Think of Paula. Think about your family. Think of your friends. Think of the thousands in that camp just beyond the fence. We both know they are being massacred. Should we join them, or can we provide a different service in their honor?" Ester grabbed the girl's hands.

"What can we do from here? We have our own problems." Frieda struggled to think clearly. The fever hadn't broken in days, a sign her body was shutting down.

"This war will end. You and I both know that. The Nazis won't win," Ester said. "We hear it on the lips of those that bring supplies to the home. They speak of the failure of the Russian invasion. Hitler can't keep this camp running while fighting the entire world. He'll have to give up one of them."

"Or he could burn this place to the ground, killing us all in one fell swoop." Frieda took a sip of water, deciding at that moment that she wanted to live at least another day.

"He can't, Frieda. He can't. We supply too much to the war effort. If that happens, Hitler loses the ability to build armaments and ship them to the front line. He must keep us alive as much as it pains him to do so." Ester smiled.

"So, we make it out alive. Then what? Where do we go? Everyone is dead." Frieda did not feel sad saying this. It was something she accepted. She could cry for her family and friends later.

"The Allies will need our help. These generals, guards, commandants will all have to answer for their crimes. Müller and Kravets will try and run; I'm certain of that. They will flee like rats on a sinking ship. And when they do, I plan on hunting them down and telling my tale. But I can't do that alone. I need help. That's why I want you to stay alive." Ester wanted the support, and when she spoke this aloud, it made sense. It was necessary to keep as many alive as possible so they could express their truths as to what happened.

"Do you promise to stay with me? I have no one. I don't wish to be a means to an end for you. Agree to love me, and I'll continue to fight." Frieda needed someone. She couldn't live in a world with no one.

"I will love you until the day I take my last breath," Ester said, leaning down and kissing the girl gently on the lips.

"Then, I think we need to get started." Frieda sat herself up, not yet having the strength to stand on her own. That kiss, not sexual in any way, gave her the courage and ability to want to press on.

"Excellent!" Ester leaped to her feet, going to her own corner briefly before returning with a small bag.

"I've been saving slips of paper for years." She

dumped some in front of Frieda, recognizing this battle couldn't be fought alone. Each slip held names, dates, stories of the men and women who had committed horrible atrocities. The maid was keeping track of everything.

Frieda took a blank slip and wrote down Ivan's name. That was her first entry into the long list that was kept until the end of the war. The murderers in Buchenwald would pay for their crimes.

CHAPTER TWENTY-ONE

The information was given in passing like one would say a simple "hello" to another as they walked by on the streets. "Your father is dead." That was how Ivan delivered the message to Karl Krueger, done with a hint of pride as though he brought good tidings. There was no remorse at all.

"What? How do you know?" Karl asked. The idea that his father was dead hit him immediately though he hid it. There was no chance the guard would see him fall apart.

Ivan smiled, sitting himself down on a rock wall. He'd offered to break the news to the child as soon as it came across the commandant's desk. He liked the emotional games he could play with the prisoners, knowing Müller despised it. Orders were easy to give for the German, but it took the Ukrainian to carry them out. He tapped his hand on the rocks next to him, calling the child over to sit.

"I'm busy. I need to work," Karl said, holding back tears as he pushed a wheelbarrow filled with the day's supplies. The longer the war continued, the more was asked of Jews. Weapons and ammunition were needed at a much quicker rate. The war had blossomed into a total war, stretching across the world, and Germany was the focus of almost everyone's ire. The Russians were coming from the east. The Americans and Brits were pushing from the west. German troops were fighting Benito Mussolini's war in North Africa. And that didn't take into account the internal enemies Hitler said were there. It became the focus to push the prisoners harder, withholding food and rest to get more supplies. If the task wasn't completed, all men in that group were shot, and more were brought in to do the job.

"Boy, I'm asking you nicely to come to sit and talk. You've just learned your father has died. It's okay to mourn him." Ivan could barely hold back a grin.

"If I stop working, the quota is not met. If the quota is not met, everyone dies." Karl stopped, looking right at the executioner. "Isn't that how you do things?" He spoke, not as a child, but as a man who understood what needed to be done. The camp had made him grow up so quickly, and though his body was now in its teenage stage, his mind and emotions were quite advanced.

"The time you waste arguing with me will result in a much worse fate. I will count from ten. When I hit one, if you are still puffing your chest and trying to be a man, I shall shoot someone." Ivan was serious. Taking a life meant nothing to him.

Karl believed him. Everyone that had contact with Ivan the Horrible would have. They all saw it firsthand, his wanton attitude towards life and death. Karl decided not to tempt fate and sat by the guard just six inches away. He could smell the alcohol and sweat, the blood caked to Ivan's boots, not cleaned so everyone was aware that his moniker was taken honestly.

"Would you like to know how Dieter died?" Ivan wouldn't wait for a response. He was to tell the boy anyway.

"You see, the SS is a stringent organization, made up of the smartest, strongest, and most loyal German men. It is an honor and a privilege to even be accepted, much less rise in the ranks of the Schutzstaffel. It's very competitive, and each and every man looks for an advantage. Once you make it, however, you must follow the guidelines given and not embarrass the SS. Your father was a dishonest man from the moment he was given the rank of Sturmbannführer. It was a mistake to reward a man who married a Jew and had a Jew child. Himmler may have believed that your father had no idea of your mother's past, but I did not. How does one not see the Jew as they lay next to them? How does he not pick up on the scent a Jew has?" Ivan leaned over and sniffed the boy, wrinkling his nose slightly.

"I've not bathed in weeks, and I wear the same

clothes every day. That's not the smell of a Jew; it's the conditions I'm forced in," Karl responded. This made the man next to him laugh.

"Very clever, very clever. You know, it's unfortunate about our current situations. In another life, you might be a good one to keep around. And because of your family name, you've survived this long." Ivan hated the politics of this business. He would one day kill the boy, but for now, it was necessary to bide his time.

"As I was saying, your father believed he was beyond reproach. He'd been given a second chance by Hitler and Himmler after his little incident. However, you cannot steal from the pockets of the elite. I come here knowing I get whatever I need. Commandant Müller does the same. He wants for nothing. But it's understood that you do not bite the hand that feeds you. Dieter was caught pilfering from the top, hiding away money so he could live life once the war was over. He was hanged like a coward, not given a bullet like all proud German soldiers deserve." If Ivan was waiting for the child to break down, he was sorely mistaken.

"Thank you for telling me this. I appreciate your honesty and hope I can one day repay you for all you've done here." Karl stood up, turning his back on the man. He waited for a gunshot to ring out, killing him but heard nothing.

"You little fucker. One day, Müller won't

care who your daddy was and who your brother is. And on that day, I will feed you to the dogs and watch as they tear you apart." Ivan was screaming, hating the lack of fear coming his way.

Karl grabbed his wheelbarrow, pushing it past a group of Jews who'd just returned from dumping their supplies. As he passed, the shot he was waiting for rang out. Blood splattered all over his face as a single bullet lodged itself in an unsuspecting Jew that had been in the wrong place at the wrong time. Karl did nothing, showed no emotion. He didn't even wipe his face, leaving the poor man's blood where it was. He would remember this day.

CHAPTER TWENTY-TWO

Gunter, may I introduce to you, Hans Krueger."
An older officer of much higher rank brought
in the young man, showing him off as a trophy
wherever he went.

"Ahhh, yes, the Wünderkind. I have heard
rumblings that you'd be joining us at Buchenwald." Müller was less than impressed with
the situation at hand. The war had turned, and
there were enemies on all sides. The work in the
camps had been increased to a faster pace than
previously necessary. Up until recently, the goal
was to create enough ammunition to continue
the fight. Albert Speer, Minister of Armaments,
had even met personally with the local camp
commanders and made sure that particular
order was understood. The Jews were a useful
source of work and Speer had no concern about
overworking them. If a thousand Jews died
providing for the Reich, so be it. Two birds with
one stone. But the killing was to only be done to
those who offered no usefulness to the war effort.
Gunter questioned it many times. How could he
believe his men weren't confused as to why the
Nazis were doing this? He, himself, would often
spend late nights attempting to find the purpose.

"Commandant Müller, I look forward to

working alongside you," Hans said, clearly excited about the prospect of being off the front line. He was willing to do almost anything that was asked of him, but cannon fodder was not something he desired to be. Too many of his mates, growing into adulthood, were shipped off, never to return again. It was the decision he made years back, to go against his own mother, that put him on the national scale as a hero. He was the young man who would sacrifice his own flesh and blood without hesitation for Germany. The past few years were perfect for him, speaking to youth groups and to local chapters of the Nazi Party. But that was when things were going well. He was on top of the world. Now it was different. This opportunity gave him some direction.

"Thank you, son. I offer my condolences. I was informed your father has passed." Müller took no joy in that news. He understood the pressures any person faced as they labored away in these camps. To be around the sights, sounds, and smells of death, though necessary for the survival of the empire, was a difficult assignment. It wasn't something Gunter would wish on his worst enemies. He could see how a man could become greedy, being around unlimited resources. He'd been careful to never skim off the top, but many, many great men had.

"He was a swine. My father's decisions, both past and present, sullied the Krueger name.

If not for the investigation, my family would have remained intact." Hans had no love for his father. He hadn't trusted him. Things were too confusing, even when he was a young teen. How was his father unaware of who he had married? And the paperwork mistake? A member of the SS did not make paperwork mistakes such as that.

"Regardless, losing a parent is never easy. However, you know that one of your family members is still alive and here with us. I hope that doesn't cloud your judgment on the task at hand." Müller was certain Hans knew his brother was here. The boy's relation to Dieter and the brother was the only thing that had kept him alive.

"I have no allegiance to the Jew, regardless of his last name. He is one of many vermin that need to be eradicated," Hans said, standing at attention. "You just let me know my role here at Buchenwald and I shall perform it to the best of my abilities."

Müller pointed to a chair, motioning for Hans to sit before taking out a bottle of whiskey and two glasses. He filled both, leaning over his desk to Hans. The boy took it and sipped, clearly not used to the burning liquid. He coughed, making the other gentleman laugh.

"As you know, the war is not going the way the Führer wished. In fact, the situation is quite dire." Müller avoided jumping to conclusions, but things were set in motion, and within two years, unless the V2 Rocket was built in much higher supply, the war would be over, and the victors would come down hard on them all.

"Adolf Hitler has a plan. I am certain of it. It was his resolve that helped the nation grow and prosper." Hans still had rose-colored glasses on, never fully realizing where things were going.

"So young and innocent. I respect that and wish I could see things the way you do. In no way do I believe Hitler doesn't have a plan. He has led us this far. But just in case of that, there have been hints of what is to be done. Do you know what has been happening in places such as Buchenwald?" Müller had dealt with the young and uninhibited several times before.

"Of course. We are using the Jews as labor, providing them with a place to stay and food to eat while the war continues. Then, when that is through, we shall push them into the Russian countryside to work as our slaves." Hans could repeat anything he read from his Nazi propaganda.

"Perhaps, instead of explaining it, you should see for yourself." Gunter had already informed Ivan Kravets that his services would be required. He had his guard wait in another room for the right moment to call for him.

"This, young Hans, is Ivan. Ivan, this is Hans Krueger." Müller introduced the men after waiting for Ivan to enter the room. It seemed as though the Ukrainian had found the liquor cabinet and helped himself to a drink or two already.

"Hopefully, you aren't a cocksucker like your brother." Ivan no longer held his tongue. What he did at this camp was a task few men chose to do. If he was sacked for any reason, Gunter would be forced to either find someone new to kill for him or do it himself. That wouldn't happen.

"Ivan, please. Relax. As you can tell, my friend here is not much of a fan of your brother." Müller attempted to ease tensions.

"That's okay, Commandant. Rest assured that my brother will get no special treatment from me. He is the enemy, and his loyalties and my own are on differing paths." Hans felt this way and had often relived this moment in his own head, though he never thought it would be the reality. The chances his brother and he were in the same place, though in differing roles, wasn't something he ever expected to deal with.

"Let's take the tour before you make that decision, boy." Ivan had disdain for Hans, much like he did for Karl and Dieter. He knew how to break a person. Each time he was brought a new person to train, Ivan heard the same speech, information that had been drilled into their heads by the Nazi Youth leadership. And it was acceptable to people looking from the outside. It was as if they either didn't know how the sausage was made or didn't want to know. To eat it when it was cooked and ready, that was the pleasurable part. It made sense. Germans wanted this war with the Jews over so they could live an extraordinary life without the invasion of the foreign element. They were just unwilling to get their hands dirty. Recruits were the same way. Hans was all excited to make the sausage without fully understanding how it was to be made.

Ivan brought Hans around the entire camp, starting with the overcrowded barracks. It would be easier to step into Hell after showing what was creating it.

"You see, it's too much. Each of these is filled to capacity, many over by double. Men, and now women, which we never kept as prisoners, stack themselves at night like cordwood. We could build more quarters, but then the government would just ship more Jews here." Ivan walked Hans around, letting him take in the smells and sights. So far, the boy didn't flinch.

"So, what do you do with them? I assume more come every day." Hans knew for a fact that this camp was one of the main concentration camps in Germany.

"We have options. Sometimes, it's easy to ship them to satellite camps within the vicinity. That allows us to bring down the numbers a bit," Ivan said, impressed with the questioning so far.

"Let's walk, shall we." Ivan ushered him out of the barracks. He led Hans to several of the workstations, making sure to steer clear of the area Karl was currently in. That was to be revealed to the child when the timing was right, and the hit would be felt hardest.

"Here's the backbone of the empire, right here. No one wants to admit we live our lives off the sweat of the Jew. If not for them, we wouldn't be discussing the war. They create armaments for the nation. Those bullets shipped to the Eastern Front are made right here. We must make sure that continues. It can take a bit of force to get the desired result, but it's a necessity." Ivan let Hans walk around and look. He could see the boy was interested, leaning down and getting in the weeds to see how things were made.

"Again, even with this role, we don't have the space for everyone. That's why when the Jew becomes too weak and useless to us, we have to find a more permanent solution. Have you heard of Auschwitz?" Ivan asked him.

"Of course. Another work camp designed to provide supplies to the German army. It's an important territory for our progress." Hans understood only what he'd been told of Auschwitz, which frequently was shown in clips at the theater. It was a known fact this was propaganda and what the government wanted the people to see.

"It is so much more. Have you heard of Operation 14f13?"

Hans thought for a moment. Those things, such as operations, were much too important for him.

"We have a subcamp called Bernburg. For those prisoners too weak or ill, it is designed to euthanize them to put them out of their misery." Ivan waited a moment and saw a look, just slightly, of shock.

"At Buchenwald, we are not fully equipped for that. Instead, we are forced to take measures that sometimes waste ammunition that could be used for war." Ivan walked towards the crematorium, knowing this was the place most people broke down. He let the young man watch the inner workings, the prisoners carrying bodies like wooden planks into the building. The smoke billowed from the stacks, the black ash falling around them, the smell burning in the nostrils and sticking to clothing.

"Many die from malnutrition or disease. We choose not to touch the dead. We force the Jews to execute that task. You see, it's better on the psyche of the German soldier not to have death become their focus. Sometimes that is unavoidable, however." Ivan called over to an old man, doing his job collecting and folding uniforms that were to be deloused and used again. The gentleman hesitated, not wanting to go, knowing what was to happen. He did listen, dropped what he was doing, and dragged himself over.

"This man does not provide usefulness to the state. He is a glorified launderer, something any woman or child can do. He used to work under forced labor, building artillery shells. We waste time and food, keeping him alive to fold laundry." Ivan took his gun out of his holster and, without hesitation, shot the man in the head.

"I do what I do because it needs to get done. It is the part of a war that no one wishes to admit happens. While everyone fights for the nation, there are the hidden heroes, like me, who do the dirty jobs." Ivan smiled, fully believing his own hype.

Hans stood, shocked. He'd spent years and years listening to the hate speech, and it made sense to him. However, this aspect of the war he despised. Hans willingly sent his mother to her grave and brother to his eventual death, and that was fine as long as he didn't think about how it happened. In the end, he was a proud member of the Nazi Party and would follow Hitler blindly, no matter the cost.

"That's what we do, young Hans Krueger. We are the ones to make the sausage." Ivan didn't care if that went over the man's head. It was accurate. Both walked back to the villa, where Gunter Müller waited for them. He was more than happy to hear that the young man decided to stay.

CHAPTER TWENTY-THREE

Hans Krueger was less than impressed with the situation at hand. He had been promised an excellent job as the poster boy for the Hitler Youth. Instead, he was sitting at a long table, going through suitcases to find any valuable items the Nazis could use to either melt down or sell for profit. It was much better than the alternative of working camp grounds; that was certainly something he had no desire to do. From the moment he watched Ivan put a bullet in the prisoner's head, his belief in what was being done for the nation was tainted. There was no need to kill a man, one who had provided services. By the looks of the dead man, he wasn't taking rations from the other prisoners. He was skin and bones, like every other man and woman who'd been here over the years. They all looked the same to him, not in a racial term like he was taught. But with the shaved heads and the uniforms, it was apparent the camp commanders were taking all identity away.

Hans hadn't talked to his brother yet though he had seen him several times. He didn't know if Karl even realized they were both at Buchenwald, though in much different positions. It saddened him to look at the once lively young boy as a tall, thin, pale skeletal figure, barely able to walk. A few times, Hans wanted to approach him, just to say hi, but he couldn't. Not only would it be frowned upon, but it would be embarrassing for him to speak to Karl. What would he say? He practiced it in his room late at night, as sleep did not come easily for him or any other guard forced to take in the sounds and smells of the camp.

"One day, this war will end, and we'll be forced to flee, you know that," Müller said one afternoon, slurring his words. The commandant was absent from the day-to-day operations and would only lumber down to inspect the separated goods, giving him the okay to ship them back to Berlin.

Hans was confused. His sense of what was real and false was upside down. He'd heard how close to victory the Nazis were and the steps being taken to be prosperous. Here, things were different. It was chaos. There was so much death and destruction, unwarranted.

"In every great victory, there is a time of peril. Much like Wagner's operas, we shall rise from the ashes to assume our places." Hans spewed his propaganda.

"Look around. You have seen what happens here. If that victory never comes and we lose this great war, how do you think we will be perceived by the victors? While not all of us have killed, we've allowed it to happen," Gunter said, sliding down in a chair. He pulled out a flask and took a swig before handing it to Hans, who drank from it as well.

"I can see men like Ivan being punished. He's a monster. I've been here only six months and seen his wanton acts of violence. He kills to prove points, get revenge, and pure enjoyment. Last week, I heard he forced two men to defile one another and then shot them for homosexual activities. He's used the dogs on innocent women, who were doing nothing but what had been asked of them." Hans spoke from the heart, something he forgot he had.

"Ivan is a product of what we've built. I am what you call an opportunist. I saw a path to money and power and took it, not because I believed the jargon but for what my support provides me. You are in a much different position than I. I grew up at a much different time. You have been force-fed this shit. It's only now that you see what was behind that kind of talk." Müller had thought long and hard about his next steps.

"Won't the Allied Powers view us differently if they knew we had never committed the act of murder? I have never killed a person." Hans was worried about his own future.

"So innocent." Müller laughed. "They don't care in the least if I killed one or a million Jews. I am the head of a camp. Under me, guards like

Ivan are allowed to commit the most horrible atrocities, and I've let it happen, all so I can reach my own level of success. I deal with the realities. If someone wants to do something, as long as I get paid, I'm happy."

"You don't believe in the race war?" Hans struggled with the thoughts that perhaps people were committing crimes for their own financial benefit.

"Not really, though, if you repeat that, it will be the end of you. I have the backing of many influential people in the party. With a click of my fingers, you'd be on the Eastern Front, fighting off snow and Russians." Müller smiled but in a way that let the young man know he was serious.

"I don't love the Jews by any stretch of the imagination. Do I think they caused chaos and discontent across the world? Not really. But being a German during this time, we all have choices. I just took the easiest road traveled. Call me a sell-out if you will, but my life has been much easier here than fighting with a gun in hand on beaches of France or in the freezing conditions of Stalingrad, that's for sure."

"But if you don't believe it, how can you stay here and remain sane? I am no fan of the Jew, but some crimes are carried out under your command. I've watched Ivan kill for no other reason than his own pleasure," Hans said.

"It's my job like it's your job. I make sure this

place runs efficiently and sends out supplies to the army. Your job is to do what I ask, which is limited in scope but much more tolerable than others. You pick through trash and find treasure. I could have you working alongside Ivan if you wish. That is something few have the stomach for." Müller was quite dangerous. He understood the concern and the moral compass this boy had. But it could not get in the way of the task at hand, regardless of the inner struggle.

"I am happy where I'm at, and you have my word that I will do anything you ask. My goal is to assure the National Socialist German Workers' Party remains the dominant party in the country. If that means giving up my life, then I shall do so with gusto." Hans spit out the rhetoric again, forgetting the moral dilemma he faced.

"Good. I'm happy you are so confident in your scope of reason. One day, I might ask you to do things that others find reprehensible. That is, unless we keep Ivan fat and happy. His happiness means we all live another day not having to do what he does." Müller handed him the flask for another sip. He could see that the young man needed it.

"You want some advice?" Gunter asked the boy, watching his head bob up and down.

"Be prepared for when this all ends. Whatever you decide to do, whether to die for Hitler's cause or not, you must be ready. It will happen,

I promise you, and while some live for the moment, you cannot. You will have to decide which hill to die on. Do you want to run? Get papers, do your research. Connect with the rat line and be ready to run, maybe forever. We will not be judged kindly. But you will need to make that decision soon, for once the dominos start to fall, it will be too late to change course." Müller stood, took one final sip of whiskey, and walked out, leaving the boy to his own thoughts.

CHAPTER TWENTY-FOUR

For years, Karl and his friends had avoided any real illnesses. Once, Abel had injured his wrists lifting a tank shell and was almost sent to the doctor. That was a place no one wished to go because in the camp, going to the doctor meant certain death. Rumors circulated that the sick were used for medical experiments, and though there was no proof by the prisoners, no one returned.

"That's silly. Why would the Germans do that?" Jakob asked one evening after their limited supply of dinner. "We provide labor that makes them money."

"You're an idiot," Chaim said, giggling. He received some looks from the others, but that didn't stop him. "We aren't really limited in quantity. Look around. There are Jews everywhere. They shoot us at random and bring in more replacements."

"Eventually, they will run out and then who will make their weapons?" Jakob liked to believe this. He and his friends had survived years, devoid of any sickness or random shooting. Fate shined down upon them.

"There are so many others to hate. The Nazis can't live without an enemy. It is us at the moment, but soon, others will feel their wrath. We just need to keep our noses clean and do our jobs without incident. We can make it. Rumor is that the war is coming to an end. We must plod through," Harta said, almost foretelling the future.

Two weeks after that discussion, an outbreak hit their end of the barracks. These men stuck together, keeping the same regimens, including bathing, eating, and checking one another for lice. Using dirty water from buckets left outside the complex, the men would wash down their beds to keep away disease. As the summer of '44 hit and the heat shone down on them, the prisoners tired out more easily. They were being forced to work longer days as the war effort demanded more supplies. Men fell by the wayside, literally dying where they worked. Some passed out and were shot later; others on the spot.

"Damn, I'm feeling sick," Samuel said, trying to work through the pain. Men always chalked it down to camp life. Fevers, nausea, lethargy . . . those were all frequent. It was still due to other issues at play. It wasn't a secret that they received minimal amounts of food that didn't meet the caloric intake for what was necessary to be healthy. This was different.

"Hold it in," Abel begged the young man. "Whatever you feel you have to do, wait until we are back in the barracks. Can you do that?" The rabbi knew what would happen if Samuel showed any weakness.

"I'm sorry." Samuel looked at them, his eyes filled with tears. He had fought very hard for both himself and his group. This was too much. With a cry, he bolted off towards a corner, grabbing his stomach in hopes not to explode. There was little pride in the camps, but even then, he did not want his friends to see him shit blood. Squatting by a building, Sam had his uniform off in just enough time to splatter against the ground. He moaned as the pain in his stomach continued, not abated by this attack.

"WHAT THE FUCK IS GOING ON HERE?" Ivan yelled, hearing the commotion. He walked over to Karl's group. The group kept their heads low, as if not to give away Samuel's whereabouts. It didn't take long for the Ukrainian to figure out the problem. With his chest puffed out, he strutted over to where their friend was, grabbed him by the back of the collar, and dragged him across the ground.

Samuel couldn't stand, his pants down around his ankles. Shit had stained the back of his legs and uniform. His knees bled as he was pulled across the dirt to where his friends stood. He refused to look them in the eye, not wanting to cause them any more trouble than he already had. His stomach hurt severely, but his pride was damaged much worse.

"What we have here is someone that can no longer handle the pressure of producing for us. Look at the Jew." Ivan threw the man down at the feet of his friends. Karl leaned down, grabbing him by the arms to help him up, but he was pushed back by two other guards that came in to see the show.

"Leave him be," Ivan said to the guards. For a moment, he put off the tiniest hint of humanity, but he feigned it well. "Go get Hans now!" He yelled at the young guard, who rushed off.

"You think you can step up and be a man? Is that it?" Ivan was looking past the soiled man and down at Karl. "I've put up with your shit for years now, holding back from punishing you for any one of your crimes. And until this moment, you and your friends have provided just enough so that the commandant would remain happy with you. But now, at my feet, is a man covered in his own shit. He is not useful." Ivan took his pistol out, examining it by holding it in front of his face, all the while making eye contact with the boy.

Hans Krueger rushed over to answer the call of Ivan, not something he'd normally do. For a moment, neither he nor his brother noticed one another. They stood, as strangers, not expecting this kind of reunion.

"Jew, say hi to your brother. It's only fair that he sees you as you truly are," Ivan said, relishing this moment. He didn't hate the young boy so much as hated being told that he couldn't use the same swift hand of justice on him as he could to others.

"Karl?" Hans said, his mouth dropping. His brother was no longer the tiny ten-year-old boy he saw hauled out of their home the day of their mother's suicide. Gone was the baby fat and the chubby cheeks. Though they wore very different uniforms, the brothers looked quite similar, not counting the years of pain and torture Karl dealt with at the camp.

At first, Karl said nothing. His mouth was open, and his lips moved, but something held his voice back. Years of anger and sadness had built up to this moment, but now that he stood so close, all he wanted was a hug. He opened his arms to reach for one but was pushed to the ground. Ivan stood between them, laughing.

"You think he wants you touching him? Do you realize who he is? Hans Krueger is a national hero and a true fighter of National Socialism. He is the envy of every other Hitler Youth. Now, he's here, helping clean up the trash," Ivan said, waving his gun at Karl. Part of him didn't care whether the boy died today or not. He only wanted to engage his brother; to see who Hans was loyal to.

"That's ok, sir. He won't get close enough anyway. There is no chance I wish to have any contact with him at all. He was a disgrace to my family and our country," Hans said, looking down at the ground, finding it hard to verbally attack his brother like that, especially seeing him in the state he was in.

"Good. Very good. But that wasn't why I called you over here. It was about what to do with this filth at my heels. Look at the Jew. He's filled with sickness. And now he grovels at my feet like a rat. What should I do with him?" Ivan was enjoying this very much, putting Hans in his place. In the real world, the boy was a huge deal, but in Buchenwald, he was just like the rest.

"If it were me, I'd send him to his barracks to clean up. We need all the healthy men we can get. This war is not won without the sweat off the back of the Jew. If we are to complete the mission Hitler has created for us, all able-bodied men must be used until there is nothing left to give," Hans answered.

"Ah, and there is the rhetoric I was expecting. All talk, no action. If it were up to you, all the Jews would be kept alive. You say you will do whatever is required of you, but here at our feet lays a man, sick and dying. He clearly has outlived his uses, but you want to resurrect him, like Jesus himself, in hopes he provides one more day of labor." Ivan pointed his gun down, looked up at Karl to make sure the boy was watching and shot Samuel in the head.

"We are asked to do things most men would run from. You are going to have to make tough decisions against your better judgment. Next time, you will kill him or find yourself shipped to the front line." Ivan turned and walked away.

"And clean up the fucking body. We don't need the disease spreading," Ivan said.

Karl stood in stunned silence, his friends close behind him. No one said a word, shocked at the events that had taken place. For years, they had avoided losing anyone and to watch Samuel, so dedicated and loving, shot for being ill, that was too hard to take.

"You son of a bitch!" Karl screamed out towards Ivan. All he received was a middle finger by the man that killed his friend.

"And you, get out. Go run back to Müller and let him know that he will pay for this." Karl looked directly at his brother as he spoke, making sure it was known these were promises and not veiled threats.

"Karl, please. Now is not the time." Abel had grabbed him by the waist, pulling him back, so the boy knew he had someone that loved him close. He let the child cry, making him turn and bury his face in the rabbi's chest.

"You should go now. You don't belong here," Abel said to Hans, not caring what his rank or title was.

Hans wanted to say something, knew he had to,

but nothing could be said that would make this situation any better. Instead, he walked away, leaving the body of Samuel lying by his friends. He refused to clean up the mess Ivan made.

CHAPTER TWENTY-FIVE

Nothing could be done to console Karl, no matter how hard his friends tried. Everyone was hurting; the pain of losing a close friend such as Samuel was hard. They'd all lost friends and family, but there was a difference now. It was hard, knowing the rumors of the light at the end of the tunnel. The war was relentless, taking so much from them. Now their friend was gone.

"We're all dead. That's it. None of us will survive." Chaim's soul was broken. He had met Samuel in a ghetto. The two men were put aboard the cattle car to Buchenwald together. For years, the two shared many intimate moments, talking long into the nights of family, friends, lost loves, and the war. Every conversation ended with discussions of how to make it through, how long it might last, and what they'd do after.

"Don't talk like that." Jakob, the young boy with angst, had opened his eyes to the world. He and Salomon had at one point been inseparable. He'd despised Karl for the longest time, not trusting the boy. Years of living alongside him told a different tale. The child was a victim, like every other Jew here. Everyone had their own story, but to watch Karl grow and accept his

Judaism, after knowing its implications, impressed Jakob.

"Why not? What does it matter? Samuel didn't need to die that way. Ivan could have shot him by the building. Instead, he dragged him out in front of us to make us watch. That's vile in itself, but it shows he'll take care of all of us before the war ends." Chaim looked at anyone for support of his theory. Up until that moment the group avoided that kind of talk.

"Please, both of you. It's not the time to debate the loss of a good friend and what it means to our uncertain future. God has a plan for us all. Rushing into judgments over Samuel's death does us no good." Abel was saddened by the death of a man he loved like a son, much like all these boys, but if one allowed himself to get bogged down with negative thoughts, many times, bad things followed.

Karl walked away for a moment, lost in thought. He'd been through so much these past few years and had accepted the reality of who he was. He no longer lied to himself or others about his Jewish heritage; in fact, he embraced it, hoping one day to continue his learning of his faith on the outside of camp walls. Until today, there was the tiniest sliver of hope that they would all make it out alive. Hope was gone now, not only with the death of a close friend but upon seeing his brother as an enemy. His heart and mind raced with feelings of anger and revenge, things he'd avoided for years.

"We must do something about this," Karl said, turning to look at his friends, not as a boy but as a man. "We have all seen what they are capable of, and if nothing is done by us, then who will stand up to them?"

"It's understandable that you're angry. There have been many things that have occurred that would cause you to be upset. But you must listen to me; if we fall out of line and cause trouble, all of us will die." The rabbi struggled to accept his lot in life. Did he want to make changes and stop the Nazis in their tracks? Of course. But what was being asked of him could bring about so much more pain.

"NO!!! You don't get it. They are killing us all and you'd rather sit idly by and watch it happen as long as we aren't the next victim. I can't do that. Today I watched our friend die for no reason other than him being a Jew." Karl was enraged, not just at those that killed, but to anyone that willingly accepted it.

"You ask me to fight back. How can I, a sickly man that has barely any strength to stand, to force myself on our enemies." Abel had had this discussion several times before. He didn't agree with the argument that God's will chose this path for him and all of the Jews.

"I ask that you stand for what you believe is

right, even at the face of a gun. Ivan shot Sam dead because he could. My brother stood and watched as we all did. No one said a word except me." Karl was crying. They all were.

"If I offer a solution, and I am not saying I will, you will have to accept all the consequences. Do you understand?" Abel looked at his friends, not just Karl. He had to get all their approval before saying anything more. He received nods from all the men, agreeing they wanted to do something.

"Have you heard of the Golem?" Abel asked.

CHAPTER TWENTY-SIX

"On the sixth day, God created man," Abel said, realizing all of the men had known the story from the Talmud, perhaps except Karl. He didn't want to assume the boy knew anything about the creation of the universe.

"It is in Genesis, the making of the man out of the earth and the life he is given. God created a living person, one that could walk, talk, think, and, unfortunately, be fallible. He's cast from the Garden of Eden for committing the sin of partaking of the apple, along with Eve. It is the first mention of how we came to life." Abel saw his friends nodding, desiring such a sermon from the man who had performed so little in the past few years. In fact, he'd avoided preaching to anyone. His faith, while still intact, was stretched to its limits as he watched men and women die in droves at the hands of the Nazis.

"Since that time, man has survived, committing sin after sin. Jews remain the focus of attacks from those that refuse to accept us as the children of Israel. We've been beaten, tortured, and killed simply due to a difference in religious beliefs. There were Jew hunts, pogroms in which our people were forced out of cities and towns all across Europe. And it was accepted. Only at certain times have we been looked at as equal. Would you believe Napoleon Bonaparte, the Emperor who took Europe by force, was the man who gave us the greatest reprieve from the violence and hate?" Abel knew the history of his people and the mistreatment throughout the centuries. The Jews were blamed for everything, from the death of Christ to the Black Plague.

"Throughout centuries, Jews have been blamed for libel, using the blood of innocent children for evil purposes and rituals. It is silly, on the face of it, but so are the many other things we Jews have been blamed for. In the late 1500s, a rabbi from Poland name Bezalel received a vision from God demanding he make a human out of clay to fight those who wished to bring harm to the Jews. By building a man, taking the proper steps, and bringing it to life, Bezalel created this being. However, it was not exactly like a man. It had many similar qualities to us yet could not speak or think on its own. It had as much independent thought as a piece of wood. Beyond the tales, there's little historical evidence it ever existed. Some stories say the rabbi used it for physical labor to do the tasks a normal man could not do. Others say it was used for revenge, to destroy the enemies of the children of Israel, to right the many wrongs thrust upon our people."

"That's an old wives' tale, Rabbi. A man out of

clay is no more realistic than ghosts," Salomon said.

"You don't believe just because you don't see it. How can you not think that the spirits of our dead roam this place? Do you not feel the overwhelming sadness and the weight of death on your shoulders at all times? The restless spirits are felt on these grounds. I promise you." Abel was confident of this, as sure as he was that he'd die before the war ended.

"But a real man made of mud? Come on, Rabbi. That's silly. He needs life; a soul does not come from nowhere but from God's graces." Salomon didn't care for false idolatry, especially claiming they could do what only God could create: life.

"Either way, how does this help us?" Karl said, not caring about the value of a philosophical discussion.

"We must be like Bezalel and find a way to stand up to those that hold us down. He was willing to risk his life to fight injustice. We must do the same. If we truly see the value in saving lives, ours cannot be the ones we are saving. We must die in the hope of seeing others live." Abel meant what he said. For years, he believed his time here was served to build up others to do the right thing.

"Last week I heard a rumor from a man that had been in Eastern Poland. He said that this past July, a group of German military men tried to assassinate Adolf Hitler while he and other Nazi officials met to discuss the fighting on the front. Hitler survived and had all of them shot or hanged, but it showed that people were willing to stand up to him, even at the risk of death. We could do the same. There is a villa where Müller stays. A good start would be to destroy his home with him in it." Abel never wanted death on his hands as he knew that by doing so, he wouldn't find his way to Heaven. However, if that meant saving lives, it was worth it.

"Interesting, but there are some quite obvious issues. The commandant has Jews forced to work for him that reside there. Are we willing to take their lives? Also, even if we do kill him, we've got Ivan to attend to, and he is so much worse. Müller is an opportunist. Ivan is a sadist," Chaim said, understanding the merits of the plan.

"What if we wait until Ivan has a meeting with the commandant there. We can kill two birds with one stone." Ittel was a man of few words, never speaking unless it held significance. He was refined, a former professor from Munich. His value as an educator did not help the Nazis in any way, only providing others to think independently. Since that wasn't what the Nazis desired, he was sent to Dachau, a camp for political prisoners. He ended up here, lumped together with these men upon the removal of men who were needed for labor. Not a Jew himself, he now identified with them.

"No, the girls would still be killed, and we can't allow that to happen. And what about Karl's brother? He would die as well." Jakob was thinking more for his friend than the girls. He could see the pain in Karl's eyes whenever his brother was brought into a conversation, especially since Hans arrived.

"My brother should not be your concern. He chose his path, and that was one of National Socialism and the hate they spread." Karl had not thought of his brother like that, but he could not allow it to dictate what the rest of them did.

"I guess it shall depend on what a life is worth to us. Is the death of the girls worth saving hundreds, if not thousands, of innocent men and women at this place? Will our revolution spread across other camps and make others do the same? We can't be certain, but let's weigh all the options." Abel didn't want anyone to die, creating a fight in his mind between what religion said about killing and what reality did.

"Rabbi, if Bezalel did create a man and use him to fight for the Jews, how did it work?" Karl asked, thinking perhaps there was another way.

"It depends on what you believe, son. I have read texts that say that one places the names of their enemies on a slip of paper and places it into the mouth of the Golem. Then those people become its focus to exact revenge. But that is only a story, a fairy tale told to young Jews at night, to make them feel like there is something out there to protect them from the evils of the world." The rabbi had studied the Golem, finding interest in the reasons for a tale like this. He'd heard it from his parents, who'd heard it from theirs.

"What if it wasn't? What if there's more truth to it than you believe?" Karl was grasping at air, but it was the first time he felt hope in months.

"Karl, it's a story. We can't make a man. Only God can." Abel was becoming nervous. He should have never mentioned the Golem to this group that needed saving. It was only to show that a Jew, feeling the need to stand up for what was right, would rebel against the wrongs of the community.

"I think we should try. Imagine having the creature focus on only Müller and Ivan. We won't have to worry about losing anyone else." Karl wanted this, more than anything. It offered hope.

"Out of the question. The Golem was a metaphor. Besides, we cannot and will not do something that only God has the right to do. I refuse." The rabbi was insistent.

"We are not one man, Rabbi. We make decisions together. I say we vote," Karl said, looking around at his friends and seeing the hope in their eyes as well. He asked them the question, and all but the rabbi raised hands. They wanted the Golem.

"Can I not change your minds? Once we do this, if it even works, there's no going back. We can't just put the Golem away like a dirty secret and act as though he never existed. It won't be that easy." The rabbi didn't want to do this. Part of him wanted to walk away and try his own plan. But he'd come too far with his friends to turn his back now. If they wished to have the Golem, they were getting it.

"Do you know how to awaken this creature?" Jakob stared at the rabbi, the thoughts of this Frankenstein monster as their savior exciting him.

"Only through stories. We will need to do this together and be bonded by this decision. Are you prepared for that?" the rabbi asked, looking around.

"To make this work, all seven of us shall participate. I will need four of you to gather supplies before we even make an attempt at it. I shall ask again, are you certain you want to do this? I want no disappointment if it doesn't work. The story is merely a wives' tale; lore to show our people that strength can come at the most unexpected moments."

"Yes, Rabbi. We do. It's the only way," Karl said, taking the lead, because even as a teen, he became one his friends looked up to. Experience had aged him.

"Ittel, Hirsch, Harta, and Karl. I will need you four to gather certain items for the ceremony," Rabbi Abel said, telling them what was needed. "Once that is completed, we will begin." He was not sure this would work and wanted to put it off as much as possible. He'd have his wish well before he expected it. The war was soon to end.

CHAPTER TWENTY-SEVEN

Abel grabbed Hirsch, pulling him close. No prisoner could hear the discussion though he was sure no other man in the barracks would have any idea what they were doing, even if they did.

"I need water. It can't be the swill we drink. It has to be clear, fresh water. A bucketful of it. One of the three necessary items is water." Abel handed Hirsch a bucket, directing him towards a pump that was used exclusively by the guards. "Everything we use must be as clean and perfect as possible without the threat of contamination."

"Ittel, you must get tinder to start a fire. If you can steal a lighter from a guard, that would be better." Abel put his arm around the man's waist. He realized that if this went wrong, Ittel could be shot. If his friends wished to go forward with this crazy plan that had little chance of working, then each must be willing to die, if necessary, for their cause.

"Harta, I need parchment paper and a writing utensil. Also, something to carve with. You must get everything. I hear there are places close to the building Karl's brother works at. You will have to sneak in, though I don't see that as a problem. Even if you are caught, talk your way out of it.

He seems to be reasonable enough." Without allowing so much as a response, he pushed Harta out the door, forcing him to get what was necessary.

"And Karl, my sweet boy, your job will be to grab some dirt and place it in a small sack. We don't need much, just enough for the ceremony. We will use other dirt to build our man." Abel had no idea if this was going to work. It sounded silly; to literally build a human out of dirt, elements, and prayer. All of what he had read and studied came from folktales, passed down from generation to generation. It gave Jews hope that if their lives were ever threatened, this creature would be around to save it.

The four men went off, each to collect their items. Instead of breaking up, Ittel and Harta went together to Hans Krueger's building and were lucky to find no one was there.

"Holy shit." Ittel looked around. There were piles of clothes in the corner. Open suitcases had been tossed to the side, emptied of anything of value. Along the back wall, art, still in the frames, leaned against one another. Watches, jewels, and tiny piles of golden teeth sat in a rusty metal bucket. It was clear that the Nazis were stealing the Jews' possessions.

"To think that, in the end, this entire operation was not about hating us as much as desiring what we earned." Harta wiped his eyes. Thousands of people that brought these belongings only to be killed like a dog in the streets.

"National Socialism was supposed to bring about a new dawn, where all those once held back would rise up. It might have started up that way, but the reasons have changed. Fucking greedy bastards. They kill for this?" Ittel slapped at the bucket, knocking the gold to the ground. He had forgotten this was a secret mission, and the noise had to be kept at a minimum.

"Shhh, come on. If this actually works, we can exact vengeance later. Now is not the time." Harta looked out the window, hoping that his friend's outburst wasn't heard. When he was confident they were safe, he rummaged around the building, looking for his paper and pencils, which was quite easy to find.

"Look in those drawers. Find a lighter or two. We can hide them if necessary." Harta pointed to a series of desks piled against one another. The place was a mess, and though it looked like there had at one time been a plan on where to put things, the massive number of prisoners brought here day by day had forced guards to throw it into piles, to go through once this part of the war was over.

It took no time at all for both men to find their supplies and return to the barracks where Abel waited. He thought a flint and rock would have been better for the ceremony to actually create fire, but beggars could not be choosers and he took what he could get.

Hirsch returned soon after, his bucket overflowing. He had snuck past guards who had been focusing on a mass shooting. If he was seen, he'd be shot on sight. It would have taken no time at all for his friends to be discovered, questioned, and killed as well. But this was the plan and he was willing to risk his life to complete it. To Hirsch, he felt he had been given the hardest of the tasks, but little did he realize, what seemed to be the easiest one became the most dangerous.

CHAPTER TWENTY-EIGHT

One handful of dirt was required of him, a symbolic gesture of the connection between God and man. It was not as if the Golem was to be created with it. Much like fire, wind, and water, the element of earth showed that all aspects of the world were used to breathe life into a soulless creature.

It was much easier said than done to find places where the soil hadn't been trodden down by years of walking. Karl had stolen a small shirt a month back in case he or his friends grew out of their old ones. All the men dropped considerable weight, their clothes hanging off them like sheets on clotheslines. Now, he had it tucked under his arm, tied in a way that allowed him to create a bag to hold the dirt required.

Karl walked for half an hour, peeking around corners, surveying his surroundings at every turn. He'd been here long enough to study where guards stood, when breaks were taken, and who might let him slip by. Some of the guards had become lax, no longer caring what happened, as long as they could live out the rest of the war without dying. Many of the newer recruits lacked the desire to kill for the cause, realizing the eventual end to this genocide. The significant sadistic figures who spread hate and death had either been transferred or disappeared, especially as word got out that the Allies were making a hard push towards Berlin, while the Russians came from the east. The pressure was felt on both prisoners, who were forced to work harder to build armaments for the continued fighting, and the commanders, guards, and operators of the camps, who were given strict orders to get numbers down.

At first Karl thought it was a mirage, a figment of his imagination. In the same place where he was shot, the body of Samuel lay. His body had not been touched, allowed to putrefy and rot. Ivan had given the orders for Samuel's friends to move him. When they'd refused, Ivan decided to let the corpse rot. Each prisoner would pass by the body each day, a reminder of what would happen to those that refused to work.

Slowly, Karl made his way towards his friend, dropping to his knees. He refused to turn the body around, not wanting to look Samuel in the face. He placed a hand on the shoulder and cried, quietly weeping so as not to be heard. Karl still had a job to do, but it was necessary to mourn his friend.

"Hey, get away from there," a voice screamed.

The command jumped Karl out of his stupor, the boy lost in thought. He reached down, grabbing handfuls of dirt on which his friend lay and shoved it into the homemade sack.

"I'm sorry, sir. I merely wished to say goodbye to my friend." Karl stood at attention. It was necessary to show the guard the proper respect. Being rude or acting deceptively would do no more than get him killed, which would ruin the operation.

"That's ok. Get back to your barracks before someone else sees you." The man approached, his face blocked by the setting sun. As he got closer, he clearly recognized the prisoner.

"Karl, what the hell are you doing out here?" Hans's demeanor changed upon seeing his brother bent down by a corpse.

Karl felt his blood boiling. He wanted to reach out and choke the life out of the man that had brought about the death of their mother, and then sent him here to this hell. Only the thought of ruining their plan stopped him from doing so.

"Leave me alone. Why does it matter anyway? If you haven't noticed, death is on the horizon for us all. Whether I die today, next week, or in a year, I won't make it out of here alive." Talking to his brother allowed Karl to pull the sack under his arm, tucking it away. This needed to be safely delivered.

"Stop that. You can't talk like that. Soon, this war will be over, and you will be free," Hans said. He'd heard the rumors as the year turned to

1945. The Germans were grasping at straws, top officials were scurrying like rats, and soon Berlin would be taken.

"Free? How will I ever be free? You sentenced me to carry this around for the remainder of my life. Even if I do survive the war, I will never be without dreams of this place. The sights, sounds, and smells will haunt me forever."

Hans reached out, trying to touch his brother. "Please, Karl, I'm sorry. I didn't know."

"Of course you did. Look at what you used to say about the Jews. You spoke of nothing except your stupid race war. You might not have known about these places, but your support and dedication helped build them." Karl pulled back. He desired the touch of his brother, but to do so, if witnessed by guards, would result in death.

"It was all talk. So many people back home have no idea what is here, created in Hitler's name. If they only knew what men like Himmler and Göring were ordering. If they heard the crimes Hans Frank and Ernst Kaltenbrünner committed, they'd step in." Hans struggled with accountability, both his own and towards the man he'd looked up to.

"You believe Hitler didn't know this would happen? You're crazy. He might not have pulled the trigger that killed my friend, but what he said and did for many years led to it. Ivan would never have shot in cold blood if not given free rein to do so. And for what? My people have done nothing to warrant this behavior." Karl attempted to keep his voice at a whisper to not arouse suspicions.

"Karl, you're not like them. I understand that now. You didn't know you were Jewish. If you had, I'm sure you'd have changed it." Hans had spent his entire youth believing in National Socialism. Up until the moment his eyes locked with Karl's on these grounds, his thoughts on Jews were quite negative, though as the war progressed, he felt sorry for them. Not enough to concern himself with their well-being but like one feels guilt for a cow being led to slaughter. The animal is too stupid to realize that its life is ending, following its path quite willingly.

"I would not change a thing. I am a Jew. My life and my friends' lives are the same. I'm no different, though that must bother you. Look at how close you lived to your enemy and never picked up on the signs. How good of a Nazi you must be to let a Jew live right under your nose and never realize it until some faulty paperwork came to light," Karl said, believing this could be the last time he and his brother could talk. When one spent enough time in these camps, it was wise not to take things for granted. Life could be snuffed out in a moment's notice.

Hans looked around at everything; death surrounding him, as ash fell from the sky. The smell of burning flesh filled his nostrils, never leaving. And what was it for? His brother had struggled with the acceptance that he was a Jew. But his own struggle was also real. For years, he was brainwashed into believing one thing: the Jew and the German could not coexist. One would have to fall for the other to survive and thrive. He heard the speeches, repeated the rhetoric, and lived the life. If Berliners and pure Germans saw what was going on at these death factories, perhaps their support would not be substantial.

"Let me help. I can sneak in food and clean clothes. You can share them with your friends." Hans was willing to risk punishment. It was much easier to admit to helping family, regardless of faith.

"Unfortunately, you can't repurchase your soul that easily. I'm sorry, Hans. I have to go." Karl turned heel and slowly walked away. Running could have resulted in being shot in the back by a guard who sat in their tower. When Karl returned to the barracks later than expected, his real family waited for him with open arms. He kept his conversation with Hans a secret, not willing to share something so personal.

"Do you have the soil?" Rabbi Abel asked, holding his hands out. He took the sack from Karl and slid it under the bed.

"Tonight, we will begin the process. If it works, we could be free of these walls by tomorrow." The rabbi was correct in his assessment. He and his group would not be hidden behind these walls much longer.

CHAPTER TWENTY-NINE

I don't understand. We have to leave?" Ivan stood at the end of the commandant's desk, confused as to what was being asked of him. "After all we've done for the Reich, we are being forced out?"

"Not forced out. This place is shutting down. Orders from Albert Speer himself. Hitler wants all camps destroyed. Some commanders were ordered to dig up all mass graves and burn the remains, but there's no time for that. We are to lock the doors and march to Bernburg." Müller already had Ester and Frieda make sure all necessary belongings were boxed and sent off to his home, where he could enjoy his spoils of war. It wasn't as if he wasn't already planning his escape. It might take years to see his family again, but Gunter had already sent money through the rat line to flee, using Catholic monasteries until he could slip out of Europe and head towards the Americas. He didn't care about anyone else, including Ivan or the two girls. He assumed Ivan would be captured and hanged for his crimes. The man was a real monster, one with no scruples or care or concern for anyone. As far as Ester and Frieda, he might turn a blind eye and let them run off into the woods during the march to Bernburg.

"What's there? It's a tiny subcamp. We won't be able to fit all these prisoners in. There's too many." Ivan sat down, pulling out a flask and taking a drag. After all these years, this is how it was ending, by running away.

"Not everyone is going with us. The weak and sick will remain here, locked inside. It is useless to attempt to drag the Jews through the cold nights. They'll just spread their diseases and die on the road anyhow."

"Commandant, that still leaves us with massive numbers." Ivan struggled to understand the purpose. "We honestly still need that large of a labor force?"

"Do you know where we are going, Ivan? Do you have no clue? Bernburg is designed as a killing area, used specifically as a continuation of the Action 14f13 program. It's a euthanasia center." Müller realized he was talking above Ivan's head. He had to dumb it down for the man. He couldn't hint at what was needed.

"Not a Jew shall survive. Everyone must be eliminated, regardless of the means. Doing that at Buchenwald is unproductive. The cost of bullets alone would be monumental. Besides, it would be impossible to procure enough in the first place. We shoot only the strongest prisoners, ones who would cause us the most difficulty on our march.

Use the remaining bullets for them. The weak, like the elderly and sick, will be left here to die of starvation or disease. Many will pass before we lock the doors to this place. The others, after the elimination process, will be forced to walk until they reach Bernburg, where they will be given a merciful death. Since I refuse to cause further damage to the young German soldier, the use of prisoners to process the Jews into the chamber and then clean them will be left to a handful of those on our march. Let them take care of their own." Müller couldn't spend much more time explaining himself.

"I will start the process of dividing the prisoners now. I do believe it would be best to bring the young Krueger boy and his friends to work the gas chambers. They are strong enough to get the job done." Ivan could not hold back his smile, and his deviousness wasn't lost on anyone else in the room. He wished to continue his punishment of Karl. It was to be his undoing.

CHAPTER THIRTY

The entire camp was awoken in the middle of the night. It would be much easier to catch Jews off guard and make sure they remained compliant. Prisoners arose from the barracks, weary and dazed, curious and afraid, as to this sudden announcement.

"This can't be good," Salomon said, making sure his friends were close.

"Relax, son. Everything will be fine. Perhaps they are letting us go," Abel said, not even slightly believing his own statement. He was more confident they would all be killed before ever seeing freedom. The rabbi had seen men pull people out of their beds, shot in the back of the head for entertainment or a show of force.

"Or maybe they realized certain items went missing," Karl said, staring forward so as not to arouse suspicion. He was not as frightened as some of the others. Death wasn't as scary as what happened each and every day at Buchenwald.

"How could they know? None of us were seen," Ittel said, but not confidently.

"I was," Karl admitted. "My brother caught me near Samuel's body." To think his brother was willing to sell him out for an ideology he no longer believed in was tantamount to the brainwashing and indoctrination the National Socialists had done.

"YOU! OVER HERE!" Ivan walked close to Karl, screaming for the boy. He seemed skittish, as though his mind was thinking about a hundred things at once.

"I want you and your friends in that line." Ivan pointed to his right. He knew that by merely motioning prisoners to a line that it would cause fear. He welcomed that, even at a time when he knew even a moment could not be wasted.

Karl stood near all of those he remained closest to. For several moments, he thought that their plan had been foiled, at least the theft aspect. Soon, however, more men and women just like him joined their line until it was over a thousand. In other parts of the camp, similar lines were formed, separating the weak from the strong. It was apparent this wasn't merely a drill or a lesson to be taught over stealing. The numbers were much too high.

Time ticked by slowly as the prisoners stood at attention for hours while the guards continued the process. By the fourth hour, Abel's knees began to stiffen. He'd hurt himself picking up an artillery shell, though he couldn't show weakness in front of the guards. He couldn't be a weak link as he was necessary to get his friends out of this nightmare. If he died trying, he needed to let them know he had tried to follow through with their plan, as crazy as it was. There was no way a man of clay could be created out of nothing, but in his eyes, God put him in this situation for a reason.

"Tomorrow, we leave this place." Gunter Müller stood in front of close to seven thousand prisoners, gathered together, watched by armed men perched on the guard towers. "Our time at Buchenwald is over. As soon as the sun sets, we begin our march to a much better place. What I ask of you is to put your greatest effort into listening and following orders. We must get there as soon as possible. Any delays could cost us our lives. The war is coming to an end; however, the horrors that shall arrive on the heels of postwar are more frightening than what exists within these walls. As we speak, Soviet forces are taking German city by German city, killing innocent men, raping women and children. If we are captured inside this camp, they shall massacre every one of us, both German and Jew. No one shall be spared." Müller didn't know if this speech was working at all. If these people did not comply, they could stay locked in and die of starvation and disease.

"Why should we go?" a Jew yelled out. Immediately, two guards leaped on him, pulling him to the side to prove a point.

"No, no. Let him go. He may ask questions."

Müller waited until the guards let the man run back into the crowd before responding.

"You go because it will lead to your survival. The Reich still needs weapons and supplies made. This subcamp has the availability to continue our labor towards the war effort. You may notice there are fewer people here than in the camp. That is because we could only choose those that are strong enough to march and work upon arrival. Believe me, when I say, we need you just as you need us. There will be no work today. I ask you to go back to your barracks, gather your belongings, and return here for some food. Once we've eaten, we will begin our walk towards Bernburg." Müller smiled and walked away. He needed to make sure all these people were in line with the task at hand. He couldn't have anyone causing chaos.

"That Jew that dared question me; can you locate him?" Müller asked Ivan, who stood close. "Once the prisoners disperse, I want him shot. I will not have disobedience." He watched Ivan shuffle off to commit his murder before heading to the villa to get his belongings. It was to be a long march.

CHAPTER THIRTY-ONE

S hit. Shit. Shit. What do we do now? We don't have time." Hirsch pulled out the bucket of fresh water hidden beneath the floorboards, along with the rest of the items. "We can sneak the lighter and even the paper. And there's always dirt. But the water? Unless we are by a river or lake, we won't have a chance. Besides, we can't carry an empty bucket." He and the small group of men huddled together.

"We could start it now. It's time for the Golem." Karl desperately wanted it to be now. If he could convince them to create the creature, no one would have to leave the camp. He wasn't stupid.

In the distance, the sounds of gunshots and screams filled the air. Those that couldn't make the journey were being massacred, never allowed to even start the march. If this Golem was real, it could save lives.

"You have no idea what you are asking. First, I can't promise it's even real. You have the desire to make this happen so badly that the disappointment will kill you. Secondly, if it does work, and I don't think it will, no one knows how this creature will react. Will it be alive? Shall he answer our prayers and fulfill our tasks to the ends of the earth? This cannot be rushed,"

Abel said, trying not to play his hand at all.

"That's nonsense, Rabbi. If we don't do it now, when will a good time be? When we are dead? Will that help anyone?" Salomon had no desire to wait either. People were being shot.

"I cannot and will not step in the way of this plan if you truly wish to do it. However, I do disagree with it. Instead of using prayers and strength, the creature could help us make it through the war. Once it's over, the legal system shall take its place to judge these criminals for their hateful crimes. But, if the Golem is what you want, then I will help," Abel said. He asked for the items to be brought forward, placing them on the floor of the barracks.

"Jakob, Chaim, Karl . . . please step forward." Abel held his hands out, motioning for them to sit on the floor around him. Ittel, Hirsch, and Harta stood behind them, shielding the view from other prisoners, all gathering their own supplies for the march.

"Chaim, pick up the water, please."

The door to the barracks busted open, and Ivan marched in. He'd been sent to look for the man who caused a scene at the commandant's speech.

"What the hell is this?" Ivan said, pushing aside men to find the group setting.

"Where did you get this?" Ivan grabbed the bucket out of Chaim's hands and threw it towards the corner, sending water everywhere.

Ittel moved forward, standing between Chaim and Ivan. "It's nothing, sir. We were just getting our stuff prepared for the long walk. That's all." Ittel tried to smile, but it was challenging to do.

"What else do you have there? Move aside." Ivan tried to push through; finally, he'd be able to exact justice on them all.

"Nothing. It's a bucket. Now leave us alone." Ittel puffed his chest out. He stood defiantly, not letting Ivan get to his friends.

"You're fucking brave. Is it worth it? You fought all this time just to die for these people. I'll give you one more chance. Move out of my way." Ivan dropped his left hand down on his holster, gripping the butt of the gun.

"Go to hell," Ittel yelled. Everyone stared in stunned silence. No one could believe this quiet man would dare do something like this, especially so close to the war's end.

"Drag his ass outside. I plan on teaching him what happens when you decide to be brave," Ivan commanded his men, who grabbed Ittel by the scruff of the neck and pulled him away.

"Quickly, grab the stuff. Now," Abel said, wishing to hide the rest of the items. Their friend had given his life so they could live. There was no turning back.

Ittel was found hanging in the square, right next to the man who questioned Müller. They were only two of the many bodies that now littered the camp. The living were forced together so they could follow the next set of instructions from the commandant. In an hour, they'd begin the treacherous winter march to Bernburg.

CHAPTER THIRTY-TWO

Ester and Frieda were placed at the front of the line of thousands of prisoners being marched through the cold German nights. Unlike the others, the two women were given proper shoes and clothing to survive the nights; Gunter had seen to that. He cared about both, though his actions didn't always show it. Most evenings, after the rapes, the commandant would talk with them, comforted by their words. He even asked for forgiveness, recognizing that what he was doing or had done was not part of his character. He wasn't a rapist or murderer, not in the least. Good men made horrible choices, he'd tell them.

They did not forgive him. Both women hated the man who kept them as slaves to his every desire. It was better in the villa than in the camp, where tens of thousands lost their lives for no reason at all. And for years, both women felt victim's remorse, connecting to their abuser, almost feeling bad for him as he wept for his crimes. That didn't ultimately change their opinion of him. He would pay once the war was over. They would cry his name from the rooftop until the German people knew the truth of their precious commandant. His issue was mere greed. But the man riding the horse halfway down the line, screaming orders at innocent people, was their focus.

"Ivan will die." Frieda leaned over to her friend, whispering promises whenever it became too cold, or her feet were sore from the walk.

"I can't wait," Ester said, giggling. It was a game they played to keep themselves busy and honest. Until she was saved, Frieda had begged for death many times. It would have been much more comfortable than living this way.

"We will start by cutting his balls off." Frieda reached her hand, grasping her lover's fingers in hers, just slightly before letting go. She and Ester had hidden their relationship from everyone, including Müller. It was not something either was willing to expose. Homosexuality was frowned upon in Nazi Germany, though two women posed less of a threat. The role of the woman was to bear children for the Reich. If necessary, both Ester and Frieda could be forced into a pregnancy. Adding homosexuality to their Jewish faith was a death sentence, especially if Ivan found out.

"We need to slit his throat, so he can't scream." Ester had seen Ivan the Horrible kill indiscriminately. He took pleasure in it. Eternal damnation was in his future, but while he was in his final moments, he was to suffer.

"Only if we need to keep it quiet. I think it

would be much better that Ivan screamed. Don't you want to hear him beg?" Frieda said.

"That's true. But would it be nice if everyone could see it? All these people who suffered at the hands of that maniac. Is it greedy of us to keep his death all to ourselves?" Ester often wondered if the hands of justice would work better, forcing Ivan to stand trial in front of the world, to describe his crimes in detail. That could be a problem, however. She'd helped Gunter pack his things and ship them out. It didn't take a lot to figure out he was going to flee when the war was over, if not sooner. How would the courts react to these people? Would Müller be viewed as a victim of circumstance following the orders of his party? Payment couldn't be left to judges and juries.

While the two women discussed how to deal with the war criminals, the men dragging up the rear did the same. Karl had no problems making the walk, though the lack of muscle or fat on his bones allowed the cold to seep in faster than he'd wished. His feet stung. The feelings in his toes were gone. But he was in a much better position than Rabbi Abel, whose old frame could not keep up as quickly.

"I don't think we're going to work," Salomon said. "It doesn't make sense. Look at how many we left behind. They just stood at the gates and watched us leave."

"Did you notice how sickly they looked?" Hirsch responded. That distinction was not lost on anyone.

"And when did these crooks ever share any accurate information with us? There's something devious going on," Chaim said.

As the march to Bernburg continued, men and women fell on the wayside, unable to continue. In those instances, guards would put a bullet in their heads. When they stopped for the evening, prisoners were given old bread and allowed to melt snow to quench their thirst. By the next morning more Jews lay dead. Cold, exhaustion, and malnourishment took their lives. There was no burial or mourning. Everyone stood up and marched on, passing the dead that littered the sides of the roads.

"Karl, may I speak with you alone?" Jakob pulled his friend back just far enough away so the other members of their group couldn't hear him. He hadn't always been kind to Karl Krueger and often tried to make it up through small acts of kindness. That wasn't the reason to approach him, however. He could tell that, unlike the others, Karl was a man of action. Through his statements, it was he that would do something about their predicament. All too often, people talked. "If I had a chance, I would . . ." or "If they do this to me, I'll . . ." Empty threats.

"Last night, I overheard some of the guards

talking. They are going to kill us. They're bringing us to this camp to massacre everyone."

"But why there? Couldn't they just shoot us all back where we were?" Karl was thinking about the logistics of removing all these people from Buchenwald. To trek thousands across the country seemed pointless.

"Bullets. They didn't have enough for all of us. Supposedly there are things at this new place to kill hundreds at one time. But that's not the only reason. They're running. The guards, Ivan, the commandant . . . all of them. They want to flee before the Russians get too close."

"They know what they've done is wrong. Those criminals think they can just leave and not be forced to stand for their crimes? Something needs to be done before we get to Bernburg. All of us will die, and they will escape." Karl was unwilling to let that happen, even if it meant his brother would be forced to pay for the crimes committed against the Jews and all those targeted by the Nazis.

"We need to convince Abel to do it tonight. We must call on the Golem." Jakob had thought about this long and hard, unable to sleep throughout the previous evening. He had very little confidence the folktale would work. There was nothing left but hope, and only the tiniest sliver of it, in the name of a Golem, was enough.

The two men caught up to the group and

explained the situation as best they could. All agreed to try it, even the rabbi, who knew his time was coming to an end. He wouldn't make the walk to the camp. He had three, maybe four, good days left before falling to the side of the road, with a bullet to the brain. That night, the Golem would arrive.

CHAPTER THIRTY-THREE

Gunter allowed his men to set up camp and rest for the evening. Even once the marching was done, the killing continued. For the next few hours, guards would find those that were too weak to continue the trip and shoot them in the woods. The commandant ordered that it no longer be done alongside the roads. He'd seen too many dead bodies piled like firewood while in Buchenwald, no matter how often he tried to ignore the crimes being committed. But it wasn't just for his own sanity. They'd be much easier to trace to Bernburg if a trail of breadcrumbs were left to follow.

"Ladies, if you could sit and join me for a drink, I would kindly appreciate it." Müller had attempted to show compassion to Ester and Frieda throughout the war, though sometimes his behavior got the better of him. In his eyes, he saved them from death. He couldn't see what he'd done. Alcohol and stress were ways for him to take the blame away from his own culpability. Gunter continued to misread the women's compliance as acceptance. He was not surprised when they sat.

"You've been very loyal. In fact, you've both been my greatest confidants. I know, I know.

You're Jewish. I get that, and the irony isn't lost on me. Because of your kindness, you've shown me that perhaps, when this war is over, we can remain friends. One day, we'll look back on this time and laugh." In his heart, Gunter believed this.

"Of course, sir. We have enjoyed serving you," Ester said, without even the slightest hint of sarcasm. She'd suffered years and years under these conditions: the beatings, the rapes. Ester did thank him for one thing, however. Because of all this, she became a more powerful person, forced to live through a nightmare to come out alive.

"And we hope to continue to serve upon reaching this new camp. We've been able to live a luxurious life in your villa. I hope we don't have to resort to the hard labor of the common Jew." Frieda did not hide her sarcasm at all. Her boss had a hard time picking up on it anyway; his regimented lifestyle forced him to do precisely as he was told when he was told to. He struggled to read between the lines.

"Unfortunately, our time has come to an end." Müller's eyes welled with tears. His voice shook. He'd established a bond with these women, and while he didn't consider them human in the literal sense of the word, they were the best and closest thing to one.

"Please, Commandant. Don't do this. Have we

not been honorable and done everything you asked?" Ester pleaded, reaching out and grabbing the man's hands in hers. "We will even do the hard labor, like the rest of the Jews. You aren't like him. Don't allow yourself to become him."

"Him?" Müller asked.

"Ivan the Horrible," Frieda said. "He's a monster. You are not."

Müller laughed. "He's not a monster. He's a sign of the times. Ivan merely does the things necessary that no normal man will."

"You are wrong," Ester blurted out. "In the past few years, Ivan has either killed or had killed close to fifty thousand people. None of them did a thing except be born into religion." She was the one crying now. If she was to die, she wanted the man to know everything.

"Do you want to know what I think?" Ester asked the commandant. She waited for him to nod his head before responding.

"You are all monsters, every one of you. From Hitler himself to the lowest ranking member of the Nazi Party, each and every person is culpable in what has happened here. We are not in a vacuum, and I am not closed off into thinking that this exact situation is not happening all across the country. If we kill off fifty thousand and another kills the same, in time, it will add up. Even if I make it out alive, I have nothing to go home to. Do I return to Austria that ran me out? They didn't want me then and won't want me now. My family is missing, and there will be no way I'll ever be able to find them. You've done this. You and your goons allowed this to happen. At no time did you stand up and say, 'That is wrong.' Instead, you signed orders, authorized killings, and closed your eyes to what was happening around you."

"I did what I had to do. Do you have any idea the pressure someone in my position faces? The orders that come in are truly overwhelming. Look at the task I currently have at hand. To march thousands of sick and dying Jews across the countryside during this time of the year, when snow still sits alongside the road and mud freezes to our boots. The decisions I had to make, the tough conclusions I came to while going through piles of paperwork."

"Like the decision to kill?" Frieda said, not holding her tongue any longer.

"You don't understand. It is not something I take lightly. War brings out the worst in people. I am an officer of the highest rank, and if given a command, I follow through, regardless of what anyone else thinks. The idea of taking a life isn't an easy one; I realize that. But it is necessary." Müller was done with this argument. These women would never understand.

"It doesn't matter anyway. The war is at its end,

and soon the world will be back to what it was. Then you can judge me."

"If we survive. That's the issue, isn't it? The fact that none of us will live to see the war come to its conclusion. Instead, we will be a statistic, number one out of the millions that have died at your whim," Frieda said, squeezing her friend's hand hard. She wanted nothing more than to lunge at her captor to choke the life out of him. She needed to restrain her emotions; it wasn't just herself that she needed to think about.

"You will survive. I am certain of that. The rest of these people, I cannot promise. But both of you will go on with happy, productive lives," Müller said, tiring of the conversation.

"You can't say that. We might not even make it to this subcamp," Ester responded.

"That is true. You won't. If you do, you have little chance of survival. Instead, I am releasing you. Once we are done with our conversation, I am calling a quick meeting of all the guards. I have left sacks of clothing, food, and money in my steamer trunk. Grab them, put on the jackets that are hanging nearby, and walk far ahead, well in front of this caravan. Wait until you can no longer see us before turning into the woods. From there, you are on your own. I will not report you missing, so no one will know you are gone." Müller felt grief as if he were losing a loved one.

"Why are you doing this?" Ester was shocked.

This man had shown compassion only when drinking or after the rapes, and this was out of character.

"Because I know what you'd face if you make it to Bernburg. I have been told what awaits every Jew there; it is death. I don't wish that fate for either of you." Müller attempted a smile. Instead, he reached forward and hugged them both together as a father would his children.

"Now, no more questions. This will be my only offer. I am going to step out, call that meeting, and gather them down the road. You will have five minutes to be gone. After that, I can't promise anything." Müller hated goodbyes. He left the tent that was set up for a man of his rank and did precisely what he said he'd do. It took the two women no time at all to do as they were told, and in less than ten minutes, they were safely in the woods, no longer prisoners of the Nazis.

CHAPTER THIRTY-FOUR

Once the others had gone to bed, the six men gathered into a circle. There was no requirement for sleep. If the Jews wished to stay up all night, that was fine as long as they could make the walk to the next destination. Proper rest was necessary at this juncture, and not having it could result in death. Death was no longer a concern for Karl and his friends.

"Let us bring out our supplies. They shall represent the elements, the four necessary items that created and maintain life to this day. Before us, we have represented fire, water, earth, and air." The rabbi laid the lighter and the bag of soil on the ground next to a puddle. He was nervous as to the reaction he'd receive when this bit of magic did not work. His friends, more like sons, would be let down. It would be easier for them to willingly accept their own death afterward, ruining any chance at what was important: hope.

"With this stick, we shall all draw the image of a man in the soil below us. This will be the same image of a man that God created on the sixth day." Abel started first, drawing the outline of a head. He handed it clockwise to the next man, who, one at a time, formed sections of the Golem.

"The earth was without form and void, and

darkness was upon the face of the deep, and the Spirit of God was moving over the face of water. This represents nothingness, the same thing God saw before the creation of the universe. Before us, we have nothing." The rabbi used the stick and drew two eyes and a mouth.

"I will say a specific line as I walk around the creature seven times. Once I have done that, each of you will do the same before giving the creature the item you hold," Abel said.

"In the beginning, God created the heavens and the earth. The earth was without form and void, and darkness was upon the face of the deep. And the Spirit of God was moving over the face of water." The rabbi walked around the area seven times, repeating this statement each time.

Chaim stood up first, doing the same as the rabbi. Once he had repeated the words seven times, he knelt down next to the creature, took a handful of puddle water, and slowly dribbled it on the man, from the top of its head to the feet. As he did this, he said the words seven times, just like the number of days God used to create the universe and all its wonders.

"Let there be a firmament amid the waters and let it separate the waters from the waters," Chaim chanted the words over and over.

Karl was afraid, but he didn't know why. Perhaps this was like opening Pandora's box, never to be truly closed again. But it had to be done. He stood, did the same as the others, and then took out the dirt he had gathered back at the camp. He dusted the entire body with it, breaking up the clumped masses so he could spread it.

"Let the waters under the heavens be gathered together into one place and let the dry land appear," Karl spoke.

Jakob followed suit, speaking the words as he circled around. Next, he held the lighter and sparked the flint. He held it to the head of the creature, expecting it to go out. Instead, a massive flame filled the entire outline of the body. Though nervous at being overheard by guards, he spoke his words seven times.

"And God said, let there be light. And there was light." Jakob looked over to the rabbi, shocked at what he had seen.

Rabbi Abel waited until his friends had completed their tasks. "Now place your hands on the body, if you will. Each and every one of us must be part of this and accept the responsibility of the Golem."

"And the Lord God formed man of the dust of the ground and breathed into his nostrils the breath of life, and man became a living soul." The rabbi said his words, and after each time he said it, he placed his mouth upon the drawn mouth and blew into it, giving the creature air.

"With this word, I bring about life." Abel used the stick to write the word "emet" on the forehead of the drawing. "This word means 'true' and is life."

For a brief moment, the drawn man glowed a bright red, brown, and blue before returning to the color of the earth. After that, nothing happened.

"What do we do now?" Jakob asked. He'd prepared himself for a different conclusion than what had just occurred.

"My child, I don't think there is anything to do. I tried to warn you . . . all of you, that this wouldn't work. Did you believe we could build a man out of nothing? God works in mysterious ways, that much is inevitable, but be not under the assumption that a human, who has flaws, could create the perfect man." Abel was saddened to know everyone was let down. He didn't want it to be that way.

A guard walked by, looking at the group and what was on the ground. He just nodded and walked away, clearly not caring about the situation. It was a sign, however, that perhaps the men needed to rest for the evening to prepare themselves for the walk. They were not being saved by the Golem.

The following morning, Abel awoke, wondering if he could walk even another day. He had hidden the fact that his knee was in constant pain because everyone hurt after walking. This morning, the rabbi was able to watch the sunrise alone, praying to himself as he often did, thanking God for the beautiful day. When his friends woke, he wished them all a good morning, like he had always done. On the ground next to them was the image of the Golem.

"What do you want me to do with this stuff?" Harta held out the writing utensil and slips of paper he had hidden in his pocket. It was not a necessity to carry them around.

"Leave them here. Maybe someone will want it," Abel said, pointing to the ground next to the drawn man, still flat, those blank eyes staring up at the sky.

"What the hell is that?" Ivan rode by the men on a horse, stopping to look at the drawing on the ground. He got off the animal, slapping its behind to send it off. There was no more concern about what would happen to him if Karl Krueger died.

"Well, well, well. Is this what you do with your final few days? Draw pictures?" Ivan stood next to the image on the ground. Lifting his foot, he swept it across the body. Even though his boot ran over it, the image stayed. Ivan did it again and again, but still, the picture remained.

"It doesn't matter anyway. You're all going to die. Nothing can save you now." Ivan pulled his gun from his holster, pointed it at the rabbi, and shot him twice, directly in the chest.

Abel dropped to his knees, the bullet lodged in his heart. He could feel his breath slowing, see all the commotion around him but could hear nothing. There wasn't pain as one would imagine, grasping his heart. He crumpled to the ground, his body laying across the drawing, his blood draining below him, pooling to the sides.

"NOOOO!" Karl rushed forward, dropping down to try to help his friend, the man that had brought him closure on one part of his life and opened the other. It was too late. He quickly realized the rabbi was dead almost immediately.

"Don't worry, my little Jewish friend, you will be joining him shortly." Ivan grinned, holding the gun up again, this time to end Karl's life.

The ground shook, the wind blew hard through the trees, and a warm breeze swept over the area. Karl could feel the space beneath him moving, and he instinctively jumped to the side. Ivan steadied himself, holding the pistol tight in both hands, still pointing it. As quickly as it began, everything stopped.

"I don't know what that was, but it only saved you a few more seconds." Ivan readjusted himself, now pointing the gun at Karl's face. He was going to enjoy this.

Out of the ground, a large brown arm shot up, grabbing Ivan by the wrist. The Golem, once a drawing, rose, pulling itself out of the muck and dirt, holding on tightly. A second arm appeared from the ground, pulling out of the primordial earth that birthed the creature. When it rose to its feet, the Golem stood eight feet tall, a large chunk of solid clay, its hollow eyes moving as if it could see. Like a large statue, it looked like no one, and at the same time, everyone. No discernable features were present on the face; no nose to smell or mouth to speak, except for a tiny slit that showed a frightful grin from cheek to cheek. Long fingers stretched, as if connected to the ground before snapping off. The large muddied chest heaved in and out, like a child gathering its first breath. The Golem knew not why it was here but was certain, it was alive.

"WHAT THE HELL?" Ivan screamed, gaining the attention of everyone close by. Before he could utter another sound, the Golem yanked Ivan's arm forward, its fingers shooting out like thick rope, wrapping around the weapon. The gun went off, burying a bullet in the Golem. It did no damage. The creature pulled Ivan's arm out of its socket and turned it, causing the man to scream. With his right palm, the monster slammed his hand across Ivan's mouth, wrapping his fingers to hold the entire face. He lifted Ivan up to his level, letting the Nazi stare into the hollow eyes. He studied the man, knowing, just knowing, he was an enemy. With only his one arm, the Golem tossed Ivan far into the woods, letting the Ukrainian's body smash against a nearby tree.

Once it had stopped Ivan, the Golem stood there, like a statue. It was alive though it didn't know who it was or how it got here. In the confusion and screams, guards rushed over, stopping in front of the Golem, staring up at the large man made of clay. Since it neither moved nor breathed, there was a momentary loss as to whether this was merely a distraction. One guard shot at it, right in the belly, to see for sure. The Golem didn't move at all or react. Two more men did the same, hoping the statue would collapse. Nothing.

"Karl, remember, we have to write stuff down and feed it to him," Harta said to him, holding the paper and pencil out. A guard, nervous as to what was around him, shot, killing Harta. The utensils dropped to the ground.

Karl rushed forward to grab the items. A gun was pointed at him, but Jakob rushed and tackled the man.

"Quick, Karl!!! Save them!" Jakob reacted suddenly, like the other men. Giving up his own life to save the others was his only concern. A butt end of a gun came down on the back of his skull, crushing it.

There was so much confusion. Karl couldn't think. His friends were dying, and he could do nothing. Dipping his finger in the blood of the rabbi, the boy wrote "NAZIS" on the paper.

"Golem, here," Karl yelled, not thinking if the creature would respond. Like a dog given an order, Golem bent down. Karl took the paper and jammed it into the slit for a mouth. The lips moved as though the Golem was eating it. Then his eyes lit. It was as if a light switch went on, giving the creature a purpose.

Looking around and scanning the surrounding area, the Golem saw its targets, glowing red. It viewed the people much differently now, moving forward. The guns offered no resistance. The Golem grabbed two guards by the heads and smashed them together with such force it killed them instantly. Other men rushed in, shooting randomly into the night. Jews died where they stood, unable to get past the bullets. The creature was unaffected, his only desire to kill Nazis. Anyone it could see with the swastika upon his or her chest was fair game. It grabbed wildly but with precision, not missing a single Nazi that came close. Men and women wearing the symbol of hate fell at its feet, not living long enough to cry and scream. Karl could only watch in horror as their creation lumbered forward, killing with a purpose. Gunshots could be heard down the line, innocent Jews being shot. It seemed as though the Nazis realized their time was up, and it was necessary to kill everyone here.

"Golem, we must save those people," Karl yelled. He started to run towards the shooting. He looked behind, seeing the Golem standing, having killed the Nazis in the area. Everyone around it was dead, Germans and Jews. Karl did not have time to mourn those he lost. He could see to that later. His only concern was to stop the shooting towards the front.

"Let's go. We have to help," Karl yelled. He watched the monster's face, the eyes move around, the expression as if the Golem was thinking. It nodded as if to agree and ran past Karl faster than imagined. In moments, the creature was out of his sight, but the screams and rapid shooting ahead told him that Golem had arrived.

CHAPTER THIRTY-FIVE

The Nazis were executing all those that stood in the front of the death march. Ester and Frieda could hear the shots ringing out in the distance. They were not seen slipping away, just like it was promised. They ran and ran, never looking back.

"I thought he'd kill us," Frieda said.

"He's many things, but Gunter is a man of his word. If he wanted to kill us, he would have. There would have been no games or luring us to a false sense of security." Ester leaned over and kissed her lover, the first time they could freely be together.

"And you don't think he'll search for us?" Frieda was scared about the future, both immediate and long term. Even as she stood, finally free in front of an empty cabin found deep in the German woods, Frieda still feared the return of her captors, reclaiming their property.

"His plan is to disappear, somewhere very different and far away from here. I've seen his papers, the collection he acquired, and hid in a safe for the appropriate time. There are tickets, small velour sacks filled with diamonds and jewels, and false paperwork. We are no worry to him, other than playthings once used for amusement. We offer no threat, as far as he is concerned. In his opinion, why would we ever turn on the man who gave us freedom? He is too vain and foolhardy to accept his responsibility and think others will either. But he is a problem for another day." Ester leaned in, kissing her girl on the neck, tasting the sweat and dirt of the long march. A nice shower and warm bed, both now within their reach, would be perfect.

Off in the distance, the gunshots still echoed loudly, cutting through the trees. It hadn't stopped in a while, something that concerned Frieda.

"We need to go back," Frieda said, pulling away and grabbing her coat.

"What?" Ester was shocked. They spent years talking of this day when they could be together and away from death, disease, and hate-filled camp grounds. Finally, they had achieved a moment of peace, and she wished to ruin that.

"I'll never be able to live with myself if I don't. You hear it too. Don't act like you don't. It's constant, bang, bang, bang. The Germans are killing them all." Frieda struggled to leave, though she didn't share this with Ester. While freedom was already incredible in comparison, there were many Jews with them that would face death. Guilt had seeped into her pores, her emotions telling her to go one way while her conscience demanded another.

"Frieda, listen to yourself. We can't go back. If we do, we die. It's as simple as that. They have weapons, horses, and dogs while we have nothing but pride. That won't serve us well as we look down the barrel of a gun." Ester grabbed her friend's hand in hers, squeezing it, begging her to rethink her decision.

"Maybe we get ahold of a gun. Even if we save one life, at least we can live with ourselves later, knowing we made an effort. Think of the nightmares that will haunt us. We have enough of those without adding any further guilt." Frieda, for once, understood what had to be done. She was no longer concerned with her own self and needs. There was no talking her out of it.

"I won't go. You want to commit suicide; go for it. Do it by yourself. I won't participate. We offer more by surviving than we do by running into a firing machine gun." Ester couldn't go back.

"I cannot make your decisions for you. I love you," Frieda said, not looking back as she walked away. She didn't go off alone for long. Within moments, Ester ran to her, hugged her briefly, and followed her into the lion's den. There was no way she'd be alone on the day of judgment.

The shouting grew louder and louder as the women got closer to where the Jews were being massacred. As they approached, screams and cries filled the air as well, making it more of a reality as to what was happening. Through the trees, bright reds and flashes from the guns sparkled.

"Stop," Ester said, holding out her arm to stop Frieda. "Listen very carefully." Amidst all the commotion, a moaning came from just beyond a grove of trees.

"Maybe someone was able to escape," Frieda said, slowly sneaking over, remaining low to the ground. It was a body. They could see the outline of one crumpled in a heap in the distance. Frieda moved a bit faster, wanting to help if she could.

"Holy shit," Frieda said, motioning Ester to come closer. "Look at this."

A smile grew across her face. Feelings of vengeance and pleasure fueled her soul in a way that had not happened in many years.

"I think my back is broken," Ivan Kravets said. He was unable to sit himself up or pull himself away. The feeling in his legs was gone, and he knew he was paralyzed the moment his body bounced off the tree.

"The poor man is injured. You hear that, Ester?" For a brief moment, both women forgot why they returned in the first place.

"Fuck off. If you aren't going to help, get away from me. I'm not going to beg Jewish whores to save me," Ivan said, defiantly, not fully grasping his situation.

"We might help you. We haven't said we won't. But you need to tell us what happened. How did you, a big strong man like yourself, find your way out in the woods all alone?" Ester asked.

"It came out of nowhere. This man. He must have been ten feet tall, at least. Those eyes! It was like looking into dark caverns. He's killing them all. Can't you hear it? Listen to those innocent boys crying for their mothers," Ivan responded.

"I'll go look. You stay here and keep our friend company." Frieda kissed her friend on the mouth, letting the injured man watch. If he died soon, Frieda wanted Ivan to know that all his hate never stopped them from loving.

It was easy to find the fighting, following the sounds. If possible, it would be wise to stay hidden. Though Frieda was willing to risk her life, that did not mean she didn't care to live. There was enough of a clearing that she could see what was happening. Littered on the road were the dead, thousands upon thousands. Death chose no sides, however. Jews and Nazis lay motionless together, for the first time in years, as equals. Instead of stopping, Frieda followed along the trail of bodies, slinking her way, just enough into the woods to remain hidden. It was then that she saw him, the man Ivan talked of. Surrounding him were guards with guns, all pointed and screaming at the creature. They shot, not just once, but unloaded their bullets into it, yet it did not fall. In fact, it didn't even flinch. It absorbed everything. And just as quickly, it darted out, grabbing one of the men by the legs. With a hard swing, it used the man as a bat, hitting the others until all were on the ground. To assure they were dead, the giant walked around, stepping on their heads and crushing them like grapes between fingers.

Frieda saw all that she needed to. She rushed back to her lover, corroborating the story given by Ivan. She assured Ester they could provide no help at all to the Jews. Many were already dead, and the giant was killing everything in its path.

"Now, you believe me. Couldn't trust without seeing it yourself. Stupid bitch," Ivan said. He felt the sole of a boot come across the side of his face, cutting into his mouth. Blood poured from the wound. He let out a cry, grabbing at his face.

"The question is now, what do we do with him? We could let him die here," Ester said.

"We *could* do that, or we could bring him back to the cabin." Frieda smiled, thinking about how they could care for this murderer.

Ester ran and hugged her hard. "You're so wicked. You know that?" She kissed Frieda hard on the lips. Stuffing a rag in Ivan's mouth, the women grabbed him by the arms and legs, carrying him off into the woods. They had plans for him.

CHAPTER THIRTY-SIX

The Golem made its way down the path, past the line of murdered Jews. It didn't know how, but it could clearly locate those that called themselves Nazis and those that were not. As soon as it found one, the monster would rush with speed uncharacteristic of a creature that size, knocking them over with a body blow. Most times, that was all it took to crush internal organs and kill the guards. Other times, it required a more personal touch. Though its sole focus was on his enemies, the creature kept one eye on Karl at all times, feeling the need to protect him at all costs.

Death was of no consequence as the creature did not understand what it was doing. It was as if a primal instinct made him do these things without an understanding of what was being done. It killed any man with a swastika, going after those that reeked of the stench of the Nazi Party. The Golem moved closer to the front of the line, attacking. He was a massive figure, one that caused panic and immediate fear within those it focused on. Guards turned their weapons to the monster, shooting in hopes it would bring it down. This reaction didn't cause alarm or anger to the beast, who felt no pain at all. Its movements were very matter-of-fact, going specifically after certain people while ignoring others. Some Jews, lucky enough to survive the onslaught of bullets, ran into the woods, escaping while they had a chance. Most were dead, never even having the opportunity to flee.

The Golem killed every Nazi in its vicinity. Not a man survived the ordeal, though many fell to their knees and begged for mercy. That was a quality the monster did not have: empathy. He had no capacity to differentiate between the good and bad Nazi.

Once it was done, the Golem walked up and down the line, giving final blows to anyone still showing signs of life.

"No one is here. Damn it, where'd they go?" Karl ran up and down the line, looking for two men in particular. One was, of course, his brother, Hans, who was guilty by association, regardless of crimes he did or did not commit. When writing the word "Nazis" down and feeding it to his creature, his brother's death never crossed his mind. Now it was at the forefront. Though he hated him, it was the only family he had left. The other man was Ivan the Horrible, the Ukrainian who tortured every prisoner who walked through the gates of Buchenwald and took the life of the rabbi. There were others, of course, such as Gunter Müller, the commandant, but he was merely a figurehead, only showing his face to give orders, never carrying them out. He'd disappeared as well. Cowards, all of them.

After surveying the front of the line, Karl slowly walked back, making sure to look at all the dead at his feet. The sheer number of the massacred Jews stretched on forever. He needed to see his friends though, the men he had called family for years. Towards the end of the line, they lay. Rabbi Abel lay sprawled over the outline of the Golem, his eyes open wide, looking up to the heavens. Karl closed them. He did that to all his friends: Jakob, Chaim, Harta, and Hirsch. Salomon still breathed, however, dying much more slowly than the others. The bullet had penetrated his abdomen, causing a slow bleed.

"You're ok. You'll be fine." Karl dropped to his knees, cradling Salomon's head in his lap. He was all he had left in the world, and would soon be taken from him.

"You always were the optimist. Is anyone else with you?" Salomon said. He could barely see; his vision was going in and out as he struggled to stay conscious.

"They're all dead. Except us." Karl was trying to stay sane, but it was difficult to do. He knew very soon, it would be only him.

Salomon let out a muffled scream, barely able to get it out. Karl watched his face, staring over his shoulder, and realized the dying man saw the Golem.

"It worked. We did it." Karl motioned for the creature to come forward. Without direction, the Golem dropped to its knees, placed his hand along the side of Salomon's cheek. It kept it there, comforting as the man died, until he took his final breath.

"We aren't done yet. You and I serve a greater purpose. If there's any chance we can save even one person, we must go to Bernburg. We'll burn that place to the ground if that's what it takes." Karl spoke to the Golem. It nodded, agreeing.

For hours, the Golem helped Karl bury his friends, scooping up the earth in which to place the men. Once it had done so, the creature carried the men to their final resting places, cradling them close as if it knew them. It had never met any of them, but it had a connection, as they were all its father. It gave Karl time to mourn, standing against a tree, surveying the dead. If it were asked to bury every Jew here, the Golem would have done so, following the orders given by its master.

When they left the site, the man and the monster walked in silence. Most times, Karl could keep up with it, though the strides of the creature were long. Eventually, after hours of marching and the physical toll taken, Karl had to stop. He collapsed on the ground, dropping to his back. He tried not to cry, not to let the death of his friends envelop him, but the grief came regardless of whether he wanted it to or not. A large hand fell on his shoulder. Karl pushed it off, but it came right back. The second time, he left it, partly because he had seen what this monster had done but also because it was comforting. The strength and force of this thing they created was massive, yet he was the only one left to see it. It was as if everything they had planned led to a situation where no one survived. That wasn't the reason for the Golem, however. It was to save lives. Karl had before him a strong force to mold into whatever he desired. He could sweep across Europe, killing all his enemies, and protecting the remaining Jews.

"We should rest for the evening. In the morning, I want to go to Bernburg. Do you know where it is?" Karl asked as if the creature knew. It offered no reply.

"Of course, you don't. You are just clay and prayers. Just know I want to be there as quickly as possible. Every moment wasted, Jews die. And we mustn't assume that every Nazi was killed here tonight. In fact, I'm certain at least one survived that started out on our journey. If he makes it to the camp before we do, his stories could speed up the process, and we will save no one." Karl spoke as if the monster registered what was being said, but that couldn't be true. The Golem was born without organs, a heart, and, most importantly, a brain, the requirement to think thoughts, independent or otherwise.

Sleep was difficult. Numerous times, Karl was able to drift off before being woken with images of his friends, riddled with bullets. He stood in their blood, the only one forced to carry on the good fight. He'd wake up screaming only to find the Golem standing above him, guarding him while he slept. Though the view made him nervous, the thought that he was indeed safe from all harm was comforting. It had been years since he felt that safety—the day his mother called him into her room to commit suicide. After that moment, there was nothing but confusion, pain, fear, and the constant threat of death, always looming close by.

There were times throughout the night when he felt like he was flying, looking down at the carnage he and his friends created. If they'd never attempted the creation of this monster, would things have been different? He never had once second-guessed the decisions made. To build this killing machine was not their goal, though he couldn't really recall what their purpose was besides surviving. Karl flew higher, cruising at a fast rate of speed, looking down where his friends lay. He sped to the front and could see how the ground was stained with blood in the shape of a swastika, the focus of the death. There was nothing but carnage. Karl tried to fly back up to avoid having to be in the center of it again, but still, he landed with a thud. That woke him out of his dream.

"Where are we?" Karl jumped up, realizing he was not in the same place he had fallen asleep. The Golem pointed to what now became apparent. They were at the gates of Bernburg, their first destination. It was not what he had expected and wondered if they were in the correct place. The gate was not made of barbed wire with guard towers used for monitoring prisoners. It was more of a wall to prevent people from seeing its community.

"Are you certain we are in the right place?" Karl asked the Golem. The creature walked towards the wall, hoisted the young man up, and let him climb over. Without even a running start, the Golem bent its knees and leaped over the wall, landing next to Karl.

It looked as if they had wandered into a university complex, a series of large buildings off in the distance. There were no barracks to be seen, and Karl wondered where all those Jews that he walked with would have slept after a day's labor. Unlike Buchenwald, the prisoner could walk freely without fear of being shot. There was no one around that he could see, no Jews or Nazis. The buildings to the back of the complex were lit up, an indication that at least people were present. Karl and Golem walked the grounds, looking into buildings, which now gave off the feeling of a hospital setting, not a government complex. Most of the rooms seemed to be empty, maybe once used, but now forgotten.

"Let's check out those." Karl pointed. As he got closer to them, a smell hit his nose, one that he was quite familiar with. There was death here; that was clear. He'd smelled the decomposing corpses that hanged from the gallows, a reminder to prisoners of what could happen to them if they stepped out of line.

"Where is that stench coming from?" Karl asked the creature.

The Golem pointed at a towering smokestack, capable of billowing out ash by the tons, spreading it along the rock paths like a blanket of snow. It was not currently working but had been used only hours before their arrival. Golem knew where the smell of death came from. Karl was curious how this clay man, living for only a full day, knew what the scent was, just like it knew who the enemy was.

In a back building, where the lights remained bright, a party was being held. It was an extraordinary occasion for the people inside. Most of them were doctors, men who had been trained for a particular task, euthanasia. It was easy, at first, on who to target. The general public would not be supportive of random acts of killing, especially since most Germans were not convinced the Jews were the evil vermin that some Nazis thought them to be. In their place, to start the task of working out the kinks for the best and most efficient way to take a life, the Germans targeted those with mental and physical disabilities. It was easier to explain to people. Resources used for taking care of what they titled "living burdens" could now be used for the oncoming war and the threats of the foreign invaders that surrounded their borders. Families were more willing to send their sick to the hospitals for care, not always realizing it was a permanent solution. The end result was still the same; the patient would die of a variety of natural ailments, and the family was sent ashes of their loved one.

In most cases, it was not known to the families that the government was using their sick relatives as guinea pigs, testing the most effective methods to kill. It was necessary to save money and the German spirit. A man forced to shoot person after person would develop specific psychological issues, something that could cost the state in the long run. Over time, euthanasia became the preferred method of killing. It cost less to kill more and was also less pressure on the German soldier. When the public did find out about this program, known as the T-4, because of its location at Tiergarten, Hitler immediately had it shut down to avoid bad press. Though that was frowned upon, especially by the Vatican, it worked.

Hitler commissioned gas vans and used them to kill many Jews by carbon monoxide. When the numbers of Jews at camps became overwhelming, gas chambers were built and used at multiple locations throughout the German Empire. There were concentration camps, like Auschwitz in Poland, that incorporated a killing center directly within their complex in Krakow. Other camps were set up primarily to kill; their only task was to murder tens and hundreds of thousands of Jews. There was no need for slave labor at Bernburg. The destination was the end. The Jews marching to this camp from Buchenwald would have faced that fate, as this was part of the death machine that rolled throughout Europe. Instead, they were dead before ever arriving.

With all the Jews kept in Bernburg taken care of and the knowledge that the newest shipment was all killed on the march there, soldiers and doctors had free time. With everything coming to an end and the twilight upon the Nazis and their reign, it was good to pass the time drinking and talking of better times. Soon, many of them would be on the run in attempts to avoid prosecution. This was indeed their last hurrah, and it was a good one. Wine cellars in the area were raided; every bottle of liquor in the hands of the locals was appropriated to make the night memorable.

Karl looked in the window, watching men too drunk to hold themselves up, laughing and enjoying their evening. Their moral compasses were no longer present, as killing had become a habit for them, like tying their shoes or taking a piss. Perhaps they were hiding their guilt behind many bottles of alcohol, but that wouldn't help them now.

"These men have to pay for what they've done. We need to destroy this place. Can you help me do that?" Karl asked. The Golem stared ahead. It would do what was asked.

"Follow me and be ready. If you see a gun lifted, attack," Karl said. He had a plan, which, if done correctly, could help end the mindless killings.

The young man had grown since he was first jailed for the crime of being a Jew. He had been so closed off to the world around him, only seeing what his father and mother wished him to see, though he didn't truly understand or accept what he was hearing. Since that fateful day, Karl had survived, seeing things in a much different way than he once had. Not only did he finally accept his Judaism, but he also embraced it and all it brought with it. He survived Buchenwald with friends to help him, though now he stood alone.

"Gentlemen!" Karl yelled, opening the door and stepping into the room where the Nazis were drinking. Directly behind him, the Golem stood, waiting.

"Ahh, a visitor. Welcome, welcome. Sit down, you and your friend." A guard pointed to a chair. Karl sat, though the Golem did not. A drink was handed down the table until it reached Karl. He didn't want to accept this, a gift from his enemies, but it was better to keep the Germans at ease. Picking up the glass, he drank the entire thing, feeling it burn his throat.

"That was very good. I thank you for that. Perhaps one for my friend here." Karl pointed behind him. He wanted the men to marvel at what stood directly over his shoulder. Instead of wonder, they just filled another glass and slid it down. Karl grabbed it, offered it to the Golem, and then drank it himself; this brought about a series of laughter from the Nazis.

"So, let's begin, shall we?" Karl had their attention.

"I am a Jew," Karl said, for the first time announcing it with such pride. He'd often heard it as derogatory.

"And I'm German," a guard said, laughing. "And he's a Pole. And my other friend is Austrian."

"Good. I am happy we are all in good spirits. Could you imagine if Hitler knew you were conversing and drinking with a Jew? Hanged with piano wire, you'd be for sure." Karl smiled.

"The war is over, *mein freund*, and Hitler is not here. There's no need to fret over that." The guard took a drink, slid his glass down the table to refill it, and took another sip.

"Does that mean no more killing?" For a moment, Karl felt something other than revenge. He looked around the table, seeing boys mostly his age. The guilt they would live with would forever follow them. He and his Golem could thank them for the drink and walk away.

"Hahaha. For a Jew, you are quite clever, you know that?" a man in a white coat, most likely a doctor at this facility, said, tipping his glass. "And since you come across as an educated Jew, you should know that tomorrow morning, as we all recover from an awful hangover, we will continue our mission until told otherwise." The doctor did not seem fazed by the fact that he killed for a living and would do it again, even knowing the war was coming to an end.

"I was afraid you'd say that. You know, for a moment, I was going to let you all live. Crazy, huh?" Karl said, looking down at the doctor.

The men around the table broke out in laughter, slapping the table, nudging one another at this statement.

"Ahh, yes. Unfortunately, you must kill us all. One tiny Jew and that 'thing' you have will do that." The doctor smiled again, though there was a bit of trepidation this time around. The mood between the two was no longer jovial. Most of the guards didn't recognize that feeling, too drunk to pick up on how thick the tension was.

"You see, Doctor, I have witnessed far too much death in the past few years, all at the hands of people like you and your friends. You kill without remorse, never once questioning whether taking another's life is the right decision. Sure, you may say things happen during times of war or that you were merely following an order, but that just makes it easier to accept your crimes. Unlike you, I've been on both sides at one time or another. I wasn't always an enemy of the state. Once, I was a future member of the Hitler Jugend, an up-and-comer thanks to my father's place in the party. That was before I found out who I really was. Someone much stronger than any of you could be," Karl said, looking around the room. Even in the drunken stupor, he had their attention now. There was no more laughing.

"So now here we sit, a Jew and dead men. I am not without mercy, however. I will give you one opportunity to walk out of here, not free but alive. Each of you will march to the next available Allied post and surrender yourselves. There you can face a criminal court, which I must say, would be better than the other option." Karl watched them all, wholly tuned in to their every movement. The Golem did as well, standing over his master. It had no real eyes of its own, but it could see all.

"Fuck you. How dare you come in here and . . ." A soldier to the left of Karl went to stand up, angry at the threats. Before he had finished his sentence, his head was smashed into the table, crushed like a grape. Brain matter and blood splattered all over. The other men went to grab their guns. The Golem jumped in front of Karl, protecting him from the bullets. "The doctor must be kept alive, please. We'll need him." Karl walked out the door, leaving the Golem to its business. He stood outside the front door, not wanting to get close to the windows. Screams and cries came from within the building. Gunshots echoed, and bright bursts of light flashed as men shot and ran for their lives. Karl waited. He whistled to himself, reaching into a bag he'd brought and pulling out some rations he'd taken back on the road to Bernburg. Something about justice made him hungry.

When the shooting and cries had stopped, Karl went back into the room. The doctor was still alive, as requested, though worse for wear. His arm was dislocated, hanging freely out of his shoulder. One entire side of his face was smashed beyond recognition. It was hard for Karl to tell if the man had an eye due to the swelling and the amounts of blood. There was a look of shock on the doctor's face, still sitting in the same location he'd been seen last. The rest of the men were dead, their bodies ripped apart and smashed together. There was blood dripping off the walls and on the ceiling. Karl delicately walked by them, wanting to avoid slipping on pieces of brain and skull.

"Now that I have your attention, I have some questions. I won't ask if you will answer them because, well, you will. Can you physically respond to them? If not, you're useless, and I'll let my friend finish you off." Karl waited. For a moment, it seemed as though the doctor was not fully conscious.

"*Ya*," the doctor said, talking out of only one side of his mouth. It was hard to understand him. His teeth were broken, a thick red mix of blood and saliva dripped down his lip.

"Good. Let's start with a simple question. What is this place?" Karl said.

"Euthanasia program," the doctor said, sharing as little as possible. He felt a large hand press down on his shoulder, causing pain in the dislocated arm.

"Jews come in here, and we bring them to the chamber. They are dead in half an hour." The doctor said it with no sadness or cockiness in his voice. It was as matter-of-fact as if it was something every person understood and had done in his or her life.

"What? You just kill them all immediately?

Why?" Karl was confused and angry. He knew Jews died when they could no longer work, but stories like this were usually nasty rumors spread to scare the prisoners at the camp.

"Because we are told to. The Jew is the scourge of the world and must be eradicated. It's not personal." The doctor's face smashed against the table as the Golem struck out in anger.

Karl stood, shocked. He hadn't told the creature to do that. He needed to keep questioning the man to see if any Jews were left alive here. Clearly, what the doctor said upset the Golem.

"Are there any Jews remaining here? If so, take us to them," Karl demanded. He could tell the doctor had little strength to walk. Both the pain of the beating and the alcohol would make it almost impossible. He had the Golem scoop him up in his arms like a baby and carry the killer around.

"By the crematorium, there are a dozen or so Jews that are alive. They were chosen to lead others into the chambers and clean the bodies out when it was safe to enter. Gold is extracted from their mouth, and then the bodies are brought to the crematorium to be destroyed." The doctor could barely keep his head upright, the pain becoming too prominent. Karl slapped him in the face to wake him up.

In the back, behind the large building with the massive smokestack, was a smaller shack. Inside, fourteen Jews sat huddled, scared, and disgusted at their role. One of them looked up past Karl and pointed.

"Golem. The Golem has come to save us." The Jew became excited, motioning to the others. Soon all of them were on their feet approaching the man of clay. They ignored the doctor in its arms, touching him, falling to their knees to thank the creature.

Karl thought about stopping them but did not. He had not had any time to figure out what exactly he and his friends had created. All he knew was the Golem was a gift from God.

"Yes, he has come to release you from this prison. Go forth and tell all the Jews you find of the Golem. Let the tales strike fear in those that have hurt our people." Karl looked up at the Golem and gave the order. Palming the doctor with one hand, the Golem used the other to tear the man in half, tossing his pieces in the woods. The Jews, both frightened and astounded, scattered, running deep into the woods to tell their stories of the monster.

"Now, let's burn this place to the ground and destroy every aspect of it that could take another person's life." Karl wanted it all gone. If he could rid the world of Bernburg, it would no longer be used as part of the Nazi death machine.

CHAPTER THIRTY-SEVEN

Karl had a plan to torch the entire complex. He was torn about this decision however. Part of him wanted to leave it so the Allies could see what the real monsters had done. For the Nazis to indeed pay for their crimes, there needed to be evidence. He was confident that it was overwhelming, no matter how many camps were torn down.

"I think if we get rid of only the buildings used to kill, we can assure ourselves that this place will be nothing more than a series of governmental buildings. No Jew will ever be murdered here again," Karl said. He had the Golem grab any wood on the grounds to throw into the gas chamber while he roamed looking for petrol. The burn needed to last for hours and hours, bringing the chamber down. In an hour, the blaze was going, crackling loudly as the man and his monster watched.

"Thank you for helping me," Karl said, forgetting the man he was talking to was not a man at all. He realized his error and went to apologize but stopped. He wasn't entirely sure, but it looked as though the creature was trying to move its mouth as if to speak. The Golem nodded and patted the young man on the shoulder as if to accept his thanks.

"We'll need to do the same with the crematorium, though it's better to use explosives. You grab some more wood and pile as much of it as you can. I'll go search for anything that can blow that son of a bitch sky high." Karl watched the creature walk away. He would have to go back into the main building and do a thorough search even though he had no real desire to see the blood and gore that the Golem had created.

As he walked away from the creature the rabbi and his friends helped to create, he wondered what was to become of it. He'd only known the Golem for a day, yet there was a bond there as if the Golem understood not only his commands but his feelings. It was not a mindless piece of clay, used only for his benefit. While it followed orders given, it showed emotion. But it killed, very violently and viciously, without even a thought, as if it was programmed to do so. How different was he really to what was happening in camps all throughout the German Reich? Doctors, soldiers, guards—all were commanded to exterminate the Jews, and they did exactly that. They didn't question or ignore the orders. Even as they led Jews to their deaths on the "path to Heaven," the loyal Nazis never thought about the short- or long-term ramifications of their crimes. It was as if the blinders were on, and their moral compasses were broken. He hadn't taken the steps they did and could never speak as if he had. But he'd ordered the Golem to kill, and it did just that. Now that the death march was no more and the euthanasia center was to soon be razed to the ground, what would become of the Golem? Was it fair to set it free, wandering in the woods, without means to care for itself or understand its purpose? Or was it better to destroy the creature he made so that no one else could get ahold of it and use it for their own motives? He had time to decide later the fate of the Golem. Perhaps he could allow it to be used for good.

"Karl?" a man said, his voice shaking.

Karl looked up. In the distance was a shadow of another human, off towards the governmental building to which he was heading. He stopped momentarily, his eye adjusting to pick up on the mysterious stranger who knew his name. He thought about calling for the Golem, just for protection, but it was not necessary. The man who'd yelled to him continued to call his name, running towards instead of away from him.

"Hans?" Karl saw his brother clearly now.

CHAPTER THIRTY-EIGHT

The fire in the cabin roared, with the smells of cooked rabbit and warmed coffee filling the home. The women had waited, patiently, for their prisoner to awake, not wanting to rush any part of this. Frieda and Ester had bathed and made love, before dressing themselves in clothing left during a seemingly hasty retreat of the former owners. It was the first time in years they both felt genuinely free. Frieda had seen what the monster had done, saving their lives. Maybe a guard who had gotten away might wander here upon seeing the smoke from the chimney. But things were different now; it was the women who were equipped with weapons. Having spent the early war years as Nazi resisters, they were both comfortable with the guns now hanging off their backs. Now, it was only necessary to wait out the remainder of the war. With an ample supply of food that was found stockpiled in the basement, that was very possible.

"Argggg." The man groaned from the living room. He was up.

"Good morning, sweetheart. I'm glad to see you're awake," Ester said, coming out of the bedroom. She walked right past the kitchen table, where Ivan Kravets lay, his arms tied above his head, the rope tightened against one of the furniture's legs. Pouring two cups of coffee, one for her and one for Frieda, she sat in a chair, close to Ivan.

"Go fuck yourself, you and your Jew friend." Ivan spat in their direction though he struggled to even turn.

"And still with the Jew-hating talk. Interesting you are willing to continue it considering your current predicament." Ester took a sip, pulling her chair closer to the table. This was something she was going to enjoy.

"You won't survive, you know. As soon as Müller finds I'm missing, he will come looking for me. Then both of you will face the hangman's noose," Ivan said.

"He's gone," Frieda responded, joining her friend. "If you think he'll come to find you, you're much dumber than we thought. Müller has disappeared, sir. He's a ghost, a shadow that cannot be seen. Unlike you, his loyalty was not to the party or the cause but to himself. Once he realized that the war was ending, he planned his escape."

"Lies. Jewish lies from a dirty Jewish whore." Ivan screamed, hoping someone might hear him. No one would, as every guard he knew from Buchenwald was dead.

Ester pulled a knife out of her side pocket and, without flinching, slammed it down with both hands into the man's thigh. Blood squirted on her face and shirt, covering her smile briefly.

"You may not feel this, but very soon, you'll pass out from loss of blood and die. Do you want to die, Ivan? Is that what you want? To die at the hands of two Jewish princesses?"

"No, I deserve a much more honorable death." Ivan knew the woman was right. He felt nothing at all but, even leaning up slightly, could see blood soaking around the hilt, which still stuck out of his leg. The entire blade was buried in his thigh. He had no strength to pull it out, and even if his hands were freed, he was afraid that he'd do more damage by extracting the knife.

"You won't receive any sort of honor in death, I can promise that. But you can have a stay of execution as long as you just listen. Any insult towards either one of us will result in me clumsily pulling the knife out. Can you promise me that?" Ester leaned in.

"*Ya.*" Ivan refused to bow to these women and would make them pay at a later date, but for now, she was entirely correct. He just needed to survive long enough for someone loyal to the German cause to find them. This cabin belonged to someone, and in the woods close to a complex like Bernburg, it couldn't have been a Jew.

"Good. Frieda, get a belt if you would, dear." Ester waited patiently, kissing her girlfriend upon her return. She could see how it bothered

Ivan, the love of two Jewish women, one that had blossomed directly under his nose. Using the leather strap as a tourniquet, Ester slowed the blood flow just above the thigh. He was going to die tonight; that much was certain.

"So, explain something to me if you would. Because it's been lost on me since I got here. Why? What made you do what you did?" Ester had to hold back tears. Even asking him brought all the death to the forefront of her memory. She had done such an excellent job at blocking it all out, not thinking about anything other than surviving. Though her path wasn't apparent, all indications were that she and Frieda would not die at the hands of the Germans. Or Russians? Maybe, but not by any member of the Third Reich.

"I was following orders," Ivan said smugly, already accepting the jargon all war criminals would use upon capture. Little did he know that excuses would be unacceptable at the subsequent tribunals where his counterparts would be brought to justice.

Frieda said nothing. She just walked over to the roaring fire, came back with a poker, the tip bright red, and pushed it directly against Ivan's neck. She held it there as the man thrashed, pulling to get his hands loose. Ivan screamed wildly, the pain almost rendering him unconscious. The poker was pulled back at the right time; enough so that he remained awake. Just.

"It seems as though Frieda was unappreciative of that answer. You have to understand something, Ivan. We've all been asked to do things in our lives, some we aren't proud of. There have been times these past few years, many times, where I was forced to look the other way while Müller and others have committed some horrible crimes. But never once did I take a life like you did so freely. If this conversation is to continue and give you but a small glimmer of hope in escaping, albeit in a wheelchair, then you'll be honest." Ester wanted to know why. She understood much of what had happened. As a German Jew, she was in Berlin when Hitler rose to power. Her husband told her it would blow over, "Adolf is a cartoon, nothing more." But her husband was wrong, and it cost her everything; her life, her home, her children. She saw the public caught up in the hype after struggling for years under the weight of the Treaty of Versailles. So, it was clear to her why ordinary Germans willingly jumped head-first into the Nazi Party and their ideals. Those people would regret it soon enough; the guilt of believing and supporting a false prophet would forever be their burden. But men and women like Ivan the Horrible, Joseph Mengele, Ilse Koch, and Irma Grese, to name a few, were more than just followers. They were killers, committing mass murders on the level that humanity had yet not seen. They took the lives of innocent people, not because it was necessary, but simply because they had the power to do so.

"Have you ever been good at something?" Ivan asked. This time he was not smirking or attempting to prod. "You know what I did before the war? I sold vacuum cleaners, and I wasn't very good at it. I had no family, no wife, no one I was close to except for the other men that I often would find at bars. I was alone and lifeless without direction. When the war came, it gave me a reason and a purpose. And, for the first time, I was not only accepted but commended for my talents."

"You call killing a talent?" Frieda asked, ready to push down on the knife.

"I do. It's not like being an artist or writer; that's for sure. But not everyone could do what I did. People begged for me to work under them at their camps. They knew I'd do things most men would be opposed to; whether it was killing one man or a thousand, the numbers matter little to me. A good Jew is a dead Jew, and I'll take that to my grave. Maybe I was born without remorse for what I've done. It isn't something I'd blame Hitler for. I'm not a fly-by-night Nazi, one who will claim he was doing what he was told. No, for me, I did it because I'm damn good at it." Ivan puffed his chest out with pride. He would not apologize for anything he'd done.

"I didn't expect anything less than that, either.

Even in your situation, you still stick to your propaganda. You honestly believe you are better than me because I'm a Jew, and you aren't. Do you realize how silly that sounds? Basing your beliefs off of something so . . . so . . . stupid. All you needed was an order to take a life. Whether it hated Jews, homosexuals, or Catholics, it doesn't matter in the least. You have the desire, bubbling at the surface, to murder. National Socialism gave you a platform to kill, and you took to it willingly. So, save your pride. You'll need all of it when you stand before God to explain your actions." Ester walked away, returning with a hand ax. She wasted no time bringing it down right below the knife, burying it deep above the knee. Ivan screamed at the sight of the blood, squirting all over him. He felt nothing as the ax came down for a second and then third time, lopping the leg off just above the knee cap.

"Your turn, baby," Ester said, handing the blood-soaked ax to Frieda.

Frieda wanted more than a dramatic effect. She wanted this killer to feel the pain for what he'd done to so many. Lifting the ax high, she buried it into the man's armpit, digging deep. This time Ivan's scream was one of severe pain. He cried out in Ukrainian, begging her to stop. She refused to listen, pulling the ax back. One more whack took the left arm off at the shoulder. Blood flowed wildly from both areas now. It was a matter of time before Ivan bled out.

"Oh, not yet, love. We have more to do." Ester ran to the fire, coming back with a shovel, red hot. Using the metal piece, she pushed it hard against the wounds, cauterizing them. Ivan screamed even louder now, wanting to die. He would not do so yet. He would have to lose more before he was allowed to die.

CHAPTER THIRTY-NINE

Staring ahead, time seemed to stop. Karl had seen his brother many times, wandering the camp grounds. This situation was different. In the past, the will to survive, and in turn, assure your friends survived as well, frequently took precedence over personal feelings. There were always other things going on at Buchenwald, screams, gunshots, and the clanking of heavy labor. Now, there was none of that. It was silence, except for the calls of his name and the crunching of the ground beneath Hans's feet.

"Karl, please, wait. I need to talk to you." Hans ran as fast as he could.

It was instinctual, the reaction Karl had. He saw not his brother, but an enemy and a real monster. This was the person who chose loyalty of a cause over commitment to his family. He was willing and quite happy to destroy the family structure over the simple fact that their mother and Karl were Jewish. Karl's blood boiled, his anger almost overflowing. Balling up his fist, Karl swung, connecting his knuckles against Hans's face. There was a loud crunch, followed by a stabbing pain up his arm.

Hans tumbled back, the force of the punch

breaking the orbital bone. He went to get up, the instinct to fight, but was sent back to the ground with a kick to the ribs.

"Wait, wait," Hans said, trying to catch his breath. He could feel his eye swelling shut, his sight in his right eye disappearing. He held up his hands, hoping to ward off more attacks.

"Now you want mercy? Begging like a dog at my feet. How dare you follow me here." Karl wanted to hit him again but didn't. He saw a brother's face ravaged by war and this physical altercation. He stopped.

"You have one minute to explain yourself. After that, you will have to face your judgment," Karl said.

"You have to run away, far away." Hans sat up, leaning on his hands.

"I think it's time for you to run, brother. I've been running for years, from my past and from who I really am," Karl said, crying.

"I'm not worried for me; it's you I'm scared for. I know what I've done, and I hate myself for it. Even when I was touted as a hero, in the back of my mind, I knew it was wrong. But, that's for God to decide." Hans grabbed his brother, pulling him down next to him.

"Have you seen it?" Hans whispered. "Have you seen the monster?"

"What?" Karl hadn't seen his brother at all since the Golem awoke.

"There's a giant, killing everyone. Rumors are spreading all throughout the area about it. I heard he's ten feet tall, breaking men in pieces with his bare hands." Hans was never one to be superstitious. He'd been sent ahead to warn other Nazis of this creature that was destroying everything in its path.

"It's a Golem, Hans. It's not a monster." Karl explained the entirety of the situation, from the reasons why to the actual awakening. "You did it to yourselves. The Golem wouldn't have been created if your people hadn't killed every Jew in sight. Now that the reckoning is here, you want to be saved?"

"Do you know how many times I saved *your* life? You assumed that by pure luck, you and your friends lasted as long as you did in Buchenwald. Come on, Karl. Did you ever take a moment to look around, really look around? How many Jews survived that weren't in your group? You can count them on one hand because they don't exist. Everyone had a shelf life except you. Ivan wanted you dead. That was no secret. Yet, you marched on. I don't ask for your help at all and won't beg you to save me. What I do want is for you to hide for the remainder of the war. Find a safe space and stay there until you can flee Europe. My life is over, but if I can help you in some way, any way, then let it be as a brother who, with his final acts, willingly helped spare the life of someone else." Hans squeezed his brother's hand tight.

"I'm not scared to die. After what I've seen, I don't worry about it. My only goal is to stop the Nazis from killing any other Jews. The decision to fight started the moment we were forced to march from Buchenwald, and it continues here. You want to help me in some way? If so, join me in finding explosives so I can blow up the final remnants of this killing facility." Karl pointed in the direction of the crematorium and gas chamber. He felt a bit of remorse for his brother, realizing that perhaps the guilt of what he'd done or agreed to would be punishment enough.

Hans agreed, and the two brothers roamed the government building, looking for anything they could use to destroy the complex. There was little talking, though Hans did attempt several times to start up conversations about the early days before the war decimated their family. Karl avoided it at all costs. While he understood what National Socialism did to young men and women, he wasn't willing to let his brother wash his hands of what had been done to the family.

"Check that room," Karl would say, sending his brother away. The buildings were much more extensive than he'd imagined; room upon room, filled with paperwork, some waiting to be shredded. It was clear to him that many of the men and women stationed here left the facility to find safety in other places.

"Over here," Hans yelled for his brother, who quickly rushed to find a room full of gasoline and dynamite. "It looks like they had the same plan we did."

"No, not the same plan, Hans. We are destroying this place to end the massacres. They were doing it to save themselves. Look at these. Take a second to read them." Karl tossed his brother a few of the files he'd grabbed in the previous room.

"It's just numbers." Hans flipped through the pages.

"Look closer."

Hans read through page after page, numbers set next to days. It became clear to him what this meant. Listed day by day were the Jews that were exterminated, a log to be preserved so future generations of National Socialists could see what the Reich did for them.

"There are thousands of pages of the same thing. These were to be burned, but the cowards left before even doing that. They were just going to blow the place up and get rid of the evidence. These are the men and women you worked for. We must leave it preserved for the Allies. Someone must pay for this." Karl dropped the papers on the ground so he could load his pack with the explosives. His brother grabbed most of the gas, though some was left in the room.

For over an hour, the two men picked through the remnants of what the Nazis had left behind. As they went from building to building, again discussions flowed into life before this. Neither man could change the present or the events of the past few years. It had all happened, and nothing could change it. No amount of apologies or promises could make up for what Hans Krueger had done or stood by and watched be done. It was silly to even entertain such a conversation, knowing that this was to be the last time each brother would see the other in absolute freedom. Karl was forced behind walls, and now, just in time for freedom, Hans would take his place, this time in the hands of the Russians.

"Do you regret your decision?" Karl asked at last, desiring the truth. Most people would lie to get out of trouble. In this situation, where trust needed to be established, he knew Hans would be honest.

"Yes and no. I do not regret following the path I took and would make the same decision every time. I was a hero in the eyes of millions of young men and women, a beacon of light for National Socialism. It would be foolish of me to say now that I would pass it all up. I have to assume that while the rhetoric would be similar, and while the speeches and laws passed might infringe on the rights of one person, it is the whole that benefitted." Hans could tell his brother was becoming angry. "I don't mean that it was the right decision. Many just like me will have to answer, not just to the Allies, but to their children as well. The guilt will weigh on my shoulders for all eternity as, once I pass on, I will still have to answer to God."

"So, what do you regret?" Karl had no anger left in him for his brother. He was a product of his environment and was shaped by his surroundings as Karl was.

"My ignorance. That's a quality I received from our father. He had no qualms about sacrificing everything for the good of his own career and wallet. Money never motivated me in the least, but the accolades, the adoration from the millions of Germans who held me high as a pillar, that was my vanity. It affected everything, including the relationships I had built. I'd like to say, if things were different, I'd take a much different path, but that isn't correct. I just wish I truly had understood the importance of family."

"I'm glad you didn't. Hans, I love you, and as mad as I am at your choices, you are still my brother. That is something that, no matter which political system steps in the way, is real. But if you hadn't made your decision, as hateful and petty as it was, I would have lived a lie. I am a Jew, like my grandfather before me. You brought out what I consider to be the best of me. I wish it wouldn't have taken the situation it did, but I can thank you for that." Karl hated what had happened to him, but it had made him into who he was. His brother had a hand into making him the man he was.

The brothers' time was limited. There would be no more happy reunions or forgiveness, except in hopes and dreams. The rest of the time they were together, Hans and Karl collected more explosives and explored the buildings like two brothers would. They talked of old times, and of what could be, without ever again mentioning what had happened. As they made their way back to the crematorium, Karl stopped at the building with the dead Germans. He walked his brother through, explaining what the doctor had said of this place. He knew it made his brother feel bad, as everything tied back to his support. None of this would have been possible without the full support of the people. The euthanasia programs, much like the killing centers, only existed because the people allowed them to survive. It was Karl's hope that his brother was able to fully accept his culpability in these crimes.

"I can't be in here anymore. We need to burn it," Hans said, dousing the building with some of the gasoline. Within a minute, the entire complex was in flames.

"We just need to destroy one in the back, and we can leave. That's where so many innocent lives were taken." Karl walked back to the ovens, not considering a threat so close.

"Karl, wait!" Hans whispered, grabbing his brother by the back of the shirt and yanking him to the ground.

"There it is. The monster. We have to leave . . . *now.*" Hans's voice shook, scared at what was so close to him.

The Golem walked back and forth, lumbering as it carried wood in its arms. Without knowing why, it piled it around the outside of the crematorium, as instructed. He followed instructions blindly, waiting for the next order. The creature had no ears or eyes, but its senses tingled. It could hear its master speaking in the distance. But there was someone else, someone that shouldn't be there.

"It's ok, Hans. It isn't dangerous." Karl stood and walked towards the Golem, smiling and waving his brother to follow him. Around them, fires burned as the flames rose high to the sky. Off in the distance, soldiers had seen the smoke and heard the gunshots. They would arrive at any moment.

CHAPTER FORTY

The Golem, a man made of clay and given life by the boy known as Karl Krueger, stood, staring at the approaching brothers. It knew nothing of Hans, though the creature had heard cries from his friend and could sense his anger. It was as if every fear that Karl had was understood entirely by the Golem. It couldn't remember where or how, but it had heard many of his stories before. However, it had orders, ones it must follow through with.

Before either man could speak, the creature ran forward with tremendous speed. His master was in danger, though it didn't know how it knew for sure. Without so much as a thought, it scooped Hans up in its arms, running off with the man.

"DON'T!!!" Karl screamed at the creature he'd created. "HE'S NOT DANGEROUS!"

The Golem heard none of that and could not recognize if the man was dangerous or not. All it could tell was that the man was an enemy, a Nazis, the thing he was told to destroy. There was confusion, however. As soon as it got far enough away, the Golem held Hans up by the throat, staring at him intently. Something about this man was familiar. Clearly, he needed to die. It could feel someone tugging against the arm that held

298

Hans high in the air. When it looked back, it saw Karl holding on, trying to pull it down.

"Please, let him go," Karl said, begging. He had understood what was going on. His brother was a Nazis, the one thing the Golem was told to hunt down.

The creature couldn't comprehend the demands. It lacked emotions to make informed decisions. It understood only the command. Without so much as an afterthought, the Golem squeezed until there was a snap of the neck. Hans went limp in its fist, his head tilting to the side. He was held for a moment longer and then dropped to the ground, dead.

"NOOOO!!!!" Karl dropped to his knees, turning his brother over, slapping him in the face in hopes of reviving him. This was a bad dream, one which he'd wake up from, fast asleep in his warm bed, with his father, mother, and brother surrounding him. But unfortunately, this wasn't a dream. He felt a hand on his shoulder, the side where the Golem stood, the same hand used to kill his own brother.

"What the hell did you do?" Karl yelled. He stood up, pushing against the Golem's chest, wishing he could take it all back, every part of it. He cried, screaming as loudly as he could at what the creature had done. Just as quickly as the anger came upon him, it left. Two massive arms wrapped around him, pulling him in. It patted his back, comforting him in ways he thought not possible.

Off in the distance, the sounds of voices filled the woods. They had heard the commotion and seen the smoke, now desiring to get a closer look. The crunching of their boots against the rustling leaves got the attention of the Golem.

"You have to go now. If you don't run away, you'll never be free." Karl looked up, his commitment to fighting and will to live gone. His entire family was dead. He had no friends, and nearby were more Nazis. Though the Golem could fight them off as well, eventually, it would be overpowered. If the Germans ever figured out how to use the creature to their benefit, there would be no stopping them. This was a force of nature, one that could easily take down entire cities without remorse.

The Golem refused to budge. Whether it was a lack of understanding or not, the creature lowered itself, sitting down next to the body of Hans, crossing its legs as if to show that it too no longer wanted to fight.

Karl could hear the voices getting closer and closer. As much as he begged the Golem, it would not leave his side, like a loyal dog. In haste, Karl stood, this time cradling the head of the Golem in his arms. He kissed it on the top of the head, in his own way letting the creature know he was cared for, and with one hand, wiped away the "e" from the word "emet" that had been written into its forehead. It was as if the monster never existed. In a moment, the creature turned to a pile of dirt in his hands, and then dropped onto the ground.

"STAND UP!" a man screamed, though not in a voice understood by the young German Jew. When the boy didn't respond, the Russian walked behind him and hit him with his gun. This got the reaction he wanted.

"Wait, wait, Dmitry. Don't be so aggressive." A man jokingly pushed him out of the way and approached Karl.

"Do you speak German?" the Russian asked. It was clear he was an interpreter.

"Yes. Of course," Karl said, realizing now that these were not the enemies he feared, though stories and rumors implied that they couldn't be trusted much more than the Nazis.

"Did you do all this?" The man pointed to the burning buildings. It was now clear how much destruction he and the Golem had done.

"Yes. I am a German Jew. It is my mission to stop the killing of Jews," Karl said, standing at attention, with pride at who he now was.

"That's what we like to hear. We are here to liberate this . . . uh . . . facility." The Russian smiled, looking at the wreckage. It was clear he and his army could continue their march.

"However, it seems as though you've done that

301

for us." The man stuck his hand out. "My name is Egor. By the looks of it, you seem to have a knack for 'liberation.'" Egor laughed, pointing to the fires.

"Do you have anywhere to go, young Jew?"

"Karl. My name is Karl."

"Karl is a much better name than the young Jew. Do you have anywhere to go, Karl?" Egor asked.

"No, everyone is dead." It wasn't said in sadness but as a simple matter of fact.

"Then, my friend, I insist you come with us. We can use all the help in liberating each and every camp. You can provide us with a welcoming face. Sometimes, people fear the Russians." He looked at his men. "I am sure you can see why."

Karl had a decision to make. He had nowhere to go, no family to go to, and no friends to stay with. If he returned to his hometown, he'd still be a pariah. It wasn't a secret what had happened to his family. At least, with the Russians, he might provide some service. He agreed, only asking for a few minutes alone. Egor was excited, informing him they could meet down the hill, where vodka and potato pancakes would be waiting for him.

For an hour, Karl sat alone with his brother's body. He decided he'd drag him to the burning building to cremate him. Rummaging through Hans's pockets, Karl took anything of value, including metals, notes, flask, pictures, weapons, and armband. He left them on the ground while he took care of his brother's body, returning to gather them all up. Next to all his brother's supplies was the pile of dirt, once the Golem. Just like his brother's body, Karl couldn't walk away without taking care of the thing he'd created. Emptying the canteen, Karl scooped the dirt up, sliding it into the container. Within the pile of dirt sat the note that said "Nazis" on it. Karl shoved that into the flask as well, not wanting to leave any remains. Tucking it under his arm, he walked down the hill to join the Russians. He would not let the memory of his friends die in vain.

PART III:

TWILIGHT OF THE GODS

CHAPTER ONE

Karl took a deep breath in, opening his eyes. He had closed them throughout most of the story. He hadn't wanted to, but not looking down at his wrinkled, old hands brought him back to a time many years ago. He'd wiped away tears from his eyes several times throughout the tale, unable to block the memories he had so often dreamed of late at night.

"Do you understand why I share this with you, Zachariah?" Karl held the wooden box in his hand, so close, as if the contents were a part of him.

Zach was too shocked to say anything at all. His mouth was agape, his brain running through each and every part of the story. He'd read about some of that stuff in his history class: the Nazis, camps, and the armed resistance to the war and murder of millions of innocent lives. He'd even met a survivor who came to the school to speak on Holocaust Remembrance Day. But in his own family, someone so close to him? To think for decades, his zayde hid this secret. He wanted to hug his grandfather, to let him know everything would be safe with him, but his teenage mind struggled to accept the story.

"This is all true?" Zach said, though it was challenging to say anything at all.

"Hand me that bottle, please," Karl asked, filling his teacup with the liquor. In a quick swig, the entire drink was gone. It burned going down his throat, causing a warm sensation in his belly. He refilled it, this time only sipping.

"I assumed that would be the reaction, and honestly, I don't blame you for it. I've hidden this part of my past from everyone, including your grandmother. My own children never knew this either. Can you imagine if your father found out his last name was Krueger and not Auerbach?" This caused Karl to giggle just a bit. It had more to do with the alcohol, but also the mere thought of how his family would react if they found out about all these skeletons.

"Why not tell people? It's such a good story." Zach didn't believe it all. It seemed too fantastical to be anything more than merely a German old wives' tale used to teach a valuable lesson.

"Unfortunately, even reliving it once, in full, has taken much out of me. You see, picture the worst thing that has ever happened to you. Every night, when you close your eyes, you dream it. It is as much a part of me as seeing my family every morning or enjoying a cup of coffee before I went to work. When I drank to block out memories, they'd come randomly. Perhaps I see a man on the street that resembles a guard

I knew or a cashier who resembled a Jew that was shot many years before. Occasionally, I'll see the rabbi, his face transforming from a cloud or television static. It comes in spurts. The one that frightens me is the figure of Ivan, that small, petulant asshole. He comes in waves, haunting me like a ghost of Christmas past, taunting me. He never says a word, too cowardly, but he watches, waiting for me to die, I suppose, where he can meet me in the afterlife."

"You don't think he's going to Heaven, Zayde. That man sounded horrible, and if anyone deserved the wrath of God, it is clearly him." Zach reached out, touching his grandfather's arm.

"That is true. The commandant will go to Hell, but sadly, I belong there with him. That was the point of the story, son. It wasn't merely to convince you there was a happy ending, even when things looked their worst. That just isn't true. Regardless of what you think of survival and the will to live, the reality is there are no happy endings. There never was, and there's no chance of it, even today. You see, I was able to go on living, fighting, and struggling through the camp system, watching so many fall when I did not. It wasn't because I was stronger or faster or smarter. It was the luck of the draw. It was as if God himself was on vacation, not paying attention to who died and who lived. Many men and women, much better than I, lost their lives to the Nazis and their Allies. But what I did was wrong. I allowed anger and revenge to exact justice, where I had no right. I am not God, and I had no right to play him." Karl had frequently told this to himself, convinced he was indeed an evil man.

"You know that is bullshit, pardon my French," Zach said, giving his grandfather a wink. "You did what you had to do to survive, and it is not just you. Because of your bravery, you saved all those people from dying in the gas chambers. You stopped that and made certain that the facility had no chance to take the life of another innocent person. You were a hero."

"NO!" Karl pointed his finger at his grandson. For a moment, he saw nothing but the anger he'd seen years prior. "Don't ever use that word to describe me. Because of me, all my friends are dead. All those innocent Jews on that march are dead. My brother is dead only because I decided to tempt fate. If I'd have left well enough alone . . ."

"If you had, every one of you would have found yourselves marching right to your deaths. You gave them the chance to fight. And it wasn't just your decision. You said it yourself; everyone wanted to stop the guards from killing. To place that guilt on yourself, only because you survived, is selfish. Don't take that away from them.

Accept their gift of giving you a chance to do what they couldn't." Zach spoke from his heart.

"That is true. But now, all I have left are some trinkets." Karl placed the wooden box on the table, slowly opening it to reveal its contents. Inside were the medals once worn by the Nazi Youth. The reds and blacks were barely faded. Next to it was a journal, filled with the musings of a German soldier and officer, one who fought bravely for the cause, even when he knew it was wrong. A dagger, engraved with the Nazi symbol of hate, lay across the bottom of the box. It was the thing hidden underneath it all that interested Zach.

"Is that . . . the canteen, Zayde?" Zach reached in, pulling out pictures to get a better look at the item. It seemed to be in pristine condition as if not a day had gone by since it was first made. As he went to grab it, a hand shot over it, holding it in place.

"That is something never to be trifled with," Karl said, snarling, the first time he had snapped at his grandson in many, many years.

"I thought you were full of shit, no offense. That can't be real." Zach was shocked. Listening to the story, he'd assumed that what was told was a metaphor for something else, like a commitment to survive. His grandfather was able to compartmentalize what he did by imagining it as something otherworldly. The creation of a man out of nothing but dirt and prayers was simply outrageous and unbelievable.

"It's all real. Did you not hear what I told you? Or did you merely believe it was the ramblings of a crazy old man?" Karl looked into the box, ran his fingers over his brother's items, and closed it up with a sigh. He hadn't come down to see these in many years, and this may be the last time anyone would ever lay eyes on them again.

"The reason I told you this story, and I didn't leave a single thing out, was to prove several points. First, you have to remember, regardless of the situation, every action has a reaction. Sometimes, it requires deep thought and decision-making that goes well beyond the norm. You see, I was angry for many years. I wanted revenge and wished to see it at any cost. It clouded my judgment, and it resulted in everyone I cared about dying. I know what you face now is difficult, much more so than I probably understand. You want blood for blood. That is easy to do. Violence and revenge are so easy to achieve, but it comes with a price. The price I paid was that I lost every friend I made at Buchenwald as well as my family. Sure, you can say I saved lives, but the war was ending, and the Russians were coming. In days, or even hours, Bernburg would have been overrun by Soviets, and the facility would have been torn down, regardless if I had ordered it. I've had many nights to think about the entire ordeal from the moment I was ripped from my home until the day I left with the Russian army to liberate camps. I bore witness to horrific conditions, much worse than I could have imagined. I think when you are in it, you fight day-by-day and close off what's surrounding you. Buchenwald was no different than others, but coming back into it, not as a prisoner but a liberator, you take on a different perspective." Karl tucked the box back in its place. He hoped his grandson had learned a valuable lesson.

"But if you hadn't survived, you wouldn't have been able to help the Russians in their quest to save more Jews. You provided a great service. I won't say heroic." Zach snickered, getting a grin from his grandfather.

"Well, thank you." Karl patted Zach on his face, then grabbed his mug and key to head back upstairs. "You just must remember that every decision you make has consequences. If you let your heart lead you, things can go awry. Let your head do the thinking and take time to really think about the potential outcome. I should have forced my brother to leave. Sure, he'd have been on the run, and our relationship would have ended without a proper conclusion, but he'd be alive. Just don't jump the gun. Let your father help you with those boys and wait it out. Eventually, they will graduate and move on. Life will find a way to kick their asses. You won't need to."

"They'll just do it again. If not to me, it will be to other people." Zach wondered what it meant to look the other way, knowing what the future could hold for other victims.

"It's funny, you know. Whether it's God or fate, the chickens come home to roost, as they say. It's like Ivan Kravets or Gunter Müller. I have no idea what became of either of them. I always watched the news about the capturing of Nazi War Criminals. Though both their names remain at the top, neither have been located. I'd like to think that they lived the remainder of their years, scared and hiding, in hopes of never being found. Can you imagine it? Running, always looking over your shoulder. Those men have paid the price over and over. One day, both will be found and brought to justice if they aren't already dead. They'll be dragged out into the public eye, old and withered. The boys you deal with will one day run head-on into something their fathers can't pay off. Believe me, it happens to everyone." Karl walked up the stairs slowly. He felt tired but good to have shared this secret with someone. It was his hopes that his tale would be cautionary and that his grandson would use it to become a more responsible and better person than he had been. Unfortunately, that was not to be.

CHAPTER TWO

Fred Ripken sat at the dinner table, his father and stepmother across from him. Since trouble had picked up, his father demanded nightly meals in the hope that discussions would help his son realize the error of his ways. Often, it went into lectures about everything he had done wrong, never once focusing on the right things.

"Nothing good comes from you hanging out with those kids. You know that, Freddy." Bunni wasn't her real name but one she picked up at the strip club circuit. Marilynn Lodgers had been with her current husband for years, well before the divorce to his fourth wife was official. She loved the money and liked Fred Senior enough. Still, her stepson always fell ass deep into trouble, bringing about unwanted stress. It was a constant headache, dealing with his antics. That was one of the problems though she didn't recognize it as anything more than "boys being boys." It was as if she refused to see how sadistic he was so that she could avoid the uncomfortable discussions.

"Nothing good is an understatement," Fred Senior said, three whiskeys into the evening. He was unabashedly open in dealing with his son. It took very little to bring about a public verbal lashing, whether in front of the boy's friends or during a meeting with the Kingston principal. Behind closed doors, it was much worse.

"Dad, relax. In a few months, I'll be off to college and won't be a burden." Fred Jr. didn't care where he went. He needed to get away, not fully understanding his father's part in his crimes. Freddy was untouchable in this city. He lacked the realization that it wouldn't translate to his college life.

"You idiot. You don't get it. What you've done has set me back years. I built my company up with my own two hands. Everything you see here is mine. It's due to my hard work. Yet you flaunt it. You use my fucking money to absolve yourself of crimes. When you leave, I will be spending years rebuilding the name, whitewashing you from this place." It wasn't wrong, what he said. Fred Senior would be spending a lot of money and time to make people forget about his son. And the worst part was that this could continue on a much larger scale. In the tiny Rhode Island town of Kingston, being a Ripken was something. Go to a campus of ten thousand students, where many families had the same wealth, and his son became that small fish in a big pond.

"Perhaps a private junior college would be best, don't you think?" Bunni frequently followed suit, drinking heavily with dinner to make it through a night. She was sick of hearing the same conversations over and over. It wasn't uncommon for her to wait until the argument became a bit too hot for her before excusing herself to go out to the pool to relax. It was much easier to disassociate from the issues rather than dealing with them. Besides, Freddy wasn't even her biological child.

"Son, this is the last time." Fred Senior leaned in close, a snarled whisper piercing from his lips. "You fuck up again; you're on your own. Got it?"

"We bein' honest, Dad?"

"Of course. Always. That's what us Ripkens hold dear. Honesty." Father puffed his chest out, delivering a statement he truly believed.

"This ain't the last time. You and I both know that. I can screw up as much as I want, and all it would take is a single call to your lawyer to smooth things over." Fred watched his father's face turn three colors of red, his lips pursed together as if he had sucked on a lemon. A vein popped out on his forehead, a sure sign he was on the verge of his heart exploding.

"You little brat. You goddamned pissant. How dare you talk to me like that?" Fred Senior hopped out of his seat, pointing a giant finger in his son's face.

"Sit down, Dad. You and I both know I'm right. It's obvious what's going on here. You've always done what you have to do to avoid sullying your good name. I've overheard many of your conversations with the lawyers or Bunni.

I wonder why you haven't legally changed my name to 'Fucking Disappointment' because that's used more than Junior." Freddy excused himself from dinner and left, going to visit Pete Saunders, the one place he could freely smoke dope.

Alfred Ripken II sat alone, his glass empty of its alcohol. He picked at his food, but he was no longer hungry. His son was correct. He was a disappointment. It wasn't just the stupidity of a teenager that bothered him but the lack of empathy. For the longest time, it went unseen. Sure, Bunni had begged him to bring Junior to the doctors to get his "head checked" as she so often put it.

"We've all done stupid things. I was sneaking beer from my parents' fridge and smoking cigarettes. How is it any different?" Fred knew full well the difference. It was a way for him to cope with the gravity of the situation.

"Hon, last week he found a cat that was injured. He kept it in the basement, torturing it. That's much more than teenage stuff." Bunni often waited until it was just them, all alone, to voice her concerns. She had been married long enough to know her husband hated to be questioned in front of others. He was much more receptive when it was just the two of them.

"I once found a dead bird. . . ." Fred started.

"No, don't do that. You know it's different. Don't start this bullshit. Your son needs serious help before it's too late." Bunni was correct.

Now, as he sat alone in his thoughts, Fred Senior wondered what the future indeed did hold for his son. It was true, his name did mean something, and for that, Junior was quite fortunate. But Alfred loved his son more than anything and was willing to go to the ends of the earth for him.

CHAPTER THREE

The home smelled mustier than usual, the result of never allowing any air to flow through. George Clement kept everything closed up and dark, never venturing outside unless it was an absolute must. His body had betrayed him years prior, and evening walks were a thing of the past. In its place was the boredom of staring at a television he had no interest in turning on or reading books he could no longer see. Instead, he sat in his recliner, coffee and cigarettes on a small wooden folding table.

"Gretchen!" George called out. In his mind, he had commanded her over in a loud booming voice. In reality, it was no more than a whimper. It bothered him that he was so weak now, a shell of what he once was. He would often speak of welcoming death, but if it came, he'd be far too stubborn and afraid to accept it. It wasn't in his nature to go quietly.

It took close to an hour, but soon enough, Gretchen entered the living room to report progress on the cleaning of the home. Recently, she was forced to come here daily, to deliver pills and to keep an eye on George. A few months back, her grandfather had fallen in his home, so unsteady lately, fracturing three ribs. It took the family many hours to convince him to get x-rays. She wished she'd never done that because now the girl was forced to be his maid, bringing him food and medicine every day.

"I could give him too many of his pills," Gretchen thought evilly to herself but quickly wiped that image away from her mind. That wasn't who she was. Besides, he couldn't last too much longer. Since the fall, her grandfather had struggled to connect past and present. It wasn't Alzheimer's; at least that's what research said. Dementia, caused by the medication and age of the patient, was more likely.

"*Hol meinen mantel*, Ester," George would scream throughout the day. Sometimes, day and night mixed together in his mind, just like the present with the past.

"Grandfather, it's me, Gretchen." The young girl would lean down in front of the old man, placing both hands on his knees to get and then keep his attention.

"Ahhh, yes, Gretchen," George would say, patting her face gently with his hand.

Gretchen would grab him a blanket, draping it over him so he could nap, in hopes that the fogginess would subside. She hated seeing him like this, but in a way it was comforting. Ever since she could remember, her grandfather was a nasty individual. He was not a loving or caring man, something that shocked her since he had been married for many years until he lost his wife.

Sometimes, when sleep refused to come, Gretchen and her mother would discuss childhood. All she wanted was answers about her family, though it seemed that her mother knew just as little as anyone else.

"All I know is he met your grandmother while working in a factory in Maine. Some woolen company, I think. He came over before the war started, running away to avoid being forced into the German army. He was placed in a prison camp in an area called the Forks, the authorities worrying that all German immigrants were potential spies. When the war was over, he went to work in mills, the only places that would hire a foreigner with no particular skills. My mother worked in a general store down the street, and she used to talk about this handsome, well-manicured fellow that would come by to woo her." Gretchen's mother loved to think of that time, giving her hope that George Clement was something other than a cold-hearted old fool.

"So, what happened? I mean, he's not a nice man. I don't ever remember a time where he hugged any of us." Gretchen struggled with these thoughts.

"At one time, maybe. I think the camp really did him in. Your grandmother would tell us that story all the time because it showed him in a very different light. I don't ever remember him being a loving father. He worked all day, came home and sat in his recliner, drinking beer, and ignoring us. When Mom died, I think it was the final nail in the coffin. If there was any sense of love, it was gone after that."

It was when her grandfather struggled with his memories that Gretchen saw what her grandmother saw. He wasn't bossy or angry. There was no force in his voice. In fact, it was sweet and caring. She liked it and liked the way it felt to be around him then. If he died with his mind somewhere else, it would leave her with good memories of him. It was often the case. When someone passed on, people tended to remember the good times and not the bad.

Much later, after the medication wore off, George would wake up again, the same angry old man he'd always been. He'd demand a dinner to be served to him at five p.m. sharp, with a bourbon on the rocks, just two shots, and a cigarette to smoke after he was done. The evening news would come on by six, and bedtime would arrive at nine, all of which would require help. George didn't know or care about the time his granddaughter left his house or whether she got her homework done. All he cared about was his needs, ones that had to be met on command.

CHAPTER FOUR

Fuck that prick," Peter said, holding in the smoke until the last possible moment, all to achieve an intense high. He had already started before Fred even arrived to join him. His drug habit had been going on for years, ever since he caught his dad smoking pot in the basement. That was the first time he tried it, a quick drag from his father to keep the secret safe. At the time, it was cool. How many eight-year-old kids were able to use marijuana with their dad and his biker friends? After that, it became commonplace, and soon enough, Pete was running drugs for his dad. His own personal mule, his father would say, giving him extra to keep Peter happy.

"Come on, man. He ain't that bad. Besides, who helped you with that expulsion hearing last year? It sure as hell wasn't your dad." Fred loved to shit on his father, but if anyone else thought twice about it, they better be ready for the backlash.

"I'm just sayin', he needs to figure you out. You don't respond well when someone attacks your manhood." Peter laughed, handing over the remaining joint, letting his friend finish it off.

"Don't matter anyway. I'll be out of Dad's hair in a few months. I was thinking of traveling to

Europe. Maybe Amsterdam for a year." Fred didn't know if that was what he really wanted to do. College seemed like the right way to spread his wings, but that was more a desire of a father, prepared to pay whatever the cost to get his son into an Ivy League school, even if the grades weren't there. Merely the fact that it was the next expected step made Fred not want to follow that path.

"Damn, that will be amazing. I'd love to join but can't. Gonna help my dad in his shop and take some classes at Rhode Island Technical College. If I want to take the business over, I need the degree." Peter sometimes attempted to think about his future, though drugs clouded it more often than not.

"I think that's a good plan. You could even move one day and start your own place, you know." Fred was more than happy to see others fail. In fact, it was enjoyable to sit back and watch others squirm over potential punishment. But his boys were his boys, and to see them struggle bothered him. Throughout his life, during the death of a baby sister, long bitter divorce of his father and his birth mom, who took off and never returned to see him, and his outbursts at school, it was Peter and Vern who stood by him. They were his true brothers, ones he would do anything for and die for. And since he'd been friends with Peter, he knew who held his friend back the most: his father. Fred knew his own father was an enabler. It didn't bother him in the least. Whenever he did something terrible, Big Daddy swooped in and took care of it. It wasn't as if Fred didn't know right from wrong. He knew perfectly well when he made poor choices. It came down to the fact that Freddy didn't care. He saw no harm in mistreating others, as long as he was amused.

Peter was different. He came from a much different upbringing. His father used his own son to deliver drugs throughout the school and local businesses. Until now, there was only smoke, yet no fire to the rumors. That was shocking to Fred. That would end, and Peter would pay the price for that. The desire for his own business or college would be gone with a conviction for selling drugs. His father would continue with his shop and just find someone else to move heavy narcotics throughout the city. Peter's best option was to get away, far away, and start a new clean life. It wouldn't happen in Kingston. Fred Senior had predicted that years ago, telling Junior he was hanging out with losers.

"Hey, want to help me out this weekend?" Peter asked, cracking open an energy drink to offset the calming feeling the marijuana gave him.

"Depends on what it is." Fred knew what was going to be asked of him. Lately, the request was becoming more and more common.

"Just have to drive some stuff for my dad.

It won't take but ten minutes, but I could sure use some help carrying boxes." Peter used to deliver the cheaper drugs with his own car but now that his father trusted him with much more than dime bags and ounces of weed, he used the van. Hard stuff, expensive stuff, was shipped in crates to be delivered to dealers that would sell for a profit. This could sometimes become a two-person job.

"Jesus, Pete. I can't get caught doing that. My dad would fucking kill me. Ask Vern this time." Fred knew what would happen if his dad found out. He was threatened with losing everything. A drugs charge by the Kingston police would push Fred Senior over the edge.

"I love Vern. You know that. But my dad, he doesn't. I'm lucky he lets me even hang out with him. Forget about him helping me run. My dad would kill me." Peter did like Vern, though love was a strong word. He would sell him out if necessary. While the Ripkens were one of the wealthiest families in the state, both of the other boys came from parents who brought in just enough to survive. They'd become friendly through Fred for various reasons. Peter once stood up for Fred when a foreign exchange student attacked the rich kid for making fun of his accent. One punch and a suspension later, the two young men were firm friends.

His connection to Vern was quite different.

He met him through Fred, who played on the same baseball team. They hung out only because Vern could throw a fastball so hard that major league teams were scouting the games before his sophomore year. That worked just fine for Fred but not for Peter and definitely not for his father. For a year, he hid the friendship until a particular incident involving harassment at school brought all three boys, their parents, and the administration into one room. That was the first time Pete's dad laid eyes on Vern Watts, and he was none too pleased. He voiced his displeasure at his son being around a boy "like that" and questioned him as to how his own friends would view this situation. Peter always knew his father had an issue with anyone of color. Though he had talked himself into believing that wasn't the reason, subconsciously, he'd kept Vern away for that reason. In time, Peter was allowed to hang out with the "black kid," as his dad called him, a more acceptable term than his father customarily used. But under no circumstance was Vern allowed in their home or even to step foot in the store. The fact that Fred brought up the idea of Vern moving drugs for his father was a farce.

"It's only Friday night. We can even go to the basketball game first so it lets people see us in public. Then, once that ends, we bring the van to my dad's shop, fill it up, and easy peasy, we're all done." Peter didn't have a choice in the matter. He just needed a hand.

"Ok, but this is it. I can't be doing this shit, even for you. My dad would kill me if we were caught," Fred said, knowing the potential ramifications of a drug bust for any of them.

"And Vern is coming. No Vern, no deal." Freddy never liked to go down alone.

Fred Ripken III was quite correct in his assessment of the entire situation. Alfred Ripken II, Big Daddy, would not be happy.

CHAPTER FIVE

Zach sat in his bedroom after helping his grandfather to his own. Thoughts rushed through his head as he lay in bed, attempting to get even an hour or two of sleep before his alarm went off for school. It would be a brutal day if he couldn't stay awake in class, and Zach had already planned to go to a movie with Gretchen that evening. He was confident that his hormones would keep him up for that, as they'd slowly ventured into the kissing and heavy petting stage. He fumbled through, having no clue what to do, but like all teenagers, his hands did the work. Sliding up shirts, touching skin. In a normal situation, Zach would spend hours overthinking if he should or shouldn't make a move like that. However, during the act of kissing, he found his hands explored on their own, much like hers did. Eventually, they'd stop, not wanting to go too far.

"The time and place need to be right," Gretchen would say, smiling at him and kissing his mouth before leaning on his shoulder to cuddle.

The boy would hold her for as long as she wished. He agreed that at this moment, he was not ready for the responsibilities sex would bring. His body did not agree with what his brain was telling him. Zach felt himself becoming excited at the mere thought of her. Now, with this lack of sleep, he might not be ready if that time was tonight.

That was not the only thought that went through his head. The story told to him by his zayde, the man he'd looked up to and trusted his whole life, was one his mind couldn't comprehend. Many aspects seemed beyond belief as if seen in a documentary or read in a book. Karl Auerbach was a Jew, through and through. That was accurate. The tale was unbelievable, and one that obviously had been explicitly contrived to teach him a valuable lesson. Was his grandfather imprisoned in a camp throughout the war? Yes, that was what he was always told to believe. But to not realize who you really were, only finding your real purpose during times of distress and the use of revenge. Those were designed to keep Zach honest and on the noblest path, he was sure of it.

It was pretty apparent that sleep wasn't coming, so Zach got up and went to the kitchen to get some milk. Searching on his school laptop, he found stories of the most surprising and questionable part of Zayde's story, the Golem. Quickly, he found site after site of the folklore of a man created by clay and mud, though the origin was suspect. This was one that all young Jewish children, especially if stuck in a concentration camp with little hope in sight, would hear from the elders to give them hope. Instead of believing what his grandfather had told him, like all untrusting teens he spent an hour researching and disproving the entire thing, not just the Golem. The items in the box could have come from any dead German, an easy task with all the bodies strewn across the continent. Maybe, over the years, Zayde created a story about those items, wholly fictional, to make himself feel more important. Dead brother? A Frankenstein monster created with nothing more than prayers? Revenge and regret. Those all were done to stop Zach from making any rash decisions when dealing with the bullies that continued to make him a point of attack, with laser focus. The most exciting part was it worked, in a way. Wherever the story came from or how it was created in his mind, Karl Auerbach, and not this Karl Krueger, brought out the necessary emotions in order to teach a lesson. Just because everything wasn't on the up-and-up didn't mean that it wasn't a cautionary tale about how to deal with unfortunate situations.

"Bing. Bing. Bing." The sound of a bell coming from the cell phone let Zach know he had received a text. It was a welcome surprise, for sure.

"Due to the inclement weather, school is cancelled for the day. All games and after school clubs will be postponed." Zach read it several times before rushing to the window.

He'd never even thought to look at the weather, and there'd been no talk of a storm moving in, yet on the ground was a layer of snow, illuminated by glimmers of sunlight just beginning to appear.

Excitement rushed over him. He could get that needed rest, and if the weather cleared up, movie night could still be a go. Zach closed his laptop, rushed upstairs, and slid into bed, where this time sleep arrived quickly, allowing him to forget all he had learned. His young mind refused to comprehend what was one hundred percent real. He'd find out soon enough what would happen when clouded judgment led him down a dark path.

CHAPTER SIX

Vern used the opportunity of a snow day to sleep in, something he did very little of. His life was spent in the gym or on the diamond. Any free time was used for clinics during the offseason to practice pitching. It was all he cared about, the competition and the desire to be the best. So the motivation was always there when the alarm clock went off at 4 a.m., just in time for the first workout of the day. Today was a welcome surprise, and a late night the previous evening made it much easier to decide to skip running in the poor weather. His parents would be pissed, especially his father, who pushed him hard to be the best. It was appreciated, and Vern knew he'd be nothing without the support. Still, occasionally, he desired to be like every other student, whose only worries were their studies or social life.

His phone had been going off for close to an hour, text messages pouring in. Most were from his dad, wondering why he hadn't left. Vern was reasonably sure the answer was obvious. All it took was a look outside to realize that perhaps running in snow was an unwise decision. He refused to answer it. Let his dad get his fat ass out there for a jog, and only then he'd listen. The others were from Fred, obviously unable to get back to sleep. Snow days were great, but if you didn't receive the call early enough, you'd be up for the day.

"What's up?" Vern texted his friend, letting an hour pass before doing so. He had no desire to go causing trouble with the shitty weather. That generally resulted in doing something stupid, and as he was approaching the spring of his senior year, Vern was coming to realize that perhaps his friends didn't exactly lead him in the right direction. Sure, he'd made his fair share of bad decisions. Still, with the Miami Marlins and Minnesota Twins potentially drafting him and pushing him to forego a college education, he needed to keep his nose clean. The first way to do that was to slowly leave the old crowd, primarily Freddy and Pete. Going for a drive on a shitty day like today had nothing but bad intentions written all over it. A slightly high friend could drive them into a snowbank, and his pitching career was all over. He'd worked too hard to lose it all now.

"Relaxing and seeing if you've got plans tonight," Fred sent back. It was quite apparent that plans were already in motion.

"Cool . . . cool. Just hanging out at home for the day. Helping my mom out." Vern lied. He didn't mind doing it either, as his friends would get on him about almost any excuse given except his family. It was common knowledge about his family's past. Murder-suicide of grandmother and grandfather, leaving behind several children to fend for themselves in foster care. Most of the siblings went down wrong paths, but Mary worked her way through community college, meeting Bill Watts in a psychology class. The rest was history, but because of her horrible past and upbringing by the system, Mary was off-limits when it came to his friends' complaints. If Vern said his mother needed a hand, it was accepted like gold.

"Nice. Get it done. Tonight, we ride." Fred left the message, not giving his friend any debate on the subject. Maybe he'd figured out what Vern was doing, disassociating himself from the group. And it was for the best, that much was certain. They were all running these drugs for Pete's dad. But no one was leaving the group.

There was no response to the last message. There was no need to be. Even if Vern had responded, he would have just extended the texts back and forth, attempting to convince him to come. Sometimes it was much better not to argue with Fred.

The rest of the day went well, with Vern spending the time being around his family, his real family, working together to shovel snow and clear a path to the oil tank out back. The chances the snow would stick were unlikely, but at least the work was done. Tomato soup, grilled cheese, and warm brownies out of the oven made for a pleasant afternoon. He was all ready to tell Fred he was not going with him that evening, but by the time the sun set and his phone rang, he'd made the horrible decision to go for that ride.

CHAPTER SEVEN

It was supposed to help heal the remaining wounds he had incurred, both physically and mentally. Sharing the story of his life, even to his grandson, did nothing but open up old scars that now bled after many years of hiding them. Karl hated the way he felt as if he had made a big mistake by even telling Zachariah anything at all. There were many other ways to teach him about resolve and revenge without unleashing such a tale as he had. It wasn't just for his grandson, Karl realized. It was also for him. To talk about something that had gone silent since the end of the war lifted a weight from his shoulders, but was it appropriate to put it on his grandson?

Karl had dealt with sleeping through the most uncomfortable positions before, both physically and emotionally. At his age, every twist or turn in the wrong direction could cause weeks of stiff joints. Some days, he'd stare at his hands, wondering whatever happened to the youth of his prior years. He couldn't remember the time when he crossed the line into what he'd become now. It was as if death came each night, taking away the remainder of his youth until there was nothing left but wrinkled skin and bones. There were many nights he'd dream of his past and just wish that death would finally have mercy on him by making it quick. He deserved it, yet wondered if this was how God punished him for his deeds. It wasn't as if he didn't want to be with his family anymore. He loved each of them more than life itself. Yet, it was the hours upon hours of sleep, where his past would come back, haunting him and scaring him awake, only to return very soon to continue their sick jokes.

"Karl. . . . Karl, wake up." A soft voice, one that seemed distant yet so familiar, called to him. He didn't want to open his eyes, not knowing what awaited him. This felt very different. He'd dozed off, partly from the emotional story, but also the alcohol that had made him sleepy. His dreams were always the same. He could smell the distinct odor of death, as if it were in the room with him instead of the scents of bar soap and clean linen. He could feel the weight of being back in Buchenwald, pushing down on his shoulders, demanding he stay there instead of return to his cushy bed. Everything looked the same as it had when he had been imprisoned there, though he heard no cries. In fact, there was always an uneasy silence, the dead walking around and through him, never noticing he was even present. He never saw his friends. It was as if he kept them locked away, not allowing them out in his dreams. He tried not to think of individuals, as it made it too real.

"Wake up, Karl. It's time for you to wake up." The voice came again. This time a hand fell on his shoulder, shaking him.

"Let me sleep in peace. Do not bother me, spirit," Karl said. He was afraid, more so than he had been in years.

"It's too late for that, Karl. You put this in motion. We must have important discussions."

Karl slowly opened his eyes, looking at the back of his wife's head, who slept so soundly. It was just senility. Nothing more. He was not transported to another time in his life, one that he begged to forget. He closed his eyes a moment longer, recognized the need for a glass of water, all thanks to the whiskey, and spun his legs to get out of bed. Standing next to him, in prison gear, was Rabbi Abel.

"Get up, son. We have things to discuss." Abel smiled, reaching his hand out to help his old friend.

"Please leave me here. You'll wake Shirley," Karl begged, not even wanting this to continue.

"She's fast asleep. If she awakens, it will be as if she's dreaming. Nothing more." Abel still held his hand out, not accepting a rejection. "So, please, to the living room. We are waiting for you there." Abel waited until the wrinkled hand fell into his, pulling Karl to his feet before turning to walk away, leaving his elderly friend alone.

For a moment, he stood in horror at what he had just witnessed. Directly in front of him, as if he never had aged a moment beyond 1945, was the rabbi who took him in and taught him his true faith. Karl knew it was just a dream, one that he could wake up from only by crawling back into bed. But something in his mind told him this was too important to walk away from. Getting his wits about him, Karl walked into the living room, expecting to see only Abel. Instead, it was filled with faces he had long buried in his memory.

"Karl, you remember Ittel, Salomon, Hirsch, Chaim, Harta, Jakob, and Samuel." One by one, the men walked over to their old friend and hugged him. Each time, it felt cold against his body. With every hug, Karl felt younger and younger until his hands had no longer seen 80 years of pain. He again looked through the eyes of a teenager, young and impressionable.

"Karl, please sit." Abel motioned towards a chair, which was taken quickly by the boy.

"Do you know why we are here?" All of the spirits had surrounded the chair as if huddling for a vital secret.

"I don't. I haven't dreamt about any of you in many years." Karl was not lying. He hadn't seen any of his friends since the day he left with the

Russians. It was as if he bottled them up along with the Golem, hiding his memories away.

"It's true. I have not heard my name spoken in a long time." Samuel knelt down next to his friend, seeing him as he was.

"This is a dream," Karl said, placing his hands over his eyes. He didn't realize they were no longer aged. "It's just because I mentioned you to my grandson. It's like opening the door to the past."

All the men laughed, hearty and loud. They were amused that he thought their appearance was due to a story or a few hard drinks.

"That is untrue," Abel said. "You have no idea what you've done, do you, Karl?" The rabbi got on his knees in front of the boy, placing his hands on his legs.

"You see, our tale remained in your mind, in a place long ago visited. My history, as well as all these people here, was ours to tell, not yours." Abel was not as comforting as Karl remembered him to be. There was a sternness to his voice.

"But . . . but I killed you all. Each one of you died because of my actions." Karl was weeping.

"How dare you?" Jakob yelled, pushing his way through so that the boy could see his face. "I made my own decisions. I also wished to create the Golem and save the Jewish people. When I died, it was not because of you but because of me. You take my death and spin it so you can have ownership of it. Do you think you were the only one who wanted to stop the Nazis? Think back and do so honestly. We, as a group, wished to make a stand. All of us here died for that cause. Don't take our desire to do what is right as less merely because we didn't live to see its conclusion."

"That matters not. It does no good to dwell on it. The issue at hand is you told your grandson of the creature we created. It would have been much better to leave that part out. Now, as a result of your ineptitude, lives will be in danger again, and many will suffer at the hands of the monster." Abel gave a dire warning.

"What do you mean? That wasn't the part of the story to pay attention to. It was about revenge and what it can do to the human soul. My Zachariah needed something to put him on the right path; to know that violence and retribution don't always lead to the conclusion one desires." Karl was angry. How dare his friends come to him to lecture him on a story he told a boy to give him hope?

Abel stood, grabbed Karl by the shirt, and lifted him off the ground. When their faces met, it was not the face of the rabbi he saw, but the eyes of a Golem staring at him. "This world does not need what we have wrought on it. Stop it before it's too late."

Karl was shaken awake by his wife, who heard

him crying in the dark. He'd not had these kinds of dreams and woken in a sweat in decades. He apologized for causing a ruckus, kissed her cheek, and excused himself so he could take a shower and clean up. Once Karl was sure his wife was back in dreamland, he quietly snuck down the steps and entered his secret place. Within the box that was hidden there were all its contents. It still hurt him to look at his brother's items. Beneath it all, the canteen lay still, undisturbed for over fifty years. Picking it up in his hand, he thought about what to do. Would it be best to release the dirt and dust into the cold night air? For a moment, the elderly man considered it and then thought better of it. It was much too cold, and he saw no need to do so. It was only a dream brought about by the mention of the names of old friends. His grandson understood the morals of his story; he was confident of that. The canteen went back into the box, returning it to its grave. There would be no Golem that evening.

CHAPTER EIGHT

The snow had stopped falling hours earlier, and plow trucks had cleared most of the roads, salting and sanding what remained of any slick areas. Much like the announcement stated, the basketball game between the Kingston Rebels and the South Cony Rams had been postponed until a later date. This took away the one real alibi the three boys had in case questions were asked surrounding their running of drugs for Mr. Saunders. It really didn't matter, in any case. Peter had to do what his father asked, regardless of games or school.

"Damn, Fred. Why didn't you do this without me? I can't get involved in this shit," Vern said the moment he approached the van that sat in his driveway. He knew exactly what was going down, and he wanted no part of it.

"If I told you where we were going, would you have agreed?" Fred asked.

"Fuck, no!"

"And that's why I never said anything. We need you, man. You're our ride or die." Fred was happy that Vern was getting into the van, even though he complained.

"Not a word to anyone. Got that? My dad would kill me if he knew that everyone was

345

going." Peter tried to hide the fact his dad was a racist asshole. His friends understood exactly what Mr. Saunders was.

"Let's just get this done and go grab some burgers after. I'm starving." Vern was hoping his desire for food would entice the others to want the same. The quicker they delivered the goods, the better. He wanted out of there as soon as possible.

The van first made its way to the shop, where crates of illegal drugs awaited the boys. To not piss his dad off, Peter asked Vern to stay in the car while he and Fred loaded it with several bulky wooden cases of drugs. Next came a few blankets and, on top of that, painting supplies. If they were stopped, it would merely look as though they were working for a painting company on their way to drop off supplies for tomorrow's job. The police would know exactly who the three boys were if stopped. Still, with a weekend on the horizon, it was easy to say it was a way to make a few extra bucks, or they were helping a buddy out.

"Are you sure we're going to be alright? I can't have a record. Fuck this. I can't do this." Vern was fidgeting, wanting to be anywhere else but there. It wasn't like he had a sixth sense, but the trouble was written all over this one.

"Relax, dude. We'll be fine. It will take ten minutes in total. We drop the shit off and go,"

Peter said, realizing that bringing him was a mistake. He should have never listened to Fred on this one and stood his ground. The fact of the matter was that the drive was the least of their worries. If they showed up with someone in an agitated state, the buyers might think twice about the purchase. Or even worse, someone could get hurt in the process of the transaction.

"He's fine." Fred turned around to look at his friend in the back seat. "You cool, man? Tell Pete you're cool."

"No, I'm not fucking cool. I'm very uncool. This could ruin my life. Pull over. I'll walk home." Vern was reaching for the side door, ready to jump out if necessary.

Pete reached behind the seat with his left hand, grabbing the sliding door's handle to hold it shut while driving with his right one. The van swerved back and forth on the road, slipping slightly on packed snow and ice.

"STOP IT! YOU'RE ACTING LIKE A BITCH!" Peter yelled in attempts to get Vern under control. His fingers were being pried off the handle, Vern pulling back each one, ready to break them if necessary.

"OK! OK! OK! If you want to go, go. But we ain't picking your ass up on the way back. And, so help me God, if you breathe a word of this to anyone, you're dead." Fred hated ultimatums, but it had to be said.

"Man, we need to get the stuff there, pronto. I told you not to bring him," Peter said, still holding tight to the handle.

"Pull over. The asshole can walk." Fred commanded Peter to slow down.

With a blinker on, Peter came to a stop on the side of the road.

"Fuck you, Vern. My dad told me never to trust you. You've really gone and fucked this up." Peter was spitting anger, his father's rhetoric flashing in his head.

"Kiss my ass, man." Vern was not going to let these two hurt his chances of success.

Vern didn't need to worry about his baseball career after that evening. He had no time to react to his decision to do the right thing by leaving. As soon as he opened the van door, he was pinned in. Flashing blue lights shone on the sides and back of the van.

"GET DOWN! GET DOWN!" A booming voice yelled at Vern, who dropped on his stomach, his hands outstretched above his head.

Soon, the police descended on the vehicle, guns drawn to extricate the remaining two boys. Fred came willingly, holding his hands high in the air. This wasn't his first time dealing with police, and it made more sense to go willingly than fighting it. Peter, however, understood what would happen to him and his family with this bust and refused to surrender. A taser to the side helped him fall out of the van and collapse to the ground.

"Gentlemen, to what do we owe this honor?" Steven Auerbach walked by the three boys, looking down at them as they sat on the sidewalk. The road was blocked off, troopers and drug dogs tearing the van apart. Several of the wooden crates had already been broken into, large bags filled with white powder exposed to the elements.

"Wait, don't answer that," Steven said before calling over another officer.

"Put your body cam on, please. I want this all recorded." The police chief waited until everything was ready.

"Boys, do you know why you were pulled over?" Steven waited for an answer. Two of the boys sat silent while the third drooled on himself. "You drove past a cop a few miles back, swerving all over the road. And look at what we found."

"Mr. Auerbach, please," Vern pleaded. He wanted to explain his situation.

"No, no. Shhhh. Let me finish before you say a word. You have the right to remain silent. Anything you say, can and will be used against you in a court of law." Steven completed the reading of the Miranda Rights, making certain all three boys were recorded listening to them. There would be no way Big Daddy would swoop in and save them this time. "Before you say a word,

Mr. Watts, remember you can stay silent until you get a lawyer."

"I want to call my dad. *Now!*" Fred said, hoping the tenor of his voice would show his anger. His dad was going to be super pissed; he knew that as soon as he saw the lights in the rearview.

"For sure, you'll get that call once we get you to the station and get all three of you processed. Do you know the shit you're in? That's a lot of coke over there." Steven pointed towards the van, hoping they understood the gravity of it all.

Though he was angry at the boys, part of him felt bad. These weren't their drugs; that much was certain. They were nothing more than mules. And the police knew Peter Saunders's father was one of the biggest dealers in the state. It was a cycle that could perhaps be stopped now.

"Listen, boys, we can do this the easy way or the hard way. You cooperate, and we can make this as smooth as we possibly can. And I don't want to see anyone hurt or lose a career over this incident." Steven looked right at Vern. He was very aware of the young boy's situation.

"Fuck off, pig," Peter said, partially aware of what he was saying.

"Got it. When we get back to the station, we can all have a nice long talk, and I hope you can change your tune." Steven called for some help and loaded each of the boys in the backs of cruisers. He made sure to put Vern in his. He would be the least venomous of the three and the most likely to give pertinent information. Hopefully, he could save this one. Unfortunately, that was not in Vern's future.

CHAPTER NINE

Zach was able to convince his grandparents to drive him to the movies to meet his new friend, who happened to be a girl. Karl was okay with it, hoping it would take his mind off the more delicate issues and onto what a teenage boy should be thinking of. Shirley took a bit more convincing, and when she found this friend was female, she demanded to meet the parents.

"It's just her mother," Zach said, hoping she would let it go. Of course, she didn't, and he agreed, after arguments, decisions, and conditions were met, that when his grandparents dropped him off at the theater, Shirley could say hello to both Gretchen and her mother. However, it had to stay under two minutes in order to not cause too much embarrassment.

"I like her. She's very nice," Gretchen said as soon as they walked away, letting her mother make idle chit-chat with the elderly couple.

"She's great. Overprotective for sure. But she loves me." Zach felt his hand open, and Gretchen's fingers wrap around it. If it could, his heart felt like it was ready to tear out of his chest. He hoped his hands weren't clammy. That would ruin the mood.

"Hey, you listening to me?" Gretchen jammed an elbow into the boy's side, just enough to break him out of his zone.

"Want to share what's on your mind?" she said giggling.

"I am just hoping they are getting along back there. Can't have our families hating one another, now can we?" Zach put his hand around her waist, pulling her against him, proud of his ability to cover up the truth. A boy's mind was a dangerous place, even when sex wasn't on the menu.

"Well, once you're done worrying, you can answer my question. Want snacks before we go in?" Gretchen pulled out a twenty from her pocket, compliments of all of the work she did cleaning her grandfather's place. He paid her nothing, which wasn't unusual. George Clement was the cheapest man she knew. Frequently, on birthdays, he'd wait until she came to clean before he wished her one. There were no cards—a waste of money, he said—or gifts. Once in a while, he'd call, but for years, he'd say it cost too much to make long distant calls, even when it was explained to him that with cell phones, there were no charges accrued. For all the work she did in that house, Gretchen saw not a dime from him. Instead, her mother paid an allowance, and one of her chores was cleaning for her grandfather. Now she watched Zach fumble in his pocket, pulling out wads of crumpled cash, most likely handed to him by his dad.

"Put it away, or you'll get hurt. It's not 1945." Gretchen kissed his cheek. "Besides, you can buy the tickets. Makes us even."

It didn't matter what film they would watch. Being under the age of seventeen only gave so many options, but Zach didn't care. Every holding of the hand or peck on the cheek sent his mind racing. He was too worried about every move and reaction to focus on a movie. Making moves wasn't exactly his thing, at least not yet. What's acceptable was a complete unknown. To have both their arms on the same armrest, touching, was an indication she wanted him around. She'd told him several times he was a perfect gentleman and tried to explain to him there was no need to worry. Still, as a teenager, insecurity was unavoidable.

"Two for *Threat at Midnight*," Zach said, flipping through the money in his fist. He did have quite a bit left over, thanks to his dad, who had left him a note and thirty dollars by his bedside.

"Good luck, champ. Call me and let me know how it went." His dad tried to be calm, and even if he wasn't, that was okay. Steve cared, and that was what mattered.

The movie went as planned. The theater was packed enough, so everything was done under a

354

jacket that Zach laid over their hands. It wasn't much, just playing with one another's fingers or touching knees together to get as close as possible, very innocent for teenagers. Still, both had reputations to uphold, and fooling around in a crowded theater would only be trouble, especially since the movie had seemed to bring out a slightly older clientele.

"We should call for our rides to pick us up," Gretchen said, smiling. "Or we can walk down the street, grab a slice of pizza and hang out a bit more. No pressure."

"Hmmm, I know my grandmother might be pissed, but I sure am hungry. Can she deny me food?" Zach slid his arm around her, leading her down the street to spend a bit more quality time with his girlfriend. He had no indication that after this night, his life would spiral out of control, bringing only heartache and pain to all those close to him.

CHAPTER TEN

Steven had already called his own father, letting him know that tonight would be an extremely late night. He hated forcing his elderly parents to take on the role of parents to his son. Neither of them complained, at least not to his face, seeming to enjoy the extra time with their grandson. The situations they'd dealt with were stressful, many times being the first to discuss the day's issues with Zachariah. That was a father's job, and Steve knew it, but a single parent with a job as time-consuming as his came with a price.

"So, Pete, want to tell us where you got the van?" Steve sat back, letting two younger officers interrogate the boys. The last thing he needed was the families coming back, claiming this arrest was personal. There would be no chance Old Alfred Senior would bail his kid out of this one, at least not without something of a permanent record.

"I don't remember." Peter didn't seem nervous at all being in this situation. This wasn't his first run-in with the law, though it was the first time he'd been arrested.

"So, you're saying you took it from someone?" Lieutenant Anthony Richardson said, observing every move. "Because if that's true, while you might get in trouble for Grand Theft Auto, it would sure be better than drug charges. One of those can be chalked up to being a stupid kid, right, Peter?"

"I'm not talking until I get my lawyer," Peter said smugly. He was not the least bit concerned about where this was heading, though he should have been.

"Great. We are in touch with a court-appointed lawyer now. He'll be here soon, and then we can talk." Richardson looked at his partner, Luis Santiago, and motioned for him to follow him out of the room.

"Whoa, what do you mean, court-appointed?" Peter held his hands up, wanting to get the attention of the officers.

"Pete . . . can I call you Pete?" Anthony sat back down, making sure that behind the see-through mirror, his chief could get a good look at everything that transpired. He didn't wait for the teen to respond.

"Well, Pete, let me explain this to you as simply as possible. You see, you have no money, and your daddy doesn't have nearly enough to hire a defense attorney to represent you. Hence, the state must provide you one, which they will quite willingly, though I don't see how this isn't an open and shut case." Anthony enjoyed watching the boy's attitude change. He loved serving the public, but also there was a thrill in backing a criminal against the wall from which there was no escape.

"But . . . but . . . but . . ." Peter stuttered. Tears welled in his eyes, for the first time that night, recognizing the gravity of the situation. It was not as simple as he once thought.

"Let me guess, you expected someone else to provide you with expensive representation. I won't namedrop, as that is quite unbecoming of me," Anthony said, playing the slightly better cop.

"Fuck it; I'll say it." Santiago slammed both fists on the table. "I think Pete here expected good ol' Alfred Ripken to bail him out. Well, here's some terrible news, douchebag. He ain't coming to the rescue. You're on your own."

"That's not what I was thinking," Peter said, trying not to show fear. It didn't work.

"Interesting because two out of the three of us in the room think otherwise. You see, when we hand over all the evidence, including the video of the arrest to your attorney, he won't fight for your innocence. He'll work on a plea, which means jail time, especially when trafficking drugs throughout the state of Rhode Island is concerned. You ever been to prison?" Santiago was ruthless. He didn't care if this was a kid or not. He'd lost a brother to drugs and had no desire to see them pushed, regardless of the age of the dealer.

"No, sir." Peter was frightened now. The mere mention of prison scared him, especially now that it was much closer in the rearview mirror than he initially imagined.

"Well, it won't be much fun for you. Maybe your dad's racist assholes can protect you." Luis grinned, touching nerves left and right. "And before you say anything, we know about that too. You see, big boy, if that ever gets out, you will be in for a world of hurt."

Lieutenant Richardson stood up, walking over and pulling a chair next to Peter.

"Whoa, relax, Santiago. We can avoid that." He placed a hand on the boy's shoulder to provide the smallest bit of comfort. Regardless of the attitude and size, the big idiot was still a child. It wasn't his fault he'd been dealt a shitty hand. Richardson patted the boy on the arm again. "Would you like to avoid that, son?"

"Yes, sir." Peter was broken.

"You and I will have a nice long discussion once your lawyer gets here. I want you to know that we are one hundred percent truthful in our desire to make this as painless as possible. I'm sure you know there is a price to pay for this, but let's see if we can work something out." Anthony liked being the good cop. It suited him.

"You ain't bullshittin' me, are you?" Peter looked into the eyes of both cops, checking to see if either flinched. "I'm getting an appointed lawyer?"

"For sure kid, for sure. You see, your friend with the pockets filled with cash has a daddy willing to pony up for the best. And up until now, he's done the same for you too. But what were his exact words, lieutenant? They slip my mind." Anthony looked across the table at his partner, winking.

"Fuck that fat piece of shit and his druggy dad. Though I could have missed a word or two." Luis laughed, enjoying the cat and mouse game.

"He wouldn't say that. He likes me." Pete was at his Waterloo now, standing ground for his final fight.

"He might. However, he's done bailing everyone else out. The drugs belong to your dad. We know that even if you don't want to admit it. And I get it. Have to protect the family. But you have to be crazy if you think Mr. Ripken won't save his son and let you two take the fall. This isn't defacing property or beating a kid up at school. This is a federal crime, and nothing Daddy Warbucks says or does will change that fact. You think Fred wants his kid to go to jail over your father's crack? Not happening," Anthony said, wanting to get the point across that this was no longer a slap on the wrist. This was a crime.

The evening went according to plan. Peter sang like a canary, with the support of his lawyer.

Vern told the truth, even if it couldn't adequately save him. And Freddy was Freddy. He danced, and he dodged, but with money behind him, he didn't give at all. He hid behind the stacks of cash, bonds, and any land his father owned. But there was anger building up inside him. The boy was done with this shit, done with the police, and done with anyone with the last name Auerbach. His father would get him out of this charge, even if his friends took the fall, but the police chief would feel some pain before this was all said and done. Freddy Ripken was correct. Everyone would feel the pain.

CHAPTER ELEVEN

The bust was all over the news, spreading quickly across Kingston. The fact of the matter was that these three boys, virtually untouchable before this moment, were now fallible. However, one of them didn't fully comprehend the gravity of the situation. Vern waited by his phone, knowing he'd receive a call from his coach about his draft status. No major league team wanted to get involved with a dealer, even if the situation was explained to make perfect sense. Plus, now that this crime was out in public, all the past transgressions, even if it was just word of mouth, would leak. Vern's life was over, at least in the eyes of a teenager.

"Fuck them and fuck Auerbach." Freddy had called them all over to his house as soon as his father bailed all three boys out. He'd said he would not cover lawyers' fees, but it didn't take much convincing to talk him into it. That was the only way they could be in the same room now, per the condition of their release. Being covered by the same set of lawyers allowed them to meet to discuss the case.

"Shut up, Fred." Vern never wanted to go with them, had outright refused to, but his wealthy friend used his mouth to talk him into it.

"What did you say?" Fred stopped picking at a bowl of peanuts, staring daggers at the ball-player.

"I said, shut up. If it wasn't for you, I wouldn't be in this situation. I can kiss baseball goodbye. No college either. All of it was tied together." Vern could feel his blood boiling, and if it hadn't been two on one, he might have knocked some teeth in.

"Jesus, you'll be fine. Poor baby might have to play in Mexico for a few years. That arm will take you where you need to go. Besides, as soon as my dad takes care of it, our records will be clean as a whistle." Fred knew he'd be fine. The fate of his friends wasn't a concern of anyone in the Ripken household.

"Yeah, sure. It wasn't my face that was plastered on the evening news. Even if we get off, public perception is still there." Vern sat back on the couch he so often crashed on. This time, it didn't feel as comforting as it once had.

"What are you worried about anyway? My dad's going to let me take the fall. I could see a serious prison time." Peter had only spoken to his father once since the arrest. It wasn't as if he hadn't tried to connect and see what their next move was. It was that the shop owner and drug dealer was washing his hands of the circumstance. If he or anyone said a word about the reality of where the drugs came from and where they were headed, a lot of blood would be shed.

"You bitches need to chill the fuck out. If we don't stick together, we're dead," Fred said, hoping to calm some nerves.

"We will *not* attack each other. That's what they want us to do. They'd rather we take the stand and play the blame game until all three of us are on probation or behind bars. I ain't selling out, and neither are you two idiots. Let the lawyers muddy up the waters and drag this shit out for years. By that point, things will calm down, and we'll be on our way to better lives." Fred didn't believe his own horseshit. He knew for a fact he'd be fine. His friends, not so much.

Peter lay back, the beers doing their work. He was in a particularly bad place, much worse than his friends realized. Not seeing his father meant that he was in a shitload of trouble when he did. His dad didn't disappear to avoid arrest. He'd deny it all and send his own kid down the river. He hid so he could blow off steam and steer clear of his son. This was very different, however. It wasn't a small issue. This was huge. Someone was going to pay for the transportation of drugs, and it was going to be Peter's ass that took the beating.

"Maybe we should just be good for a while. You know, keep our noses clean until things settle down. I'm with Vern on this one. We can't risk everything. Let your dad do the legwork, and we do whatever time we need to, if necessary." Peter leaned over and slapped Vern, letting him know he was with him on this one. He didn't receive much of a response, which wasn't shocking. It was his drugs, more or less, and he and Fred had roped Vern into it. He was just as pissed as the other two, but it made more sense to let things happen over time.

"Be good? That cop fucked us again, and you want to sit back and take it up the ass?" Fred said. The constant enabling did nothing but give the boy a feeling of invincibility. He saw no long-term problems that would arise out of this incident; the drugs were not a big deal, and even if they were, it was all on Peter Saunders, to begin with.

"He didn't fuck anyone, man. It's on you two. I told you I didn't want to go. And if you wouldn't have driven all over the *God damned* road, we wouldn't be in this predicament." Vern was no longer going to listen to his friends, always leading him down the wrong path. He wondered if he honestly had time to reinvent himself and his reputation.

"Well, I tell you what I'm going to do. I'm going to make Auerbach regret not minding his business. I'm sick and tired of that asshole coming after us." Fred watched Peter perk up.

The thoughts of doing the right thing had gone out of the window.

"Let's beat the shit out of his kid again. Like really beat him. He can't come after us if his kid's in the hospital." Peter was ready. It had been a long time since he had taken his anger out on someone.

"No! No more beatings. I won't do it. I'm done." Vern went to walk out. He couldn't do this anymore.

"YOU STOP RIGHT THERE!" Fred leaped in front of Vern, pushing him back without much success.

"Get out of my fuckin' way, Fred. I'm only telling you once." Vern balled his fists, ready to do whatever was necessary to get out of there.

"Alright, if I promise not to do anything to that little prick, will you sit and listen to reason?" Fred had to keep him there. If any of them sold out, the other two would be screwed.

"I'll listen." Vern released his fists and sat back down.

"I won't harm a hair on the boy's head. But I do plan on scaring the shit out of him." Fred smiled, taking out his cell phone to send a message.

CHAPTER TWELVE

Things tend to escalate quickly when teenagers refuse to understand the limits of their actions. Take, for example, the child that cheats on a test. When he's approached, caught red-handed, he denies it. There's rarely an acceptance of guilt. It's a fight or flight reaction. The child is backed into a corner and wants to get out without a scratch. Even the most courteous and most honest kids fall into it too. Eventually, they tend to break and take the punishment. But all too often, young adults don't really understand the gravity of their decisions. A young boy, recently giving his heart to love, reacts in ways that adults would not. It matters not how often wiser people gave him advice.

The call Zachariah Auerbach received sent him into a rage. He'd been angry before, even livid. He'd always thought of ways to fire back, really get at those guys for making his life a living hell. Trying to stop his father from reacting was not working; though, to be honest, he understood why his dad went after them. Those three deserved it, and once they left school, each one would go on to torture other kids. It just wasn't going to be him. The school's reaction was also understandable. Principal Collins continued to attempt to help him. It just wasn't working when the students had the backing of a lot of money and influence in the community. Even his zayde tried his best, talking him off the ledge. This was different.

"Zach?" A voice choked back tears.

"Gretchen, what is it?" Almost immediately, the boy could tell something was very wrong. Just the mere mention of her name sent the girl over the edge; sniffling and crying made it hard to talk.

"I got a call from that asshole. He said . . . he said." She could barely finish the sentence.

"What did he say?" Zach tried to control his anger. He knew immediately who she was talking about.

"He said . . . that I either put out willingly or he's taking it. Told me he'd be over to my house tonight."

"That's rape. You need to call the police." Zach would call his dad if he had to, though the cops proved unsuccessful time and time again in their handling of these boys. Hell, heavy drugs were being driven around town, and the assholes would only get a slap on the wrist.

"My mom isn't even home. What am I going to do?" Gretchen was scared. Though she'd always been independent, this was different. She knew those boys would be willing to step over the line. That was apparent. The fact that Fred

Ripken would be ready to call and threaten a rape only days after an arrest was a testament to his willingness to pursue his evil intentions of hurting the Auerbachs. She was just in the line of fire. That was more than she bargained for when she started dating Zach.

"Go to your grandfather's place. If you come here, they'll expect it. Can you get there?" Zach was fighting back tears, but they were of anger.

"Yes. I'll go right now. He's not expecting me, but lately, he has no idea what's going on," Gretchen said nervously.

"Good. Leave now. I'll see what I can do." Zach knew what he was going to do as soon as he received the call. It had been in the back of his mind for days.

"And, Gretchen, I love you." Zach didn't know if he actually did have those kinds of feelings for her. Everything was so new to him. It just seemed appropriate to let her know, at this time when everything was so wrong, that there was a tiny glimmer of hope and love.

"Thanks. Promise me you won't do anything stupid." Gretchen waited for him to agree before hanging up the phone. She was angry: at Fred Ripken, at the situation, and at Zach. How dare he drop that word at a time like this? To think, at a time like this, her boyfriend was using this opportunity to get her approval.

Zach seethed, his body shaking, his head racing

a mile a minute. Initially, he picked up the phone to call his father so he could handle the situation. It would do no good. If the threat was through a phone call, everything could be denied, and only after the rape would things have been handled. What good would that do? His grandfather was asleep in his recliner, snoring over the news. It would serve no purpose to wake him, burden him with problems, and all for no real solution except "turn the other cheek." It was that moment, through all the disbelief, that Zach decided what he was to try.

It felt like he was floating down the basement steps, the particulars a blur, even much later when he reflected on the events. He didn't care if his grandfather or grandmother, who was cleaning dishes after dinner, heard him. This wasn't the first time he had thought about coming down here. Ever since he listened to the tale, Zach had the idea floating in his head. In fact, after a particularly dense meatloaf, he was able to slip the set of keys away from his grandfather enough to run down the street to the local Walmart and make a copy. He was never questioned, though he often wondered if Zayde ever knew they were missing. If he did, it wasn't mentioned.

The door opened without a creak, willingly allowing him down, almost inviting him to do so. He closed the door behind him, hoping no one would see it slightly ajar. Using only a small flashlight, he found the small room he had been led to, slipping in to find the table, chairs, and everything in the room cleared, again, as if fate had deemed him worthy of taking on the task. Placed right where it had been a few nights prior was the small box, also locked tight.

"What the hell am I doing?" Zach said, sliding the key into the lock. In seconds, he had the box in his hands, its weight much more cumbersome than he thought, as if thousands of souls hid inside. The teenager quickly placed the box on the ground, wanting it out of his possession. It felt so dark. Even with the feeling of dread, Zach still picked through it. In no time at all, he located the canteen, hidden again beneath pictures and awards and the other trinkets that meant so little to him; to his grandfather, they were gold.

Without so much as a second thought, Zach unscrewed the cap of the canteen, something that took a bit of work. Years and perhaps God wanted to keep it closed tight. Turning it upside down, he dumped what looked to be sand and dirt into a pile. Within it, crumpled up in a tiny ball, was a piece of paper, one he did not notice. Using his ring finger, Zach wrote the following word in the pile of dirt, "EMET."

CHAPTER THIRTEEN

It felt good to turn his friends away, especially when they left without so much as a whimper. Sure, there was a racial slur or two directed his way, but nothing he hadn't heard in the past. He knew that if push came to shove, neither boy would stand up to him in fear of getting their asses handed to them. Sometimes, all it took was a bit of bravery to make the change.

Vern hated being stuck home alone without anything to keep him busy. His mother was forced to work an extra shift, and his dad was out again with friends. All too often, Vern had spent evenings drinking, smoking, and causing trouble. Finally, it was time to make the right decision. He grabbed a book out of his bag, lay on the couch, and did something he didn't often do, homework. It was then that he heard a bang from the backyard, causing him to get up to check.

"Hello?" Vern opened up the screen door, leaning out to see what caused the commotion. It was too dark to see much, except what looked to be a large animal in the yard.

"Get the fuck out of here," Vern yelled, grabbing a rock from by the door and throwing it hard in hopes of scaring the creature off. The stone hit its target hard, but it did nothing to move it.

"HEY. I SAID GET OUT OF HERE!" Vern turned on the porch light to get a better look. It was not an animal that was by the shed but a figure of a person. One thing Vern didn't want was rabies, but seeing a human there changed his demeanor.

"Listen, man. I'm going to go inside and grab my baseball bat. If I come out and you're still here, I'm beating your ass with it." Vern issued the warning, hoping that when he did return, the figure would be gone. He had no desire to be hauled into the police station, even if it was self-defense. With the current charges being levelled against him, a brutal beating of a stranger would do nothing to help his case. When he returned to the backyard, however, the shadowy figure was still there.

"Ok, I guess we gotta dance. You're going to regret this, motherfucker." Vern held the bat, ready to swing as he left the porch, defensively walking towards the figure. It was as he got closer that he realized the size of what looked to be a man was much more prominent and taller than he was. For a moment, fear rushed through his head, but that dissipated. He was a significant prospect and had made a living out of playing baseball. He could swing the bat with such force that it wouldn't matter how big the person was.

"Fuck this. I'm counting to five, and then I'm swinging for the fences." Vern still couldn't make out much about the person's features. Something seemed off. "Five . . . Four . . . Three . . . Two . . ."

Before he could reach One, an arm shot out, grabbing the weapon. Without any trouble, it held the bat in both hands and bent it as if it were a piece of silverware. The arm and hand were not normal. It was like mud.

"What the hell?" Vern spun on his heels. He needed to get inside and call the police. Running as fast as he could, the young athlete got indoors, slamming the door shut. He both locked and bolted it. That would stop whatever was out there. It did not. The wood on the door cracked as the creature punched its fist into and then through the door. In seconds, the man was inside.

For the first time, Vern saw his stranger in the light and felt his bladder let go. It wasn't a man at all. It had no real features other than holes that looked to be eyes and a line where a mouth should have been. On its forehead, a random series of letters sat above the eyes. It wore nothing yet had no features of gender. It was a giant man of clay. He tried to punch it once, but his hand crunched against the creature, breaking his fist. He screamed in pain.

"GET OUT!" Vern demanded, running through the house to find a safe space. There was nowhere to go. Tossing items in front of him to stop the Golem, Vern made his way upstairs to his bedroom, a place where he had a few surprises. Under his bed was another bat and a few knives he'd used to kill a stray cat. He refused to be a sitting duck, letting this thing come at him. Hiding in his closet, with the knives in his hand, he would make sure he wasn't the only injured person. He planned on killing that thing.

It was eerily quiet, and only the sound of his breathing was heard. It was as if everything he'd been through in the last few minutes were nothing more than a weird dream. Vern waited and waited, time passing by, holding his broken hand. He could stay in the closet, hoping his parents came home, but if that monster got to them, it would kill them both. He had no choice. He had to confront it if it was still even in the house. Grabbing the white closet door, he slowly opened it, just enough to see if he was alone. Staring back at him, waiting, was the Golem. Before he could close the door again, the creature reached in and wrapped his hand around Vern's neck, lifting him off the ground and then out into the room.

"Help, help help." Vern could barely make out any words, his throat being forcefully closed. With all his might, the boy lifted the knives in the air, bringing two down into the arm of the creature. It didn't even faze it, not loosening the grip at all. Instead, it became tighter as the

fingers of the Golem pulled closer and closer to one another.

Life was slipping away, everything he'd done coming to him in waves. He wondered if this was just a bad dream, in which he paid for all his wrongdoings. Every time he began to drift off, he saw the face of that thing looking into his soul. It frightened him, knowing he was going to die. He could even feel himself floating across the room, his feet not touching the floor as his throat closed. Before he realized it was happening, he was flying in the air, thrown out the window at tremendous speed. Vern hit the ground, his neck snapping upon landing on his head. He was the newest victim of the Golem, yet he would not be the last of the evening.

CHAPTER FOURTEEN

Peter sat in the driver's seat, shoving a greasy hamburger into his mouth. He and Fred were both beyond angry Vern refused to join them. It wasn't contentious in any way, but they wondered if he'd sing like a canary if given a chance. All that didn't matter now. What did matter was that Zachariah Auerbach and his father would both feel a little bit of pain for fucking with them. It was as if the potential drug charges were gone, out of sight, out of mind. Alfred Ripken II, Big Daddy, sure recognized the damage and had begged his son to stay home, at least until names were cleared. Freddy refused to listen.

"We're just going to grab a bite to eat and then come back here. Promise," Freddy said, only following through on half his promise. Both boys had burgers, fries, and milkshakes; that wasn't the lie. However, instead of returning home, a truck sat parked across the street from Gretchen's home, waiting for her to leave.

"That bitch won't stay there. There's no friggin' way. She and that prick are going to meet up somewhere." Pete saw a light turn off in the young girl's home, and he became excited. He knew what his friend's motives were, even if it was told to him that it was merely to scare them.

There was no chance Freddy would have all the fun.

"And here she comes. Stupid girl. It's like clockwork. Follow and don't get too close. I don't want her to figure out what we're doing." Freddy had no idea how far he was willing to go.

The truck crawled along at a snail's pace, never once turning on its lights. At any time, the police could have pulled them over and ended this entire venture. It was as if fate designed for everything to happen for a reason.

"Where the hell is she going?" Freddy said, watching the girl run up a path walkway to the front steps of an old gray, modest home that sat in a cul-de-sac of a retirement community. This wasn't the Auerbach house, and Freddy had no idea whose home it was. Regardless, the desire to cause some shit overpowered his conscience.

"Ok, you wait here. I'm going in. Don't come in until you see Zach. Got it?" Freddy gave his friend a thumbs-up for approval. Pete returned it, not saying much as he finished off a handful of fries.

Peter sat in the darkened car, slurping his shake as he watched his friend disappear into the darkness. The thought of what could happen never entered his mind. The understanding that he could be in trouble if his friend committed a crime was foreign to him. It was like everything else, Peter ran on emotion alone. If he was hurt or in pain, others would be as well. It was a top-down plan. His father beat his ass, so Pete, in turn, beat someone else's. This year it was Zach Auerbach; that was his flavor of the month.

Even though Fred told him to be quiet, sitting by himself, listening to the crickets in the dark, made him nervous. It wasn't as if Freddy was his boss, Peter thought, as he turned on the radio to listen to Country Gold on 97.4, home of Providence's premier country station. As Johnny Cash sang in rough tones, it was enough to block out other sounds, especially one of footsteps as they approached the truck.

Peter had no time to react to the hand that came in through the driver's side window, sending shards of glass shooting into his face. Blood sprayed on the dash and ran like rivers down the boy's face. With force, Peter's head was slammed hard into the steering wheel, breaking his nose and embedding the glass deeper.

"Arrrgggg," Peter screamed, his mouth barely opening as blood poured out. His face kissed the wheel again and again until he no longer made any more noises. An eye hung from its socket, the pressure of the attack forcing it to pop out. His nose and mouth were a jumbled mess of blood and meat, exposed. Teeth lay scattered on the dashboard and floor. Peter had no need to concern himself with drug charges or poor decisions. He'd made his last one.

Fred Ripken never heard any commotion coming from his friend's truck. He had one focus at the moment, and that was to turn the Auerbachs' lives upside down. If that meant stepping over the line, then so be it. At this point, he'd resigned himself to the fact that he was in trouble in some form or fashion for the drug charges. Even then it wasn't set in stone, though he hadn't really informed anyone else that his father planned to frame the other two boys in the van instead of him. That was what money would do for you, and before his friends realized what was going on, he'd be off to college and far away from any retribution.

The house was surprisingly dark, an indication that perhaps Gretchen Clement was hiding already. He'd threatened rape, not something he was prone to do, though Freddy couldn't promise himself that he wouldn't get caught up in the moment. That was sometimes a concern for him. When Fred reflected on his future, it looked surprisingly bleak. He'd seen the movies and read the stories about the rich and elite falling. It wasn't the 1950's, where money bailed you out of everything. If he fucked up, his face would be plastered across neighbors' televisions. Even the drug bust, as harmless as that was and easy to write off as innocent, was all over the news. Even if he wanted to be good, it wasn't in his nature. Fred knew that from an early age. He had a sadistic streak in him, one pointed out by therapists and doctors. His parents blamed the divorce and the pressure of being a Ripken, but everyone knew the truth.

It was hard to sneak around the home, looking in windows. The place was locked down like a fortress it seemed, all windows closed up, and shades drawn. It actually looked as though the windows hadn't been opened in years, piles of leaves, pine needles, and dirt collected on the outside of the sill. It was no use even attempting to jar those loose. Maybe one of the doors would be unlocked. He made his way to the backyard.

"Asshole, you need to leave." A voice demanded Fred's attention. Zach stood off by a tree, close enough to the porch to be seen.

"Well, well, well . . . if it isn't the brave hero. Come here to protect your princess?" Fred laughed. The threat sounded canned.

"Go home, Fred, before it's too late," Zach spoke more confidently than he ever had. He felt powerful, controlling this force so unnatural to the human world. This entire situation was playing in his head like he always wished it would. Many nights he stood in the mirror, watching to see how it would look to be brave.

"Ahh, I see. Don't want to wait until it's too late, now do I?" Fred walked away from the home towards the Auerbach boy. He was going to give the kid a lesson in humility. Usually, he had his buddies back him up, but beating up this little shit didn't seem like a tough task. Besides, in his pocket, he had a little surprise just in case it came down to it.

"I'm warning you, Fred. Get out of here." Zach stepped forward, not back. He'd not seen his protector since he'd summoned it. He hadn't known it would work; the lie his grandfather told him. Or so he thought. As soon as he wrote the word in the pile of dirt, a high wind blew in, forcing him to shield his eyes. When he was able to clear his vision, Zach saw the creature standing before him, groggily rubbing its bear paws over what looked to be eyes, as if waking out of a deep and very long sleep. There was no attempt to communicate at all. The Golem was there for protection only and revenge. Zach had written three names down on three separate slips of paper, all to feed to the monster. It wasted no time waiting for instructions before lumbering up the steps and out of the house.

"And if I don't. What if I stay and go fuck your girl? What are you gonna do? Watch?" Fred slid his hand into his front jacket pocket, feeling the cold steel against his fingertips. "You freak. That's why you came here. To watch me do your girl. Zach, you're one sick dude."

"Guess you won't listen to reason. I'm really sorry." Zach held up both hands in the air, introducing his next guest. Behind him, loud crunches could be heard moving closer and at a fast rate.

Fred pulled the gun out of his pocket as soon as he saw it, this massive figure that stood directly behind Zach. It was at least eight feet tall, and though he could only see the shadow of the monster, it frightened him, nonetheless.

"HOLY SHIT!!!" Fred pointed the weapon in the general direction of the boy. As soon as the gun was raised, he was rushed, the creature coming at a speed so unlike something of that size. Two shots got off, neither one wounding the monster. It kept moving until it reached Fred, leaning in to shoulder check the boy with such force, Fred's shoulder completely dislocated as he flew across the yard. He crumpled to the ground in pain for the first time in his life, feeling absolutely helpless. He cried for help, hoping Peter would hear the shots and come running. That would not happen this time. When he looked up, it was the face of the creature that looked down upon him. Fingers wrapped around his entire head, lifting him off the ground.

"I told you to go home, but you wouldn't listen. You're too arrogant to think anything could happen to you." Zach approached the Golem, standing next to it. He didn't understand the full power and force of what his monster could do. It wasn't real to him.

"Why are you such a total asshole, Fred? You

have everything you want, but you don't care. You just let your fat fucking daddy bail you out. But one day, he won't be able to help you, and that day is today. What would he say if he were here now, seeing you pissing your pants like this? Do you think he could pay off the Golem? How much would it take for the Golem to leave you alone?" Zach walked over and slapped Fred's stomach to keep his attention directed at him.

"I'll tell you. Nothing. Nothing Big Daddy can do to help you. All the money and power in the world can't stop this. So, beg. Beg me for forgiveness." Zach was still angry, even though the entire situation had been stopped in its tracks. All the beatings, verbal attacks, humiliation caused to him by the one boy, more than the other two, was something he struggled to get past. Now that he was the one on top, the man with the power, it was time to show who was boss.

Fred tried to do just that, to beg. That wasn't above him to do so. But he could do nothing. The creature's palm covered his mouth, making it almost impossible to breathe. The smell of rotting leaves and dirt filled his nose, gagging him. If the grip wasn't loosened and soon, Fred would suffocate. With all his might, using his injured arm, Fred lifted the gun up, pointing it at the Golem. It squeezed tighter, his head crushing in the monster's palm. Fred could feel himself drifting off, his arm falling to his side. It was then that the gun went off.

"Ooof." A noise came behind the Golem. Zach dropped down to his knees, a red stain quickly showing on his white shirt. In his belly, a bullet lodged itself.

With force more magnificent than it showed, the Golem threw Fred as hard as it could. It didn't matter where the young man landed. He was dead as soon as the decision was made to throw him, the neck snapping immediately at the brainstem.

As Zach lay on the ground, bleeding out, he realized his grandfather was right. Revenge only brought about pain. Then the world got black.

CHAPTER FIFTEEN

Karl leaped as soon as he heard the phone ring, a task much harder for a man his age. He had no idea who or why someone would ring this late, especially on the house phone. The boy had his own number, compliments of a father who wished to give his son privacy. Since then, except for churches asking for money, Karl and Shirley's phone wasn't active. The older one gets, the fewer friends are around to contact them.

"Hello?" Karl said. He could immediately tell something was wrong.

"Mr. Auerbach? Is Mr. Auerbach there?" A girl's voice shook, fighting back the tears.

"This is he. Can I help you?"

"Zach needs help. He's in trouble. Those boys are here." Gretchen Clement blurted out anything that came to mind, not caring if she made sense at all. She knew her boyfriend had told her that contacting the police was futile. Still, upon hearing the commotion, she had no choice in finding help, calling his grandfather.

"Slow down, slow down. Tell me what's going on. Don't leave anything out," Karl said though, when he thought about it later, he wished he hadn't.

Gretchen explained everything. She described the threats of rape, the rushing to her grandfather's home for safety, and the screams. She was confident her own grandfather had no idea what was going on anyway. He barely recognized his name or what year it was.

"Ok, stay where you are. Don't go out there, no matter what you hear. Keep your door locked and make sure you and your grandfather stay away from the window." Karl gave her instructions, taking down the address.

As soon as he hung up the phone, he felt sick to the pit of his stomach. It was as if he already knew what had happened before he even checked. The door to the basement, cracked open, made everything come into focus.

"Oh no," Karl said, descending step after step, quickly as he could. Even when he saw the box sitting on the floor opened, Karl still had to check. But his worst nightmare was real. The open canteen and the cap that sat next to it told him all he needed to know. Rushing back to the phone, he called his son, who was already busy on another call. Apparently, a teenage boy was injured and presumed dead. At least that was what the operator told Karl after taking down the information.

"Tell Steven to get there now. There's no time to waste." Karl slammed the phone down. In the other room, Shirley sat in her chair, knitting and singing to herself. He'd wished he was more honest with her. She deserved to know everything about him, including his past. It was something he never wanted to surface again. Now, there she was, having no concerns in the world. This would be the last night she could feel that way, closed off and comfortable without a care in the world. There was no knowing where this night would lead or if this was the end of him. Karl didn't care about his own life. He'd lived one several times over, but at least he knew what he was getting into. This would all be so foreign to Shirley, things she'd never even thought real. How could she trust him if he hid his past? He walked over to her, kissed her on the head, and excused himself.

"Steven needs me to pick up something for him," Karl lied, hating himself for it.

"This late? Do you want me to come with you? You know how hard it is for you to drive in the dark." If Shirley could sense anything was off, she didn't show it.

"I'll be fine. I'll even call on my way home." Karl hoped he could do that, to hear her voice. Then, and only then, after this was over, would he explain everything: the war, the camps, the Golem. Even as he drove to the location given to Steven to meet him there, Karl kept going back to what would happen when everyone found out about his secret. It was the sound of a gun that brought him back to reality, the shot ringing out loud in the cold, crisp night air.

Without even putting the car in park, Karl opened the door, jumping out to run towards the sound. He was filled with fear and dread, not wanting to see where the noise came from. Moans led him to the backyard, and for the first time in many years, a lifetime ago, Karl and the Golem saw one another.

"No, no, no." Karl's whispers became louder as he made his way towards the Golem. He could see someone on the ground next to him.

"Get away from him. Now!" Karl yelled at the creature, who watched him intently. It did as it was told, seemingly having completed the tasks it was ordered to do. The elderly man dropped down, lifting his grandson's head in his lap.

"Zach, son, wake up. Wake up." Karl slapped the boy on the face, looking for any signs of life. It took a moment or two, but the child did awaken enough to smile at his grandfather.

"Zayde, you were right. I should have listened to you," Zach said, barely able to speak.

"Shhhh, don't worry about that now. You need to hold on. Do you understand? Your father will be here any minute." Karl could see where the bullet had entered, though hopefully, it had avoided any major organs.

"I'm fine, Zayde." Zach's face was white, his

brow beaded with sweat. He felt no pain at all, just a warm numbing feeling.

"I'll stay with you until your dad gets here." Karl ran his hands through his grandson's hair, praying everything would be ok. It was his story that made this possible. If he'd only kept his mouth shut, the Golem would have been lost to history. The Golem . . . was gone.

His concern wasn't a monster, even if it was created by him. It was his grandson, dying in his arms, moving in and out of consciousness. This was all his fault, the entire thing. The stories he told were to teach Zach about forgiveness and what happens when a person focuses on revenge. Instead, he gave away a vehicle with which to unleash anger and dispatch enemies. It wasn't supposed to be this way.

A scream from within the house caught Karl's attention. He could see where the door had been kicked in. "I can't leave your side," the man whispered towards his grandson. He would not be forced to make a decision. More screams came out of the house; still, Karl ignored them. He knew the Golem was inside though for what reason remained unknown.

"Zayde, please go help her." Zach looked up, barely able to keep his eyes open. There was a chance if help did not arrive soon, that the boy would die.

"I won't leave you. The police will be here

soon, anyway." Karl was not moving from this spot, even if he blamed himself.

"Gretchen is inside. Don't let it kill her, too." Zach's statement sent a shiver up his grandfather's spine. Before, it was assumed the monster did the damage. To know that it had killed already during its short time back brought about a whole new wave of fear. There was no indication of the state of mind of the Golem, who had been asleep for decades. There was also the unknown of if and how it decided who lived and died. If it wasn't stopped by him, for good this time, the creature could fall into the wrong hands, and that would be the end of civilization. No one could keep the Golem contained, and the use of its strength was beyond what any weapon or set of human hands could do.

"I'll go help if you promise to stay alive. Can you do that, Zachariah?" Karl said. He would not leave without it.

"Go. Before it's too late," Zach begged.

Karl removed his grandson's head from his lap, lay it on the ground, and covered him with his jacket. He had no desire to leave Zach's side, but could he live with himself if more died because of his decisions? The Golem needed to be stopped.

CHAPTER SIXTEEN

Karl followed the screams of a young girl frightened by what she saw. All the lights were still off in the house, making it difficult to navigate, especially for someone with advanced age like himself. It was quite strange, however, that even as old as he was, Karl felt more youthful than he had in a long time. It was as if laying eyes on the Golem gave him some sort of strength he'd forgotten he had.

"LEAVE HIM ALONE!" Gretchen screamed at the creature that attempted to push past her to get to the elderly man she had hidden in the closet and under blankets. The girl had heard the fighting outside and the gunshot. Though it was difficult, she was able to get George Clement into the closet, where he'd be safer. She was expecting a crazed teen to walk in, intent on raping and harming her. She wasn't ready for what entered in his place.

"STOP! NOW!" Karl stepped into the bedroom, standing in the doorway. He saw the back of the creature, muscles pulsing. The old man, after decades of ignoring the truth, realized what brought this creature to life. It wasn't just mud and a prayer. It was much more.

The Golem turned its head around, looked

at Karl, and started to grab at George Clement again. For some reason, it was determined to get its hands on him. Karl yelled again and again. The monster kept its pursuit.

"Abel, stop. Please," Karl said, now knowing what brought life to the Golem.

This time, the Golem did stop. He turned, looking at Karl, tilting its head to the side. One of its two eyes twinkled very quickly.

"But you aren't just Abel, are you? Hello, Sam," Karl said. The dirt used to create the creature was soaked in the blood of his good friend. And when Abel was shot, he fell upon the place where the Golem was. Their blood and their souls helped form the monster, bringing it to life.

"You don't want to do this. You need to stop. No more blood shall be spilled." Karl walked over to the Golem, grabbing its hands in his to pull it away. He wanted to appeal to his old friends, at least what remained of them in this empty vessel. The Golem refused to move. Instead, it pulled away from him to get back to the closet.

"Please. Why are you doing this? Haven't you done enough?" Karl pleaded. This time, when the creature did stop, it shoved fingers in his mouth, pulling out a tiny crumpled piece of paper, one Karl recognized.

"NAZIS," Karl said, looking first at Gretchen and then towards the closet. "Golem, stop." The creature listened this time.

"Gretchen, who is your grandfather?" Karl asked.

"What?" Gretchen was confused. They stood next to this monster, who would kill them all, and this old man wanted to know about her family.

"Grandfather. Who is he?" Karl asked again, everything becoming clear.

"George Clement."

"Have him come out," Karl demanded. He could see the trepidation on her face.

"Abel. Samuel. Sit here. Do not move unless I tell you." Karl was in complete control. He held in his own hand, the paper he'd written years ago, the first and only order he ever gave the Golem.

Gretchen went into the closet and came back, holding the hand of a gentleman that made Karl seem young. George Clement was hunched over, no longer the tall, strapping lad he once was. The memory of the war and his role in the Holocaust might have faded in and out, unclear of what year it was. But it was him. Karl could tell immediately.

"Commandant Gunter Müller?" Karl could see the once-mighty Nazi, now a withered shell.

"*Guten tag*, Hans Krueger." Müller shot his right hand in the air, giving his visitor the proper Hitler salute. He'd clearly mistaken Karl for his dead brother. It made it no easier to accept, but the proof was there.

"I am not Hans. I am Karl Krueger. My brother is dead. My friends . . . dead. All because of you." Karl felt that same anger his grandson had swell back into him. After all the years of hunting Müller down, to know he was so close, right underneath his nose all the time, made it harder to accept.

"Ahhh, young Karl. I'm so happy to see you. How is your brother?" Gunter was not who he once was. He was dying. His brain was riddled with disease. He remembered little, forgetting statements made moments before. He did, however, remember the past.

"You killed him!" Karl said again, this time with more force. This caused the Golem, so docile, to sit up. It did not take its glare from the Nazi.

"Leave my grandfather alone. He's not in his right mind." Gretchen begged Karl to stop. She'd always assumed he had a checkered past. But a Nazi? That wasn't something she was willing to accept.

"Unfortunately, my dear, he has just enough memory to remember me. When you are ready, I will share the entirety of this criminal's story. But today is not the day. Today, it is his judgment day, and he shall pay for all those he ordered to be killed. The men and women at Buchenwald demand retribution." Karl's words rang true. He looked back at the Golem, who stood up. Instead of rushing forward, it walked to Gunter and scooped him into its arms like a baby.

"PUT HIM DOWN. YOU'RE KILLING HIM," Gretchen screamed.

"No more will die today, my dear. But he will pay for his crimes." Karl walked out of the house, the Nazi war criminal carried behind him. In the back, Karl could hear the girl screaming. It did not matter. Police sirens blared. His son was here.

CHAPTER SEVENTEEN

The next several weeks were confusing and difficult to accept. The morning after the massacre at the Clement house, the elderly man appeared tied and on the doorstep of the police station, with a folder hanging over his neck. Within the hour, all news stations had released the information of the infamous Gunter Müller, Commandant of Buchenwald and number one on the FBI's most-wanted list of war criminals. Though his family fought to deny it, Gunter was too far gone to remember much about himself except his war years. His health was failing, but it didn't matter to the German government. Within the month, the former Nazi would be extradited back to his homeland to stand trial for his crimes. He'd die in jail, awaiting trial.

The death of the three boys was shrouded in mystery, and the story had holes, but it was one the general public accepted. Fred, Pete, and Vern had all been busted driving drugs around for Peter's dad. If any of them had sung at court, which would happen if given a chance, the entire operation would have been destroyed. In retribution, each was shut up. It wasn't implausible, but with the rape allegation being spread by Gretchen Clement, Alfred Ripken II thought it better to accept what was given as the reason to avoid bad press. Several men were arrested for the brutal crime, including Peter's father, though there was no physical evidence. In time, people lost interest in the facts, moving on to new crimes in the news.

Zachariah recovered from his wounds and was lucky the bullet missed any vital organs. However, the night's events were a blur. Due to blood loss, he did not remember anything. Unlike his grandfather, he would not have the deaths of three men on his conscience. That was something he wouldn't have to live with. Revenge did cost Zach so much though, including the girl he loved. She and her mother went to Germany to support her grandfather and never returned. It was too painful.

Karl never wanted any of this. He tried to think of ways to explain everything to Shirley or his son, but what good would it do? The only person he ever told the real tale to used it to bring about more destruction. Instead, he lied to both. He spoke of his time in the camps and his connection to Gunter Müller. This time, there was no creation of a Golem. During the confusion of the death march, Karl was able to slip into the woods, where he ran into and joined the Soviets until the end of the war. Shirley cried, asking him over and over why he kept this to himself for so long. Steven said nothing, confused about so many things.

"It was too painful to burden others with my story," Karl responded.

It didn't matter. No one needed to know the truth. It was better if the stories died with him. At least that was the way he wanted it to be. Upon returning to his home that night, Karl saw the Golem, waiting for him, with Gunter Müller sleeping on his couch. What would have his friends thought, seeing this? Their enemy curled up like a dog, comfortably away in a different world.

"Leave him at the station and return here." Karl gave the order, tying the folder around the criminal's neck. In an hour, the Golem came back, as commanded. Since the moment he saw the creature again, Karl thought about what he was to do with it. It did not belong here, not on this earth anyway. He needed to destroy it, and wanted to, though something had stopped him, much like it did once before.

This time, it would be different, he told himself, as he watched the Golem in the backyard, digging a hole, as instructed. When it was done, Karl returned the creature to dust, as it should be. There would be no good if he let the wind take it. Would it remain dead if in the atmosphere? And hiding it where someone could find it was dangerous. Karl went downstairs, grabbed the canteen, and filled it again with the remains of the Golem. Karl would bury it in the backyard, where he could keep an eye on it. No one would find it, as long as he were alive, and hopefully, the truth would die with him. This time, before sealing it away for good, Karl took out a sharpie marker and wrote "sleep" on a slip of paper, sealing it in the canteen. His last real order to the Golem was to rest. Before he buried the Golem for good, Karl used the marker one more time, putting the word "MET" on the top of the canteen. This time, the Golem would stay dead.

Center Point Large Print
600 Brooks Road / PO Box 1
Thorndike, ME 04986-0001 USA

(207) 568-3717

US & Canada:
1 800 929-9108
www.centerpointlargeprint.com